ELEMENTAL OUTCAST

PARANORMAL OUTCASTS BOOK 1

SEAN FLETCHER

D1736139

Come hang out in the **Fantasy Fiends Reader group** on Facebook! We chat, recommend YA fantasy reads, and get into mischief. It's the best place to learn about new book releases, exclusive ARCs, cover reveals, giveaways and more.

To receive two FREE YA fantasy books and be notified of new releases, **Join My Newsletter.** No spam, and you can unsubscribe at anytime.

You know you want to. We've got magic and stuff. :)

CHAPTER ONE

My blood pooled on the tile floor, turning the stark white into a canvas of smeared red. The smell of it turned my stomach and made my already weakened legs tremble. If I hadn't been dying, I'd have been upset at the mess I was making.

"Riley…"

My best friend's voice was a terrified whisper. Iris crouched behind one of the sinks of the fairground's bathroom, eyes wide, knuckles white.

"You're hurt. He…he—"

"You okay?" I asked through gritted teeth, keeping our assailant in my peripheral. Even speaking those two words sent waves of fiery pain from where the guy had driven his knife into my side.

"I'm…I'm…"

She seemed physically fine. Just emotionally traumatized. I wished she'd scream. I wished I could. Maybe somebody from the rest of the fair would hear. Maybe they'd batter down the door this creep had locked behind him.

Mr. Stabby himself stood in the way of our escape. I'd tried to get a good look at his face the moment I'd noticed him follow us in here, but he wore a deep hood. The little of his face I could glimpse beneath was wrong. Half-formed, mushy, and clay-like. Burned, maybe.

But he was smiling. I could see that much.

I pressed my fingers harder against my wound. Blood leaked through. "Okay, creepazoid. Last chance. Let us out."

I tried not to shake. I tried not to let him see my fear.

The guy smiled wider. He raised his knife and brought it down straight at my heart.

※

"RILEY!"

I pulled my eyes away from the Ferris Wheel to see Iris waving at me from one of the food stalls.

Ho-boy.

"Deep. Fried. Butter," Iris said when I went over. "We gotta try it."

"Uh…" I looked at the chef. He seemed *way* too proud for someone who moved his customers' date of heart attack thirty years closer. "Are you sure that's the most appetizing thing here? You haven't found the fried scorpions yet?"

Iris rolled her eyes. "Come on. You only turn seventeen once. Better eat it now while your arteries can handle it. Two please," Iris told the stall owner.

"Your birthday coming up?" the man asked as he wrapped Iris's and my future stomachaches into wax paper.

"Today, actually," I said, smiling at him.

"And tonight's a surprise celebration!" Iris snagged my arm and pulled me close, pretending to wipe a tear from her eye. "My little girl's all grown up."

I *had* been totally surprised when Iris had shown up at my house and dragged me out to Cliffside's end-of-summer-fair. If I was being honest, I hadn't expected much, if any, celebration. Most of my few other friends were still gone on summer trips or internships. I'd kind of expected my parents to do something, but they'd been...weird the last few weeks leading up to my birthday. Don't get me wrong, they were always weird. But this bordered on paranoia: insisting on driving me to school; wanting me home *way* before curfew; texting me in the middle of the day to ask if anything was wrong.

Like *that* wasn't ominous. They'd been so clingy I was glad I'd snuck away with Iris tonight. She was right: you only turn seventeen once.

The stall owner handed us our fried butter on sticks, then held up a hand when Iris tried to pay. "On the house. Er...cart. For the birthday girl."

I smiled again as we thanked him and blended back into the crowd, meandering between the booths of games and more heart-stopping fried delicacies. Joyful screams came from the direction of the rides we'd promised to hit later.

"Mmm..." Iris polished her butter off in a flash, then eyed mine. "Are you..."

I took a bite (*Helloo* taste buds!) and handed her the rest. "All yours."

She took it, grinning. "I knew you were my best friend for a reason."

She proceeded to scarf mine down until there weren't even crumbs left. Not that she had to worry about a little thing like gaining weight. Iris' muscles were insanely toned from all the days she spent competitively swimming. Her chocolate hair was braided with three strands, hanging almost to the middle of the skirt she wore over her tights.

I stopped in front of one of the game booths, the kind where you had to knock over some obviously weighted bottles to win a prize.

"That," I said, pointing at an enormous stuffed panda, nearly as big as I was. "If you were trying to decide what to get me for my birthday, wonder no more."

Iris showed me her butter-stained hands. "Napkins first. Then I can get you that monstrosity you'll dump on your poor parents when you leave for college."

She disappeared into the crowd in search of a place to wash up. I approached the booth and handed the woman running it a few bucks.

"Anything you have your eye on?" she asked as I took the three balls and lined up to throw the first.

"The panda up there. It's destined to be mine."

The woman nudged her head to the cereal-mascot-looking tiger beside it, his fur obnoxiously orange. "Feel like that one would match you better."

My first throw went embarrassingly wide. I gave the woman the side eye.

"Because of your hair," she added, as though what she'd been referring to wasn't the most obvious thing in the world.

My hair was the kind of fiery red that made me think God had turned the saturation up to eleven on his divine Photoshop. It was always frizzy like I'd walked out of a thunderstorm, and I had to keep it tied back in a messy ponytail or else it'd blow all over my face at the worst times.

"The panda's just fine," I said. I wiped my hand on my torn jeans and lined up again.

"Whatever you say," the woman answered right as I threw again. I winged the bottles. They jiggled but didn't fall.

I threw the last one before the woman could distract me again, and as I did I felt a prickle on my skin. Not the kind that told me a thunderstorm was coming (I'm *that* kind of weird), but the kind that said I was being watched. Stalker sense.

"Better luck next time," the woman said cheerily, but I'd already swung around to scan the crowd. The fair had grown far busier than when we'd first gotten here, jammed thick with hundreds of screaming kids, stressed parents, and couples. The lights from the rides dazzled in every color, glinting off the metal beams of the stalls.

A boy was staring at me.

I easily picked him out, even surrounded by dozens of people, as though my eyes had been drawn right to him. He stood in the dead center of one of the main thoroughfares, but everybody breezed right by him as though he wasn't even there. I don't know how they couldn't notice him. Even this far away I could practically feel a strange sort of energy crackling off him. His gaze was the very definition of *intense*.

I took a step toward him, right as Iris reappeared. "You would not believe what one of the stalls is selling. Wait for it...Fried bubble gum."

I looked over at her for only a second, but when I turned back the boy was gone. Vanished just like that. Like he'd never been there at all.

"Riley? Are you all right?" Iris said concernedly.

"I'm...Did you see someone just then? In the crowd?"

Iris squinted where I pointed. "Well...I see a lot of someones. Anyone in particular?"

"It was..." I felt my cheeks heat just a little. My first day as a seventeen-year-old and I was already imagining boys shooting me smoldering looks from across fair grounds.

"Oh...I get it now," Iris said, mentally filling in what I hadn't said. "*Rawr*. You're a real vixen."

"Oh shut up," I said, giving her a playful shove.

"Riley," Iris continued in a mock serious tone, "when a girl reaches a certain age—"

"You..."

She laughed again as I tried to grab her. I chased her toward the rides until we started walking again. I grinned over at her, expecting her to crack another joke, but she looked strangely serious now. "So *do* you...I don't know, feel any different?"

"Iris, I swear, if you're asking me if I—"

"Not *that*." She rolled her eyes. "I mean, do you feel grown up? Like I said, different?"

Did I? Besides my parents' odd behavior, I didn't feel anything about me had really changed. My friends and I had begun to grow a little distant through the summer, and especially now with our senior year coming up. The only thing of note were the weird dreams I'd been having: dark skies, complete with booming, disembodied voices speaking things I couldn't make out. I often awoke with only the barest recollection of them, and they never really bled into my everyday life. Nervous symptoms, I was sure, of having to make a final decision on colleges. But other than that?

"Nope," I said. I beamed at her. "Same old me."

I could have sworn Iris looked sad when I said that, but for the life of me I couldn't guess why.

And just like that the Iris I knew was back and we were chatting away as though nothing was wrong.

After debating which rides we wanted to go on, Iris said she needed to use the bathroom and hurried off. I lingered at a picnic table, totally not scanning the crowd for mister tall, dark, and intense whom I'd seen earlier. It shouldn't have been too hard to spot him. After all, he'd practically jumped out at me the first time.

Another prickle on my skin. I casually turned around to look, not trying to seem too eager. No one was there. Then I heard the thunder rumble in the distance and sighed. Of course. It was just my built-in Doppler radar.

I got up. If a storm was coming then I didn't want to be outside when it hit. I didn't mind getting a little dirty, but I'd never liked rain, even as a kid. It always made me feel crappy and sluggish. A little under the weather. Pun intended.

I looked for Iris. She was taking a long time, and if we were going we'd have to leave soon. My parents had probably found out I'd taken off by now and would have a talk about responsibility waiting for me when I got home. Definitely wasn't looking forward to that.

I found the nearest bathroom one thoroughfare over. It looked completely deserted. Like the boy, dozens of people walked right around it as though it wasn't there.

Okay, that was weird. My skin was prickling again, and not in a good way.

I entered the girls' bathroom.

"Iris? Not that I wouldn't *love* to say I told you so, but if that fried butter's giving you trouble—"

I froze when I spotted her taking shelter behind one of the sinks, whimpering.

"Riley, he's—"

I heard the door close behind me. Heard the lock click into place.

I spun just in time to see a hooded man lunge at me.

⚜

Now I barely moved out of the way in time as his knife flashed past. My side screamed as I twisted the wrong way. More blood pooled through my fingers. I slipped a little on the slick floor as I backpedaled toward Iris.

This was bad. Bad, bad, bad. We'd been in here for over five minutes and nobody was coming to help. Thanks to my parents' insistence that I take self-defense classes, I'd been able to survive this long. The classes had taught me a lot, but this wasn't sparring on plush mats in an air-conditioned studio. This was real. This was so, so real.

My vision began to split in two from the pain. I felt Iris' shaking hand grip my arm. "Riley..."

"When you see an opening, run," I gritted out.

"No, I can't! I—"

"I'm telling you to."

"I—"

"You will. Please, Iris." I looked down at my best friend. She was many things, but a fighter wasn't one. If this creep finished me off she'd be next. "Run when I give you the chance."

Then I charged straight at our attacker.

That threw him off. Score one for me. He'd probably thought he'd found easy prey. But if I was going to die here, I'd make it far from easy.

I rammed my shoulder into him and shoved him into the nearest stall. "Now, Iris!"

There was a horrible moment when I thought she would stay behind. Then her shoes squeaked as she took off, fumbled with the lock, threw open the door.

Then she was gone, and I was alone.

I stumbled back as my attacker swiped again. I felt so sluggish. How much blood had I lost? At this rate, my only chance at survival was to avoid him long enough for Iris to come back with help. All I had to do was—

My foot slipped on the blood. I felt an intense bite of pain and looked down to find the attackers' knife protruding from my stomach.

Well. Crap.

Bright lights glared down at me as I collapsed. I could make out the shadowy outline of the man as he loomed above. My skin was prickling again. But not like I was being watched or sensing a storm. A heat was building from somewhere deep inside me. My skin grew warm, then unbearably hot, until I thought I was going to combust.

The walls flickered orange and red. My head spun as I looked over and, as out of it as I was, I realized that somehow a fire had started inside the bathroom.

I gasped again and the heat rushed from my skin, collecting into a ring of flames that shoved my attacker back. The stall doors melted, the mirrors shattered. I heard the guttural roar of some enormous creature that couldn't have possibly been real. Too feral. Too loud. Like something you'd hear in a nightmare.

Another wave of pain rushed over me. My breath hitched. The fire shrank back and the room went silent. Black was creeping into the edge of my vision. I heard the light footfalls of something walking over to me. I grew hot, but comfortably so, as whatever it was stopped beside me. Something licked the side of my face. It felt like sandpaper.

The black rushed in and I saw no more.

CHAPTER TWO

"Arise...*Arise*...ARISE!"

My alarm clock sounded different than usual. Either that or waking me up in a booming voice was my dad's idea of a hilarious joke. Give me five more minutes and I'd roll out of bed and tell him—

I gasped awake, my eyes snapping open. I lay on an unforgivingly hard floor in...was it a cave? A tunnel? I wasn't sure. All I knew was that it was nearly pitch black and frigid. Wonderful.

I'd just started picking myself off the ground when torches flared to life along the walls, startling me. It *was* a cave. Thick with roots dug deep into the walls and fang-like stalactites sprouting from the ceiling. The damp cold air tightened my lungs—

My lungs.

I looked down. Oh yeah, I was breathing. And those knife wounds...

I pulled back the sliced parts of my shirt where the guy had stabbed me. My skin was healed and unmarked. That hadn't been a dream. I could vividly remember the attack. The fair. The boy. Iris making her escape.

I relaxed a bit at that. Iris had escaped. She'd probably gone to the police and they'd taken her to safety while I...

Was somewhere. And apparently still alive. My wounds were miraculously healed, though something still felt off. Something other than *everything*. Though I could breathe and feel and see, it still felt as though something inside me was missing.

That, and I realized I wasn't alone.

I whirled around to face the back of the cave. Only, it was no longer a cave but a wide, ancient hall. Instead of torches, the immense clay columns on either side were lit by bowls of fire. On the walls beyond the pillars I could see intricate markings, almost like the hieroglyphics I'd read about in school. Flowers bloomed over the drawings, sinking their thick vines deep into the earthen walls. Chrysanthemum and lantana, lilies and something that had to be oleander.

But none of my surroundings held my attention—or made me worried. That honor belonged to a panel of shrouded figures at the head of the hall. I squinted but could only make out their vague shapes. Whoever they were, they'd better have an explanation for the weirdness going on.

"Where am I?" I asked.

"She's awakened!" one of the figures said.

"At last," said another.

"A manner most unorthodox," said a third.

"But it *did* work; you can't deny the results."

"But is she worthy? Was it worth it for *her*?"

"You saw what she did."

"Luck, nothing more. I don't believe she's worth our time—"

"Hey!" I said, breaking into their group therapy session. "I'm right here. What's awakened? What did you do to me?"

I took a step toward the panel. The instant I did my stomach lurched. I blinked and found myself exactly back where I'd started. An uncomfortable, unsettling idea I'd ignored up to this point was taking shape. This wasn't possible. None of this was possible. And yet...

"Look how unprepared she is!" The panel had started up again. "The others—"

"All had their own challenges to overcome."

"Challenges? Ha! This is insurmountable."

"She is the first, she must be the one."

The one? I frowned up at them. I couldn't explain what was going on, but I was already sick of being left in the dark. "Someone needs to tell me what's—"

"*The Thirteenth one shall be the key,*" the figure in the center said. "*The remedy to Outcasts' strife.* She is the one. Unorthodox or not, uncertain or not, there will be no more debate."

Some of the other figures grumbled at this. I was still rolling the central figure's slam poetry around in my mind. Thirteenth what?

The central figure stood and immediately vanished.

"You probably have many questions."

I'm not ashamed to admit that I let out a squeak of alarm. That's what happens when somebody suddenly appears beside you without warning. Almost like it was...

"You have no idea," I said when I finally managed to get my throat to work. "And I hope you're going to answer them."

The woman smiled, crinkling her already crinkled face. If I thought witches were real (not that I did, though I was beginning to question everything I thought I knew), then she'd have been the witchiest witch who'd ever witched. Long, crooked nose, complete with warts? Check. Slightly greenish tint to her skin? Check. Flowing, unflattering black dress? Check. The only things that didn't fit the stereotype were that she carried no broomstick, and the kindly smile she was giving me.

"I'm not going to answer your questions," the witch said. "You'll learn in time. It is the Sisterhood of the Chosen's job to weigh worth and pass judgement, but we will not affect your path after that. That is for you alone."

"You can't even tell me what's happening?"

"I cannot."

"And you won't tell me—"

"I will not."

I tried to resist putting my head in my hands. But witch lady wasn't done. She stepped close and lowered her voice, as though she didn't want the others to hear.

"In your blood runs centuries of power. In your blood runs hope. Don't fail."

"Don't fail *what?*" I hissed, now far past annoyance and red-lining it toward exasperation. "What the hell am I supposed to do?"

The witch reached out a hand. "Lead."

I started to back up, but the witch's finger touched right over my heart. I gasped as my heart thudded hard, like an engine coughing to life after being dead for years. It seemed to jump as she pressed again.

"Stop!" I gasped. "Whatever you're doing, stop!"

"I can't," the witch said. "I'm giving you a second chance."

The next heartbeat was the hardest yet. The black that'd swallowed me before swept over my eyes, and almost immediately fled again.

I was in a new place, open and brightly lit, lying on a soft bed. My heart wasn't beating painfully, but its normal, consistent rhythm. I sighed. This I could make sense of. I was in the hospital. I'd survived the attack and they'd brought me here. That dream of witches and ancient, epically intoned, prophecy-sounding words were just that: a dream.

I let out a long breath.

Right as the boy from the fair appeared over me, fury in his eyes.

CHAPTER THREE

I instinctively lashed out, punching right at his face.

The guy easily leaned back, dodging my blow as though I was moving in slow motion. He still looked furious, but he was smirking now.

"Please. You couldn't hit me if you tri—"

I kicked out from beneath the covers, catching him in the side of the knee before scrambling to the other corner of the bed.

The guy had barely flinched at my kick. Now that I got a good look at him, three things were immediately apparent: he was definitely the guy from the fair; he was unbelievably good-looking; and he was glaring at me like I'd just murdered his best friend.

His jaw was model-sharp, shoulders broad and fitted in a black T-shirt. His hair alone would have been a marvel on any normal guy—black as midnight, strands staked across his forehead while the rest appeared perfectly tousled—his lips full and still tilted downward in a pissed curved line. But I couldn't stop looking at his eyes. His irises were red as roses—or blood—and seemed to suck me right in...

I managed to free myself from his gaze. What was wrong with

me? This guy had clearly kidnapped me and all I could do was stare at him? At his near-perfect face, at his mouth…

He smirked again and I saw his teeth. His *teeth*. It couldn't be…they couldn't be…

The guy moved faster than was possible, appearing on my side of the bed. I tried to punch again but he caught my wrist.

"Let me go," I said as calmly as I could, trying to break his iron grasp.

"How did you manipulate the prophecy?" he said.

Prophecy? "I didn't manipulate anything. Now. Let. Go."

He relinquished his grip, but almost immediately leaned closer, way into my personal bubble. My heart (which was *definitely* working again) stuttered into overdrive. If it wasn't obvious before, I knew with certainty now: there was something predator about him. Like a snake. Or a wolf. Or a…

Vampire? My disbelieving mind offered, looking again at his teeth.

Yeah, like a vampire.

"Don't lie to me," he said. "The witches spoke it to all of us before sending us here. How did you fool them? Did the Northern Pack set you up to it? Maybe the Deathless?"

"I don't…I have no idea…" I managed to shove him away and again scrambled to the other side of the bed to put some distance between us. I knew what this was. This was a hallucination. I'd gone totally bonkers, and my dream guy and my nightmares were colliding into some freakish collab from Hell.

"You're not real." I pushed as much confidence as I could into my voice. If I fought back, focused my mind and really *believed*, he'd go away. I was sure of it. "You're just my imagination. I'm not looking at you. I don't see you. You're not real…"

He stalked closer, immediately shattering my illusion. "Oh I'm very real. Dangerously real. And there's a lot more that's even more dangerous than me out there. You've stumbled into a whole different world, little girl. Vampires, shifters, the undead, and those are the least of your worries. Now I want you to answer my questions—"

"Jasper!"

A young woman walked into the room and the guy, Jasper, lazily leaned away from me. I felt a small sense of relief. Wherever I was, at least this girl seemed to have my back. She looked like she put the capital T in Tough. Her hair was short and sculpted. Tattoos and faded white scars clawed up her arms while her ears held a window display's worth of piercings.

"Ari," Jasper nodded. He crossed his arms as though he'd been doing absolutely nothing wrong. "You're late. She was awake a while ago."

"And you're already terrorizing her." Ari punched Jasper on the shoulder, then gave me a kind smile. "My name's Arianna, but call me Ari. And I apologize for him. He never learned how to talk to girls properly. Or anyone, really."

"I wanted answers," Jasper said. He glared at me. "Still do. They sent us her. She can't be…"

"You're the boy from the fair," I said. It was the only thing I could think of to say. Maybe because the fair was the last time anything in my life made sense.

"The fair?" Ari said. "Wait, Cliffside's summer fair? What were you doing there, Jas?"

Jas?

"Investigating a magical disturbance." His eyes remained locked on me. "And I think we found it."

Ari looked thoughtful at that. "You think you sensed her before—"

"Okay, that's enough."

I swung my legs out of the bed and got to my feet. I realized I was still fully clothed, blood, shoes and all, as though I'd been sent straight from that witch's hall right to…wherever this was. "The last few hours I've been attacked, stabbed, electrocuted by the Wicked Witch of the West—"

16

Jasper frowned. "Wicked Witch—?"

"And now kidnapped. I'm done. I'm out."

Ari gave me a sympathetic look. "I get it. Really, I do. All of us were confused when we first arrived at the Loft. But I promise you weren't kidnapped, you were sent. There's a lot to explain, and I imagine it's a ton to grasp for someone like...well, someone..."

"Human," Jasper cut in. "Weak."

"Whatever," I said, not even trying to conjure up a response to that. "I'm going home."

"Riley, please." Ari stepped in front of me, hands up. "I know it's a lot, but this is your home now."

"No, my home is with my mom and dad." Who were probably freaking out right now. "Out of my way."

"Riley—"

I shoved past her, only to feel Jasper's iron grasp on my arm again. "Ari's right. You can't go home. They won't—"

"Let me go," I said, voice dangerously low. "I'm warning you..."

My skin was growing hot. It grew within my center, rose to coat my skin.

"Not until you listen to what we have to say," Jasper said. "And I get my answers."

"Jasper..." Ari warned.

But it was too late; the heat had grown to a furious burning. "Hands off!"

I ripped away from him, throwing my arms up to push him off. All the heat pushed out. A ring of fire exploded from my body, blistering the air in a blinding flash of light before crackling away to nothingness.

I stared at where the fire had gone, trying to catch my breath. Trying to make sense of it. How had I done that? *What* had I done?

"Still think she's not one of us, Jas?" Ari said.

But before either of them could stop me, I rushed out the door.

※

THE LOFT, or whatever that girl Arianna had called it, happened to be right in the heart of Cliffside, slotted alongside the other outrageously priced condominiums and towering skyscrapers. I had no clue how much time had passed since the fair, but it was mid-day, the sky gray with the threat of rain. My skin prickled.

I walked as fast as I could away from the Loft, accidentally shouldering into pedestrians and muttering half-hearted apologies as I did so. I felt like if I walked fast enough I could forget about what had happened.

About the fire that'd leapt from my body.

About Jasper's teeth, and the figures in the hall.

Magic. Vampires. Witches. Real. All of it was real.

At last I leaned, exhausted, against a crosswalk button. A few people gave me concerned looks, right before the light turned and they started to cross. I'd wearily pushed off to follow them when my eyes snagged on someone. They stood out of the flow of foot traffic, hunched and shrouded in the shadows between two buildings. I couldn't have said why they'd caught my eye.

Then they turned my way and I glimpsed their face: sunken, hollow eye sockets; peeling flesh; tongue lolling out over sharp teeth.

I swallowed a scream and hurried across the street, but now my senses were on full alert. Everywhere I looked I caught snatches of things I never had before. The glint of sharp fangs. The pointed snout of a wolf peeking from beneath a hat. The words to a spell drifting out from a nearby pawn shop.

I squeezed my eyes shut until the wave of disorientation passed and the noise of the crowd returned to its usual dull murmur. That stupid Jasper, he'd put these ideas in my head.

Scared me into thinking danger and the impossible lurked around every curve.

I finally relaxed when I stepped onto the L train. Things were starting to look familiar. This was the usual route I took from school back home to my neighborhood on the north end of Cliffside. I kept my eyes on the passengers at each stop, but none of them looked out of place. Nothing wolfish or sharp-fanged about them. Just normal, tired commuters on a normal, battered L train in a normal city.

I eased against the window as we began passing over the river, the foothills of Cliffside slowly rising to greet me as though an old friend. A slice of coastline formed the inlet that the train was passing over. On the opposite bank was the fairground I'd been at with Iris. I wondered if the police would still be searching for me—

I pressed my face harder against the glass, looking at where the fair *should* have been. All of it was gone now, the lot as vacant and bare as it usually was most of the year. I was no carny, but I knew you couldn't pack all the rides and booths up in only a few hours.

I yanked my phone out of my pocket. Completely dead. I looked around the train car, finally finding an older man reading a newspaper. I spied the date at the top and felt my blood go cold. A week. It'd been a week since the fair.

I braced my arms against the center pole. The man looked concernedly up at me. "You okay?"

"Just fine," I said, forcing a smile.

I had to get home.

Once I reached my stop at Knob Hill, I rushed off and practically sprinted from the platform. All I could think was how my parents must be feeling. A week. I'd been missing an entire week. They must have thought I'd been kidnapped (technically true). They must have thought I was...

I swallowed, not wanting to finish that thought.

I turned onto my street and spotted the house I'd lived in since birth. Just seeing the brick front and meticulously manicured lawn my dad kept in order filled me with a sense of calm. In all the craziness, here, at least, was something that had remained the same.

Only...As I stopped running and crossed the front yard, I noticed that not everything was how I remembered. The hedges had grown thicker and wilder than their usual, impeccably trimmed appearance. I had to push aside a pile of packages that'd been left nearly toppling at the front door.

Feeling a bit uneasy, I tried the front door handle. They'd thankfully left it unlocked and I stepped inside the brightly lit foyer.

"Mom? Dad?" I yelled, my chest nearly bursting with relief. They'd be beyond overjoyed. I would be too. This entire nightmare could finally be over. We'd hug and cry and put this entire thing behind us.

My smile slowly wilted when nobody came running to greet me. *"Mom? Dad?"*

They'd left the door unlocked, so they had to be here. Where were they?

I checked the living room, then upstairs. Their bedroom, like the yard, had been left in unusual disarray. My room, however, looked the exact same as the night I'd left it. I picked up one of the plushies I kept on my dresser—for sentimental value only, I swear—and hugged it. A second after I did, I thought something moved in the place where it'd been, but when I stared at the spot, I couldn't see anything. I put the plushie back. Everything remained eerily silent save for the sound of the air conditioner outside kicking on. There was a distant rumble of thunder. I went back downstairs and checked the kitchen.

"There you guys are!"

My parents sat at the kitchen island, papers spread out in

front of them. I could tell my dad had been crying based on the red splotches covering his cheeks. My mom too.

"Guys, hey!"

I ran forward, partly thinking that something was very, very wrong, that there was no way they'd missed me come in, partly just wanting to hold them, to let them know I was okay and they didn't have to cry anymore.

I stumbled past my mom as I tried to hug her. I blinked, not comprehending why I wasn't holding her right now. I stared at my arms, wondering if I'd somehow forgotten how to use them. Had I just missed?

I tried to hug my dad.

And passed right through him.

"No. Nonono. Guys, look at me. Look at me!" I grabbed for my mom's hand but it was like grabbing mist, my hand drifting through hers like she wasn't even there.

Or I wasn't.

"I called Chief Ryans and he says there's still some hope." My dad's voice was thick with tears. He sounded broken, and that nearly broke me. "They've checked all the potential suspects, all the places she might have gone."

"Nothing on the Amber Alert?" my mom said, pushing aside some of the papers. I saw my junior year's yearbook photo plastered on most of them.

"Nothing," my dad said with a defeated sigh. "He did say...He did mention the possibility that she ran away—"

My mom slammed a fist on the table, spilling her mug. "She did *not* run away. How many times do we have to tell them that? Iris was there. She saw the man with the knife."

"He was real," I said. I raised my voice. "You hear me? He was real, and I'm *right in front of you.*"

"But nobody else did," my dad said, and I sank back, horrified. "There was blood in the bathroom, but no man. No sign he'd ever been there, and nobody saw him leave."

21

I couldn't stand this any longer. I didn't know what kind of magic—yes, I'd admit it, magic—had done this to me, but I wouldn't let it take me away from my parents. I would *make* them see me.

I picked up my mom's mug and smashed it on the counter. The sound was satisfyingly glorious.

My parents didn't even flinch.

How could they miss that? I couldn't touch them, but I could obviously touch other things. They had to have noticed.

But when I looked at where the mug had sat, it was there again, completely untouched. How…?

I reached over the counter and, with one huge move, swept all the papers off. I watched them this time. Watched as they fluttered past my parents' unchanging faces.

Then the papers *changed*. It was like I was seeing double: the papers I'd touched, fluttering in the air, but also the papers my parents must have been seeing, unaffected where they'd always been.

Then my papers vanished and it was as though nothing had been touched.

I opened all the cabinets, broke all the dishes against the floor, turned on the sink faucet, threw their spice rack, *anything* to get them to look at me. None of it worked. By the end of my tirade I sank against the counter, out of breath, with everything I'd just messed up back in its usual place. I felt tears threatening to break free and pressed my arm against my eyes until they retreated. As much as I wanted to, crying wouldn't help. Those jerks Jasper and Arianna had done something to me. They'd trapped me here in this between. Alive, but not fully.

I looked up as the front door opened.

"Mr. and Mrs. Jameson?" Iris called.

"In here," my mom called.

Iris stepped into the kitchen and my hopes soared, only to

plummet even deeper than before as her eyes passed right over me. "Still nothing?"

"Still nothing," my father said.

Iris nodded. She gave my mom a hug. She didn't even glance my way.

I walked out before the tears could force their way back.

✻

I HID myself among the hydrangea bushes on the side of the house. Not that there was any point. Anyone walking by could apparently see me, just like the guy in the train. Or the man with the peeling skin on the street corner.

Anyone but the most important people in my life.

I sat for what felt like hours until all the sunlight drained from the lawns and the streetlamps came on. Until thunderclouds growled overhead, opened up, and dumped rain on me.

Flippin' great.

I squeezed my knees tighter into my chest as I began feeling weak and lousy as I always did. I had no idea where to go. I could stay here. I could obviously physically touch things. But the thought of hanging around while my parents mourned my absence was too painful to bear.

I hung my head between my legs, on the verge of feeling sorry for myself.

I sensed the presence of someone else. I looked up to find Jasper standing over me. He hadn't made a sound as he approached. His hands were thrust into his pockets, red eyes slightly glowing in the dusk.

"It's a curse," he said. His tone was strangely soft. Maybe even...consoling? "The same magic that sends us to the Loft also keeps our loved ones from seeing us."

"How?" I managed to say.

He shrugged. "Ancient magic. It just knows which ones we're closest too. Which ones will hurt us the most."

That didn't make me sad; that made me furious. "But *why?* Why me? Why do that at all? What's the point?"

Jasper looked as though he was going to answer. Then his expression hardened. "If you come back to the Loft, you might help us figure it out. But I doubt it."

"Gee, thanks for the vote of confidence."

"Just being honest. You don't have a clue about our world. I could see it on your face. And all of us there? We've been stuck a long time."

I moved my legs to get some feeling back into them. They trembled a bit as I pushed myself into a crouch.

The corners of Jasper's lips tilted down further. "Don't expect me to carry you."

"Don't expect you to be a nice guy, either," I snapped. "And I can't go back with you. I'm not one of you."

"One of what?"

I waved a hand in the air, not believing he didn't get it. "What you were growling at me about earlier. Magical. Paranormal. A vampire."

Jasper let out a deep chuckle, though there was something primal and not funny at all in it. He continued giving me a humorless grin, showing every bit of those sharp teeth. "I wasn't being entirely truthful earlier. The thing is, if you were sent to us, it means you're not human, either."

CHAPTER FOUR

I slept like the dead.

I realize the irony in that.

Despite his insistence that he wasn't going to help me, more than once Jasper steadied me on the way back to the Loft. The rain had really done a number on my strength. The rain and, well, pretty much everything else. A couple times I must have fallen asleep, only to wake up with him supporting me as the L train rocked. I watched his eyes scan the nearly empty car, but for what I didn't know.

Call me crazy, but during those times I'd felt...safe. I thought vampires were supposed to be cold, but he was warm, and smelled slightly of pine and petrichor, like he'd just emerged from running through the woods after a rainstorm.

Then he'd noticed me looking at him and quickly leaned me against the center railing, lips tilting down into their usual frown.

"Get ahold of yourself. You're acting like a drunk."

My hero, ladies and gents.

Somehow (I'm not admitting Jasper helped me anymore), I made it back. Ari immediately directed me to a room they had set aside. I'd flopped face down on top of the plush comforter and fallen asleep.

Now that I was awake, not even a lingering headache could keep me from noticing how nice the room I'd slept in was. Clean, bright, with windows overlooking one of the quieter side streets of Cliffside's downtown. There wasn't a single sentimental item in sight, though. I should have grabbed a plushie from my room. Maybe two.

The thought of my room, my parents, my old life, threatened to overwhelm me, so I shoved all of it to the back of my mind and focused on the here and now.

I cleaned myself up in the bathroom. Used some makeup that someone (probably Ari; I couldn't imagine Jasper being that thoughtful) had left. Finally I threw my hair in its usual messy ponytail and called it done.

I took a moment to stare at my reflection in the mirror. Other me looked exhausted, definitely a little scared. But I was here. And I'd take things one at a time. Before I'd fallen asleep, I'd heard Ari tell me to meet them in the Gargoyle's Roost when I was ready. I hoped the name was just an artistic choice. But with how the last couple days had gone I'd have to be prepared for anything.

My stomach growled.

Right. I needed food first.

I left my room and almost immediately got lost in the maze of hallways. It was clear this "Loft" place wasn't broken up like any downtown apartments I knew of. My room was one of many, set in a cluster of hotel-style hallways full of windows that every so often gave me a view of a central lobby of sorts one floor below.

More than once I felt eyes on me, only to find nobody there when I turned around. Jasper had mentioned there were others living here, but the place appeared deserted. Still, I couldn't shake the feeling I wasn't as alone as I thought.

The feeling of being watched came back. I turned again and

spotted a pair of eyes staring at me from the crack in the door of the nearest room.

"Uh...hi?" I said hesitantly.

The eyes continued staring. I could make out a shaggy head of hair clamped down with headphones, lit up from the glow of screens behind him. He still didn't speak; just kept watching me. I began to grow a little nervous. Surely they wouldn't let anybody *dangerous* in here, right?

"Do you know where breakfast is?" I said. "I'm new here and kind of starv—"

The door slammed shut. From somewhere else in the Loft I heard a loud screech. What might have been a battle cry. Or a scream.

I'd...just keep moving, then.

I eventually found my way downstairs to the central living room. And I had to admit, from down here, the place looked pretty cool. Exposed wooden beams crisscrossed the arched ceiling. Expansive windows shouldered either side, each letting in a view of both Cliffside's skyline and the shoreline. Two couches had been shoved together along with bean bag chairs in front of an immense fireplace that two of me stacked on top of each other could have stood in. Finally, a kitchen on the other end tied the whole thing together, complete with a bar on one side.

I didn't have a clue where I'd ended up, but if these were the perks, I could get used to that.

I dug around in the kitchen's refrigerator—fully stocked with every kind of food I could imagine—searching for something that looked good. There was a baggie of celery sticks with COLLETE'S—DON'T TOUCH, ELF sharpied neatly on the front. Stroopewafels, which definitely didn't need to be refrigerated, were beside them with RODGE taped on the front. I could see Ari had left pre-mixed protein shakes sitting in the door.

I looked for anything with Jasper's name on it, before remembering that his snack of choice likely came with two running legs attached.

I shuddered and grabbed a yogurt drink as I closed the door. It wasn't much, but it'd tide me over until I could get some answers.

I chugged down the yogurt as I walked around the rest of the room. I spotted a slab of rock over the fireplace I hadn't noticed at first. It was made of a rich obsidian, fitted into the surrounding rock like it'd come built into the place. Two lines of familiar text were etched in fiery letters on its face:

The Thirteenth one shall be the key
The remedy to Outcasts' strife

That'd been the same thing those stupid witches had said to me. I had the strange, unsettling feeling they thought *I* was this thirteenth one. This "remedy.".

Yeah, right.

Directly beneath the text was a faint symbol: it was tough to make out, but I could have sworn it looked like a jagged Y. Or football posts. Or a wishbone.

I needed answers. To all of this.

I polished off the rest of the drink and took the second set of stairs back upstairs. I had no clue where the Gargoyle's Roost was, but I imagined it'd be above me. I didn't see any more eyes peering out from the doorways I passed, but I did hear voices as I reached the fourth floor. A door at the end was open, directly opposite a second kitchen.

"You seem more worried than usual," Ari said. Her words were followed by a loud *thunk*. "This isn't the first time a new outcast has shown up."

"No, but it's the last time," Jasper said. "She's the thirteenth."

I peeked in, being careful to stay out of sight. It was obvious this was a planning room of some sort, with an enormous table in the center and whiteboards all around. In one corner were piles of books, candles, and other things I could only guess the use to.

Jasper stood at the windows on the other side of the table, hands in his pockets. Ari lounged in one of the chairs, tossing knives into the already badly scarred wall.

"And you think she's this 'key?'" Ari said. She threw another knife. *Thunk.* "The one the prophecy talks about?"

"No idea. Surprisingly, two lines and years of debate among the other paranormal leaders haven't made it any clearer. I do know that word of her arrival is already spreading."

"*How?*" Ari said. "She just got here."

"I'm guessing somebody on the outside has eyes and ears on us at all times. The Northern Pack and the Deathless want answers. Even the Horde is trying to get involved, and they don't care about anyone other than themselves."

"Not much different than the others, then." Ari sighed, balancing another knife on the tip of her finger. "They all know to leave us alone. We'll handle them like we always have."

Jasper turned away from the window, muttering under his breath. His face was drawn, uncertain. "I thought when the last outcast arrived we'd finally have answers, not more questions. Now I'm more confused than ever."

"Don't get all growly," Ari said. "It's not her fault. Remember how you were when you first got here?"

"And you?" Jasper shot right back.

Ari grinned. "Exactly. We all start somewhere. I'm sure she's powerful. But also ignorant, untrained—"

"And right here," I said, unable to listen in any longer. "I want answers."

"*Jasper,*" Ari said, grinning at him. "She snuck up on you!"

Jasper glared at me like it was my fault his vampiric senses or whatever had failed him. "I was distracted."

"What were those groups you were talking about?" I said, not willing to let them get off topic. "I'm the thirteenth what?"

"Outcast," Jasper said.

"It's what we call ourselves," Ari explained. "Or what the other groups call us. I can't remember which it is. We're the Outcasts of all groups, belonging to none but ourselves."

"The other groups of what?" I said.

Jasper's eyes narrowed. "You know what."

I swallowed hard. "I do, but I want to hear you say it."

"You—" Jasper started.

"Paranormals," Ari said.

Of course. *That.* "Like vampires and witches and—"

Ari stood and changed right before my eyes. One second she was there, a normal—well, semi-normal—two-legged human. The next, a cheetah stood in her place, lean and fierce-looking.

My mouth dropped open. The cheetah's lips quirked up in what might have been a cat-like smile. *"Shifters. Yep."*

I heard her voice in my mind, clear as if she'd been standing beside me.

Ari did a sudden, lightning-fast sprint around the room, then rose on her back legs and in an instant was human again, clothes and all. Thankfully.

"I should have done my morning workout," Ari complained. "I feel as energetic as a coked-up weasel."

"Right..." I drew the word out. "And shifters. Are there any other paranormals I should be worried about?"

"Oh, plenty. There are lots more kinds of paranormals like us," Ari said cheerily, unaware that she was shattering the final fragments of my previous reality.

"And some of you are here, in this Loft."

"There are twelve of us who live here," Jasper said, clearly impatient that they weren't explaining this fast enough. "Now thirteen."

"The Outcasts," I said.

"The Outcasts," he agreed. "Some from the same paranormal race. Others..." He continued staring at me, daring me to fill in the blank.

"And what am I?" I said.

Ari shot Jasper a worried look that she quickly tried to conceal with a smile once she noticed I was watching. "We're not entirely sure yet. But it's no big. We weren't totally certain Rodge was a dhampir until a few days after he'd arrived. Even he didn't know."

That wasn't the most reassuring thing to hear. Whoever this Rodge guy was, I had a feeling he'd at least known this entire magical world existed before he'd been thrown into it.

I caught Jasper staring at me and resolutely stared back until he smirked and walked over to one of the white boards. I was sure that my ignorance about all of this was one of the main reasons he disliked me so much.

The rest...I didn't know. He was just a jerk.

"I know you think I'm this key or whatever," I said. "But I honestly have no idea what I'm supposed to do."

"None of us do," Jasper said. That made me feel a little better at least. "An ancient coven of witches cast an immensely powerful spell to create the Outcasts. Each of us in some way nearly died before being chosen and sent back here."

I choked. "Wait, you all *died*, like me, to get here?"

"Nearly," Ari amended. She shrugged. "But for whatever reason, the witches and their curse thought we should be here."

"And now you're trapped," I said softly. "And you can't see your closest loved ones."

Jasper's arms tensed as he squeezed the end of the table. "Yeah. As you saw, as an Outcast we can still interact with the world like we used to." He threw me a sardonic glare. "But we can't interact with our loved ones. We can't talk to the people who mattered most to us in our old life."

I jumped as the table cracked. Jasper quickly let go of it.

"Great. I just replaced that after Leon's display during the last meeting," Ari complained.

Jasper grunted. He uncapped a marker and started writing. "Listen up. I'm not going to repeat this: Because we came so close to death, we have a better connection with the Horde—the race of the undead—and other specters like them. The other paranormal groups like the Northern Pack of shifters and the Deathless vampires understand and respect our...*unusual* position."

"Usually," Ari said, leaning against the table, arms crossed, one eyebrow cocked. "The fact that the Loft is stuffed to the brim with protective hexes, geas, and charms probably helps."

"True," Jasper said. He finished writing the names of the other paranormal groups on the board. "They leave us alone, and occasionally call on us to help with various odd jobs."

"So, what, you guys, like, run errands for them?" I said.

"In a manner of speaking," Ari said. "Them and other paranormals not associated with any group. It's not glamorous but it keeps us busy, and many of the Outcasts have magical abilities stronger than most. Up until you arrived, we were also spending time searching for clues to answer the prophecy."

"But you got nothing," I said.

A muscle in Jasper's jaw twitched. "Obviously. Don't suppose you have any bright ideas? Maybe an answer or two from those fiery hands of yours?"

I looked down at them. "No. Not really."

Ari put a comforting hand on my shoulder. "Don't worry, we're not expecting you to know everything. We've waited this long. We can wait a little longer."

"Maybe not." Jasper had turned back to the board. He circled the three main groups and began drawing lines off them. "Like I said, now that she's here—"

"Riley," I said, glaring at him. "The name's Riley."

"—there's an expectation for something to happen. The Conclave has been patient with us, but they won't be for too much longer. With all thirteen of us present, they'll want us to split our allegiances soon."

"You already know what the other Outcasts think about that," Ari said. "Shifter, vamp, whatever, we stick together."

There was so much passion in Ari's voice that, despite being as confused as I'd ever been, I couldn't help feeling a strange sense of pride, too. Jasper had the personality of a venomous cactus, but he and Ari truly seemed to care about the group. A group of which I was slowly acknowledging I'd become a part.

"I'll help you figure this prophecy out," I said, stepping up to the white board.

Jasper glared at me. "You'd better—"

"*Thank you*, Riley," Ari said, giving me a little hug. "We've looked for ways to solve it, but now that you're here, things should start making more sense."

I gave her a weak smile, hoping that was true. And hoping that whatever I did would eventually help me and the others see their loved ones again.

I looked at the different groups Jasper had written, then to the blank circles beneath which he'd drawn lines. "What are those for?"

Jasper tapped the marker against the board, still staring at me. His vampiric gaze was so intense I could feel my skin heating up before he finally turned away. "There's something we're missing. Remember that assassin last month, Ari?"

I perked up. "Hold up, *assassin?*"

"How could I forget?" Ari said, unflustered. She pulled up her left sleeve to reveal an angry red slash on her forearm that looked a little fresher than her scars. "Nearly got me a couple times."

"Wait, I thought you said the other paranormals respected the Outcasts," I said, my voice coming out thin.

"Most. Not all," Jasper said. "There are some against the entire idea of prophecies and Outcasts. Some who think we're holding on to some secret power we refuse to share with anyone else."

Oh, wonderful.

"Jasper, I told you that guy was just an outlier," Ari said. "Not every paranormal's associated with a group. They can't monitor what rogues will do."

Jasper grunted. He continued tapping the empty circle. "Now that she—Riley—" he added, catching my eye, "is here, and word's getting out, it'll be interesting to see if attacks like this increase. And if there's something more behind it."

"I'm not sure interesting is the right word," I said.

"You're paranoid," Ari sighed to him.

"You're too trusting," Jasper said. "She's intrigued a lot of very dangerous and important paranormals. Riley."

I blinked and Jasper was right in front of me, his eyes mesmerizing up close. I remembered reading in some books that vampires had the ability to compel you to answer them and follow their every command. I wondered if that held true in reality.

"Personal space," I said, pushing back against his hard chest. "It's a thing."

"How did you nearly die?"

"Whoa, let's not go digging into that just yet," Ari said. "I'm sure it's still a sore subject—"

"A creep stabbed me," I said, unflinchingly meeting Jasper's gaze. If this was his attempt to rattle me, then it wouldn't work. "Multiple times while we were at the fair you were stalking me at."

"And had you seen him before?"

"Of course not."

"And did he seem keenly interested in you?"

"Of course not..." I paused. When I thought back to it, like really considered it, I couldn't deny that it was a possibility. Iris had been gone a while before I ever showed up, and yet my attacker hadn't managed to hurt her. Or hadn't tried to. I could almost believe that he'd waited for me to arrive before locking the door behind us.

"He...might have been," I admitted. Jasper shot Ari a triumphant look. She rolled her eyes.

"There's no way he could have known she was an Outsider, or even a paranormal. *She* didn't even know."

"Still, something's up." Jasper wrote *Assassin* in one of the empty circles. "We should tell all the Outcasts to be on alert until I figure this out."

A door slammed. I heard rapid, stomping footsteps heading our way right before a girl burst into the room.

At first I thought a model had somehow missed the runway and wound up here. She was inhumanly beautiful, wearing tight workout clothes that hugged her perfectly proportioned body. Her lips were the color of ice chips, her blonde hair straight as a sheet with not a split end in sight.

"Collette," Ari said. "We didn't know you were back."

"Hey," I said, extending a hand. "I'm Riley—"

"So you're it?" the girl said, and my mind immediately switched to, *Crap, not another one.*

"The thirteenth key or whatever?" Collette went on. Her eyes scanned me up and down. She was so beautiful that for the first time in a while I found myself strangely self-conscious of every wrinkle in my clothes and every frizzy strand of hair out of place.

"I guess I am," I said coolly.

"Then go ahead, break us from this curse." Collette flourished one hand in the air. "Tell off those old, dead crones who did this to us." When I didn't answer she stepped closer to me. "I don't even feel any of your magic. What are you?"

I stood up straighter. "I'm not sure yet."

"What powers do you have?"

"I'm...not sure yet."

"Do you have a clue about the Grand Laws? Do you plan to

call a Conjunction? What if the Conclave tries to move against our little enclave? What will you do then?"

What, what, and what?

"That's enough, Collette," Jasper said. "Did Maxime take your celery sticks again?"

I shot him the side-eye. Not that I wasn't grateful he was defending me, but the gesture was pretty rich coming from him.

Collette stepped back, smirking. "She's totally clueless. And we're totally screwed."

She turned, waving over her shoulder. "Hope you guys like the way things are now, 'cause it's not changing anytime soon."

She walked out.

"Goodie, another member of my fan club," I muttered.

CHAPTER FIVE

A ri and Jasper had to head out on some mysterious errand right after, so I spent the rest of the day wandering the house, avoiding Model Girl and trying to figure out what type of paranormals she and the rest of the Outcasts could be.

Jasper: vampire, obviously. Ari was a cheetah shifter. I hadn't known there were any other kinds of shifters outside of were-wolves, but then, a list of what I did know about the paranormal world could possibly fill a sticky note. A very small sticky note.

I'd have to learn. And fast.

The next morning I continued meandering the halls, senses partially on alert in case I ran into Collette again. I'd spotted her earlier that morning up in the Loft's massive gym-slash-sparring room (complete with an eclectic choice of non-lethal practice weapons) and steered clear ever since. The house seemed *way* bigger on the inside than it looked from the out. I'd found a game room, a *third* kitchen, an enormous garage that could probably fit ten cars, and a rooftop terrace that any of my high school friends would have loved to throw parties on. The entire place was a monstrosity. Some real estate agent had made a killing.

I didn't spot any of my new housemates until later that

morning when I went down to the kitchen to grab breakfast. I was surprised to find a dining table in the center of the living room. The table had already been set, a plate piled high with croissants and bagels in the center. In the kitchen, Ari was chopping up fruit and putting it into a bowl.

"Mornin'!" she said when she saw me. "Hope you like your breakfast processed, because it was Leon's turn to do the shopping and that guy has no clue what a proper diet is."

"Can I help?" I said.

"Sure can. Stir that oatmeal. Should be close to done."

I went over to the stove and stirred the pot that'd started to bubble. Ari finished the fruit and started pouring orange juice. "Miss Maisy, our goblin housekeeper, usually cooks, but I like to do it every so often. It centers me, you know?"

"I totally get it," I agreed. I used to help my dad cook on the rare mornings I got up early enough before school. We'd crack jokes and he'd juggle eggs, only stopping when he'd drop one on the floor or mom walked in and gave him the stink-eye.

Spooning the oatmeal, pouring my drink, sliding a bagel into the toaster, all normally mundane things had a strangely calming effect on me now. I felt tears of what I'd lost threaten to come up again, but I wiped them away and helped Ari bring the last of the breakfast over to the table.

"There's a lot here," I said when we finally sat down. "I didn't really see too many of the others around."

"Some are out and about," Ari said. "Others are abroad and you won't see them for a while. Unless there's an Outcast emergency, we all kind of have our own schedules."

She dug into the oatmeal and washed it down with a swig of her protein shake. "But the ones who are here will eat, picking away at it during the day like the vultures they are."

Sure enough, I was halfway through my fruit when Collette walked in. I tensed, prepared to snap back against another verbal lashing, but she barely spared me a glance as she took a bowl, loaded it up with exactly three strawberries, and started to walk off.

"Where's Sienna?" Ari asked, clearly not expecting her to stay.

Collette shrugged. "Dunno. Probably *swimming.*" She couldn't help shooting me one last glare. I did the mature thing and made a face at her.

"She's not usually like that," Ari assured me when Collette had left.

"I'm not taking it personally," I said, really trying not to take it personally. "It's probably been a while since you guys have had a new Outcast."

"It has," Ari agreed. Her ears perked. I heard a small noise and turned in time to see a slim shadow retreat back into the darkness of the hallway upstairs.

"Sawyer, come out and meet our new friend," Ari said.

Sawyer remained hidden. I wondered if it was the same person who'd been peeking out at me yesterday.

"*Sawyer,*" Ari said.

"It's fine, really," I said. "I'm sure I'll meet everyone eventually."

Ari gave an exasperated sigh. "Sure. Sawyer's always like that so it's whatever. But the others…"

I felt a prickle on the back of my neck and looked up as Jasper appeared directly beside me, reaching over my right shoulder for a glass of orange juice. I resisted the urge to jump at his sudden nearness, but he must have been able to tell he'd spooked me because he flashed a devilish grin. "Got you."

"No, you didn't."

"Your heartbeat says otherwise." He leaned in closer. "I can *hear* it."

"Trying to get back at me for sneaking up on you yesterday? That's petty."

Jasper merely took a sip of the orange juice and began sauntering out.

"Oh no you don't." Ari stood. "We're all going to sit and have breakfast as a *family*."

Jasper cocked a lazy eyebrow at all the empty chairs. "Maybe another time, Ari. The bayside centaurs need some help finding one of their missing foals. I'll probably be back tomorrow."

I glanced out the window as Jasper left and Ari sat back with a defeated sigh. "He goes out during daylight? I thought vampires, you know, combusted if they did that."

"Jas is a little different from most vampires," Ari said. She speared one of the strawberries violently with her fork. "There are two types of vampires; the Bloodsworn and the Forsworn. Jas is a Forsworn. He's stronger than most normal vampires and can resist sunlight almost as well as a human. He also drinks magic instead of blood."

"Wait, magic, like...the kind we have?"

Ari paused with a strawberry nearly to her mouth. "Technically. But he doesn't do it to any of us. He doesn't talk much about how he feeds. I only know he'd never hurt anybody to do it."

"I didn't know vampires even had a choice on what to eat."

"It's not an easy existence," Ari said. "Most who try to forgo blood and change end up dying in the process. Most never even attempt it."

I looked at where Jasper had disappeared. "Did he say why he did it?"

Dishes scraped as Ari scooped hers up. "He told me, but we've been friends for a while. If he wants to, he'll tell you."

Somehow, I doubted that would happen.

※

I CLEANED up my own dishes and headed back to my room. I'd nearly made it when I turned the corner and ran face first into someone hurrying the other way. Cold water splashed my front, shocking me.

"*Oof!* Sorry, didn't see you—" The girl paused, mouth agape, as I stumbled away from her. She was completely drenched from head to toe. "Britches and brimstone—you're the new girl!" she said in an airy, breathless voice. "The thirteenth Outcast or whatever that dusty old prophecy says."

"Yes…" I said warily, still a bit shocked from the sudden encounter.

The girl let out a shrill squeal of delight and embraced me in a hug, ensuring that every spot she hadn't soaked on first contact was wet now. "Sweet, sweet, sweet! About time there's another girl here my age. Ari's awesome, but she's, like, intense sometimes, you know? And Collette…"

The girl wrinkled her nose. "Well, if you've met Collette, you know she can be a little snippy sometimes."

"I've met Collette," I said. "Believe me, I get it. I'm Riley."

"Sienna Landry," the girl said. "Fourth Outcast and witch extraordinaire."

She must have just noticed we were both wet because she waved her hand and I was immediately dry again. Another wave and she was dry, too, freeing the multicolored strands of her hair. She smoothed out the frills of her dress over her jeans. I could smell something on her; incense or candles and a hint of chalk, like she'd been near a bunch of blackboards.

"I was just coming back from swimming," Sienna said.

"I didn't know there was a pool," I said, then clamped my mouth shut before I could follow up with, "Do you often dress up to go swimming?"

"Yeah…" Sienna said, sounding like she knew what I wasn't asking. "It's, uh, a private pool. Anyway, you're new here. Let's grab a drink."

Decision made, she latched herself onto my arm and pulled me back the way I'd come.

❦

"They can all see you, you know."

Sienna broke into my thoughts as I gazed around the café we'd taken a seat at, only a little way down the street from the Loft. Sienna had ordered tea and a heaping breakfast platter of eggs and potatoes, which she'd promptly sprinkled more herbs onto from a little bag tied at her waist. I'd only gotten hot chocolate and clutched it while I continued staring at everyone else. I hadn't been an Outcast very long, and learning that we could still leave the Loft and do seemingly normal things was a huge relief.

"I did the same thing, too, when I first got here." Sienna dug into her eggs. Her earrings glinted in the sunlight. "My sisters and mothers of the Coven couldn't see me so I thought I was practically invisible. Stuck in the between, you know? So I stripped and went running down the middle of Birch street."

I choked into my hot chocolate. Sienna grinned like that was exactly the reaction she'd been hoping for. "Yeah, people saw me. Leon and Ari won't let me live it down, either. See, your transition is already better than mine."

Pretty low bar to set, but I was cool with it. I wiped my mouth, chuckling. "I don't think anyone told me about that. I think I would have remembered."

"It was a while ago," Sienna said dismissively.

"Really? How long?"

Sienna took another large bite of her eggs, chewing thoughtfully before washing it down with a swig of tea. "Must be going on ten years now."

"Wait." I peered closer at her. I knew a little more about witches than I did the other paranormal creatures. At least I thought I did. There were the crackly ancient ones who danced around bonfires and cast prophecies, and then there were those like Sienna, the ones who could steal youth and bewitch humans.

"You don't look any older than me. Were you a kid when you got here?"

"The Outsiders don't age," Sienna said.

"Oh. Wow." I took another sip, thinking over that. "So you can't age, you can't see your loved ones, you can't leave…"

"We can leave," Sienna insisted. "Daniel, Andres, and Maxime travel all over the world, and Kaia spends most of her time with the Horde. But they're always drawn back here eventually. Something about being an Outcast, I suppose. The Loft and the magic here calls to you. I suppose it's part of the curse. It's not *all* bad," she said, seeing my dour expression. "At least we have each other. I'd have hated to be Jasper."

"I wouldn't say that," I said, remembering his little prank earlier that morning. "He seems to like being himself plenty enough."

"True." Sienna laughed. "But he was also the first Outcast, Ari said. She didn't arrive for a few more years after. Can you imagine that, trying to figure all this stuff out by yourself?"

I couldn't imagine. If that were me, I may have gone a little crazy like Sienna had. When I looked at Jasper that way, it was almost understandable why he was a bit rough around the edges. Almost.

"Well, now that I'm here, maybe I can help," I said. "I don't know *how*, but I'll try."

"Oh, that'd be amazing!" Sienna said. "Any clues yet?"

I thought back to something Jasper had said. "The prophecy has to have some answers. But other than that…" I leaned over the table, lowering my voice. "Jasper told me a little about how the other paranormals view the Outcasts. He also said there have been a couple assassins."

Sienna swallowed a particularly large swig of tea. "Well…I mean…assassin is a strong word…"

"Have there been?"

43

"I wouldn't call them assassins. More like outsiders. We didn't want to scare you."

I wasn't scared. Not exactly. Maybe Jasper was right and these groups that wanted us gone needed to do it for a reason. Maybe there was something we hadn't discovered yet. Something they didn't want us to know.

Sienna was peeking around the crowded café like the next assassin would pop up from behind a menu. "There have been a few attacks against us over the years, but nothing we can't handle."

"Collette said something about a Conclave. Well, she more like yelled it at me. But could they know anything that might be able to help us...?"

Sienna was shaking her head hard, making strands of her multicolored hair flick around her face. "The Conclave's just the governing body of the three biggest paranormal groups in Cliffside. They wouldn't know anything more than we do, and honestly, you don't want to get them involved."

"I got the feeling the Conclave was supposed to help you guys?"

"Technically..." Sienna sighed. "Paranormals or not, we all have human tendencies. That's to say some of us definitely have ulterior motives. That goes double for those in the Conclave. Each of the races there are always looking for ways to expand their influence."

"And what about the Grand Laws?"

Sienna wrinkled her nose like the idea of anything involving rules put her off. "That's right, you wouldn't know about those. They're the laws all paranormals follow, no matter if they're rogue, part of a group, whatever. And if you break them..."

She trailed off, leaving the punishment up to my imagination. "The laws are pretty basic when you think about it. One, no revealing ourselves to mundanes—that means humans—without approval from the local Conclave. Two, no attacking mundanes.

And three, all paranormals stay on their own turf. Otherwise we'd have turf wars right and left. There are a couple more laws, but those are the big ones."

She waved a hand over her tea and it began to steam again. "I appreciate you taking this so seriously, but you've only been here a little bit. Take some time to settle in."

I knew Sienna meant well, but I couldn't do that. I was taking this like I'd been taught in self-defense—as much as *that* had helped me: adapt to the situation, act on the situation. I was stuck here and wouldn't get to see my family unless I did something. Even more than that, there were other Outcasts relying on me. Ones who had been kept away from those they cared about for much longer.

Sienna suddenly stood and waved over my shoulder. "Leon! Leeeooon!"

I turned to see a massive Samoan dude with a motorcycle helmet tucked beneath his arm making his way toward us. "Would you pipe down?" he grumbled as he reached us. "Believe it or not, some people want to eat in peace."

A Pe'a tattoo covered one of his massive arms. Fine hair draped across his head, some of it coming down the sides of his face to frame it like a mane. He didn't make me nervous exactly— the complete opposite, in fact—but like Jasper there was an underlying sense of something primal beneath his human exterior.

"Your name's Leon, so let me guess...Lion shifter?" I said.

Leon gave an approving growl. "What gave it away? The hair, or that my parents might as well have named me Simba and taken all the mystery out of it?"

I liked him immediately. Unlike a certain vampire I knew.

"Glad our thirteenth has arrived," Leon said, giving me a rough pat on the back. "Now those other paranormals can finally shut their traps."

"Was Yu giving you trouble again?" Sienna said sympathetically.

"Yu and his furry pests are always causing trouble. Every delivery I hear something new. This time it's that Lukas has lost patience with us. Says we're a waste of space and resources that they should do something about."

I swallowed. I didn't know who Lukas was, but it probably wasn't worth mentioning that someone had nearly done me in apparently trying to "do something about it." And Jasper didn't think they were finished.

"They won't mess with us," Leon went on. "Not when they find out what our thirteenth can do. Speaking of which, what *can* you do?"

I resisted shrinking under Sienna and Leon's expectant gazes. "Um, I'm not sure yet. I cast a little fire—but I can't really control it."

"Maybe you're a witch!" Sienna said.

"Huh. You didn't know you were a paranormal before you joined us?" Leon said.

I shook my head. "I always thought I was human."

"Huh," Leon said again, and I wasn't getting a good feeling from his reaction. "I'm sure Lukas won't mess with us. Probably. Maybe keep the fact that you thought you were human a secret. Some paranormals are weird about that. See you both later."

And before I could press him to explain what he meant, he put his helmet on and lumbered out.

※

THERE WAS a boy waiting outside the Loft's front door.

Sienna had gone around the outside to do a quick "ward check" since according to her, "Jasper and Ari were good at many things, but maintaining defensive wards isn't one of them."

"Can I help you?" I asked the guy.

46

He turned, flashing me an easy smile. He wore a jacket emblazoned with red and gold, his skin tan, muscles like ripcords where he'd pushed the sleeves up. His chocolate hair had been pulled into a short ponytail. "Thought I'd be stuck out here forever. You must be the new Outcast. I'm Hayes."

I shook his offered hand, trying to place him among the dozens of names of Outcasts and paranormals Sienna had thrown my way over breakfast. "Riley. Is it locked?"

"For me, yeah. I'm an idiot and forgot the charm to dispel the locking mechanism." He winked. "Think you could work your magic?"

"Can't help you much in the magic department, I'm afraid," I said, stepping past him and trying the door. Jasper or Ari must have given me whatever charm Hayes was lacking because it opened easily and I stepped inside. "Come on in."

"No magic whatsoever?" Hayes said, following me into the living room.

I bristled, expecting a reprimand but he sounded genuinely curious.

"I have some. Nothing too crazy," I said. "Some 'key' I've turned out to be, huh?"

"I guess that remains to be seen," Hayes said. His eyes scanned the empty living room. "Anyone else here?"

"Sienna's right behind me." I paused. Something about the way he looked around at everything felt off to me. He acted like someone who was seeing the inside of the Loft for the first time. "I don't think Jasper mentioned you."

Hayes shook his head. "Of course he didn't. I swear, you leave for a couple months and it's like you're dead to them."

I relaxed. They had said a few of the Outcasts traveled all over. Hayes must have been returning from a long trip and simply readjusting to being home.

"They've changed the place quite a bit since I was here last," Hayes said. "Where's the planning room again—"

"The weirdest thing," Sienna said as she stepped inside and closed the door. "Never seen a protective ward go down that fast—"

She froze when she spotted Hayes.

Hayes grinned at her. "Busted."

Then he pulled a knife and put it against my throat.

CHAPTER SIX

For a moment I seized, my mind slowly catching up with what was happening as Hayes wrapped his arm tighter around my throat, bringing the knife closer.

"Seriously?" I rasped as it became harder to breathe. I tried wedging my hands between his, buying me some room to breathe. "Another flippin' guy with a knife?"

"Just hold on, Riley!" Sienna had her hands up in what I guessed was a spellcasting stance, her eyes full of fear.

"Let's not do anything too hasty," Hayes said. He held the knife up as though we needed a reminder. I began trying to angle myself to break free, but his grip on me was strong.

"Let her go," Sienna said. I resisted rolling my eyes. Bless her, but was there any less effective thing to say to an attacker?

"I'm warning you…" Sienna's hands glowed with magic. "You dare hurt her and I'll mess that pretty face up real quick."

Hayes chuckled. I could feel him grin against the back of my head. "I wouldn't dream of hurting such lovely ladies such as yourself. I'm only here to send a message, that's all."

Sienna's eyes flickered to me. She seemed to be trying to tell me something. "Yeah? And what's that?"

"Is that a natural hair color?" Hayes said, and for a moment both Sienna and I stopped moving, dumbstruck. "Or did you dye it yourself?"

"Are you...an idiot?" I wheezed.

Hayes shrugged. "Just curious. Looks good on her. The highlights really bring out...well, everything, really."

Sienna shook from her stupor. The magic in her hands brightened to an angry red. "Let her go or I'll—"

I didn't wait for her to finish, biting down on Hayes' arm right before throwing my head back into his face. He grunted in pain. I forced my arms beneath his and broke free from his hold.

"You *bit* me," he said, lashing out with a kick I was forced to backpedal from.

"And you tried to cut my throat!" I said, spitting out the taste of his arm. "Call us even."

Hayes dodged as Sienna sent a couple bolts of magic at him. He fired a couple bolts of magic right back that exploded over my head, washing me in a burst of heat.

He was another witch. Wonderful.

While Sienna distracted him, I knocked over the dining table and took cover behind it. A moment later Sienna vaulted over to join me. "Nice going! He'll think twice about taking you hostage again." She launched a volley of spells at Hayes before crouching again. "He's got some moves. Pretty snappy spells, too. I think he's a warlock."

"Which means what?" I said, inching around the edge of the table to get a look at where Hayes was now.

"It means he can use magic, but he uses more charmed items than spells to conjure it."

I peeked out.

Only to immediately retreat as Hayes launched a spell at me and set the side of the table on fire.

"But he can use spells plenty, too," Sienna said.

I quickly batted out the flames that'd started creeping up one of my pant legs. "What was that about not hurting us?" I yelled.

"You haven't seen me try yet," Hayes yelled back. "I thought you said you had some magic. Seems the thirteenth Outcast isn't much more than a mundane."

I cringed. The way he said it made it sound like an insult.

"I'm in touch with a few people who'd be interested to know that," Hayes added.

"I can't get a good angle on him," Sienna said. "Think you could give me some cover?"

"With *what?*" I held up a broken chair leg.

"I meant with your magic."

"I can't use magic."

"That's not what Jasper said. He saw it. You just have to relax and concentrate. I know you can do it."

Another of Hayes' spells slammed against the table.

Relax. Right.

But I closed my eyes and took a deep breath, trying to center on that prickling feeling I'd felt right before I'd summoned my fire before. I could feel my skin start to grow hot, warming little by little. I focused on that, focused on the rising temperature.

Only to have it vanish.

I sank back, exasperated. "No good. Sorry."

Sienna patted my hand consolingly. "Chair leg it is, then."

"Wait." I spied one of the bean bag chairs, sitting lopsided just past the cover of the table. I scrambled around Sienna and pulled it beside me. "When I throw this, hit it."

Sienna understood. She leaned back, like a shooter preparing to nail a clay pigeon. "Go!"

I heaved the bean bag into the air, angling my throw so it went right toward where I assumed Hayes was. Sienna's spell streaked through the air and obliterated it, sending an obscuring cloud of beans in every direction.

I wasted no time in lobbing the chair leg in Hayes' direction, then sprinting to the kitchen while Sienna fired off more spells to keep him busy.

Talk about feeling useless. I hadn't been keen on having magic before, but it would have been really helpful now. Instead, I dug through the drawers until I came up with a chef's knife, grabbed the oatmeal pot from this morning, and charged back into the fight.

Hayes saw me coming and launched a spell my way, but it was way wide and I easily batted it aside with the pot. Maybe he *wasn't* trying to hurt us. Or maybe his aim sucked.

Sienna slid over the table and she and I advanced on him. "We've had enough fun for one day. I suggest you leave," I said. I held the pot and knife higher for emphasis.

"I haven't said my piece yet," Hayes said.

"Then start talking," Sienna said.

Hayes started to lower his hand, then lunged at Sienna, barely missing and cleaving the air beside her. I'd anticipated it and sprinted at him, my own knife nearly cutting across his arm as he spun out of the way too fast for me to follow. Like my earlier fight, I was unprepared for this one, and a second later I found myself pushing back atop Sienna, Hayes looming over us with his knife pointed at my chest.

"This is the message: disband the Outcasts. Each of them needs to join their proper paranormal group or there will be consequences."

"If we do that, do I get to be in your group?" Sienna groaned, trying to move from beneath me. "You've got some pretty good moves. I wouldn't mind watching you work."

"Sienna!" I hissed. "Fight him, don't flirt with him!"

Hayes grinned. I gripped the pot tighter and leapt up, swinging toward him but Hayes moved out of range. I blinked and he was gone. The front door slammed.

"Well. That could have gone better," Sienna said.

I waited a moment to make sure Hayes was truly gone before

helping her up. "Did he really mean that?" I said. "About us having to abandon the Outcasts?"

"Maybe." Sienna dusted off her skirt. She saw my expression. "Don't worry, it's not the first message we've gotten like that."

She whistled as she took in the damage. I nudged a scored armchair with my foot. There was a gasp behind us.

Ari stood in the doorway, tank top slightly sweaty like we'd just interrupted an intense workout. I realized only then just how bad the carnage must have looked.

"What...What..." Her blazing eyes seared into us. "Start. Explaining."

CHAPTER SEVEN

On the count of three, I helped Ari heave the dining room table back up. There were multiple ugly scorch marks across the top, and what might have been a missing chunk of wood in the leg where I'd dug my nails in. For a guy who'd claimed he hadn't wanted to hurt us, Hayes' attacks said otherwise.

"It's not too bad," I said optimistically. "The damage gives it…character."

Ari grunted. She shifted into her cheetah form and started brushing up the beaded entrails of the bean bag with her tail. I retrieved a broom from a nearby closet and helped her.

"Miss Maisy's going to have a fit when she sees this," Ari said when she'd shifted back.

"I'm so sorry," I said, feeling terrible. "I'm the one who let him in. I'm guessing he needed an Outcast's permission to bypass the wards."

"It's not your fault," Ari said, some of the bite draining out of her voice. "You didn't know."

"No, she didn't."

Collette stomped inside, nearly letting the front door slam on

Sienna who followed right behind her. "And that's gonna get us all killed."

"Don't be so dramatic, Collette," Sienna said, glowering at her. "We were fine."

Collette daintily rubbed one of the singed parts of the carpet with the toe of her shoe. "Obviously. She's ignorant and entitled and she let him inside without checking to make sure he was even one of us. How do we know she's not a spy?"

"I'm *not* a spy," I said. "And I'm not entitled. I don't even know what I'm entitled to!"

Collette threw her hands up. "Exactly! And you don't know who the hell is even supposed to live here—"

"Enough!" Ari's words sounded more like a warning growl. She glared at the two of us, which I found a bit unfair. I'd screwed up, I knew it. But I also couldn't be expected to take verbal abuse without defending myself.

"Collette, Sienna, thank you for resetting the outer defenses. Hopefully they won't be tested anytime soon," Ari said.

"Yeah, *hopefully*," Collette said, giving me a look that made me want to calmly strangle her.

"I'm going to talk to Riley now," Ari said. When neither girl moved, Ari nudged her head. "Alone. Go on."

Collette let out a huff and gave a professional-grade eyeroll. "Whatev."

Sienna crossed her arms, remaining firmly in place as Collette left. "Whatever you need to talk about, I can hear it, too. After all, I was fighting, too."

I felt a rush of gratitude toward her. Ari was fair. I doubted I was in any serious trouble; but still, it wasn't like I wanted to face this alone.

"Very well," Ari said. "Riley, the guy that just attacked you…"

"Hayes," I said. "He said his name was Hayes."

"Hayes," Sienna reiterated, albeit in a much dreamier voice than mine.

"Sure, Hayes," Ari said. "I'm thinking it's a little too convenient that he showed up so soon after you arrived. I want to know, was he the same person who attacked you at the fair?"

"What?" Sienna said.

I totally hadn't thought of that. Despite his stated mission, he definitely seemed like he'd been trying to kill me. He'd had a knife. But even though my memory of the attack was sparse, I was pretty sure the man who'd gone after Iris and me had been wearing a hood, and what part of his face I'd seen had looked mushy. Then again, Hayes could have modified it with magic. I was sure that was possible.

"I'm not sure," I admitted.

"It couldn't have been him," Sienna said. "Hayes was probably here because Riley's the thirteenth Outcast. How would he know who she was before that?"

"That's what has me worried," Ari said, thinking. "Because if Hayes *was* the same attacker..."

"It means that he knew who I was before I did," I finished.

"That's crazy!" Sienna said. "None of us knew we were special before we were chosen as Outcasts, and only the witches determine that. You know, *after* we nearly die?"

The idea that somebody could have possibly had tabs on me, watching me, waiting to strike, made my skin crawl.

"Are there people who might know that?" I asked Ari.

"I don't see how. Then again, you are the key, so there might be stipulations to your presence here that don't apply to the rest of us. I'm not..." She finished with a shake of her head. "I just don't know. I'll have to ask Jasper when he gets back."

My stomach did an uncomfortable flip at the thought of stern Jasper learning what had happened. "Do you have to?"

Ari smirked as though she knew exactly what I was thinking. "He may act like a jerk sometimes, but he'll want to know. I promise he doesn't bite—" She stopped. "Well...never mind."

"I can ask Sawyer to look into people who might want to hurt Riley," Sienna said.

"That's a good start," Ari agreed. "In the meantime, until we get a handle on things, you need to stay in the Loft at all times, Riley, unless you're with someone else."

"What?" I practically exploded. The Loft was nice, sure, but I couldn't be trapped here. "I need to help search for clues to the prophecy. How can I do that from in here?"

"I get it," Ari said. "But now that we're on the alert, the only way someone could reach you is if you leave."

"That's a risk I'm willing to take."

"We'll *I'm* not. And I'd bet all the other Outcasts who are relying on you to solve this prophecy would agree with me!"

I couldn't believe what I was hearing. Ari was usually so level-headed; the older, wiser one amongst us. Couldn't she see that me sitting around doing nothing was the worst thing we could do right now?

"In case you forgot," I said. "I won't get to see my family again if I don't help. And not you or anyone else is going to stop me from that."

Ari's eyes turned to slits. "Believe me, I think you understand those consequences the least."

And then she stalked off before I could come up with a retort.

Sienna laughed nervously. "Staying away from the bad guys. That's not such a bad thing, right?"

I didn't answer. I was still too busy fuming.

"I know I shouldn't think so, but did you see how cute Hayes was?"

I threw Sienna an incredulous look, not unaware that her attempts at distracting me were working. "He tried to stab you, Sienna."

"I know," she said dreamily. "He was cute when he tried."

The front door opened and Leon walked in. He sniffed. His gaze brushed over the remnants of the destruction.

"Did I miss something?"

I stomped upstairs, too angry to answer.

THE GYM WAS WIDE OPEN the next morning. I was grateful Collette wasn't there. I didn't know what that girl's deal was, but I wasn't in the mood to butt heads with anyone at the moment. I'd lain awake most of the night stewing over the events of Hayes' attack and Ari's chastisement after.

I'd found some workout tights and a tank top in the dresser of my room. Both fit perfectly, which was nice and a little creepy that someone knew my size. Not that I had another choice. Apparently I wouldn't be leaving to buy my own clothes anytime soon.

I slammed my fist against the punching bag as I passed, heading for the cardio machines. The gym was divided up into the gym side with the weights and treadmills, and the sparring mat, practice weapons, and a jungle gym-looking apparatus I couldn't begin to guess the use to.

I looked at the practice weapons as I started up the treadmill. I needed to move. Needed to burn away these disgruntled thoughts and just exist in the moment of exercise ecstasy.

I ran until my breathing was ragged, my legs letting me know they'd make me pay later. As I stepped off, my eyes drifted back to the weapons. I didn't know the first thing about handling weapons. My self-defense had been focused on what we'd usually have on us at any given time. Which would not be...

I perused the rack. A sword. A staff. Was that a scimitar? And nunchucks?

Somebody's fighting tastes were...varied. I couldn't master all of them, but if I really was a target, it couldn't hurt to try to learn one.

I picked up the staff, which looked the easiest to use. A giant stick. No problem.

There was a scuffed, sad-looking practice dummy at the edge of the mat and I went at it with a fury, bashing every available inch I could hit. Apparently I wasn't completely gassed yet. My frustration at this entire situation fueled me. I whacked the dummy's chest like I was holding a baseball bat, then slid my hands up and jabbed it in the face. I could tell my form was crap, but it felt good all the same.

"I hope you're not pretending that's me."

Ari stood in the doorway of the gym watching me, her expression casual and yet uncertain.

"No." I gave the dummy another solid whack. "Of course not."

Ari grimaced. "Your grip is wrong. If you want to really hurt an inanimate object that's in no way a personification of me, you need a better hold." She walked over and held out a hand. "May I?"

I tossed it to her and she deftly caught it, spinning the staff around her body in something I would have called helicopter style. "Each weapon, no matter its shape, is an extension of yourself." She thrust her arms out in a stabbing motion, and I could see it, the staff in perfect alignment with her body. An extended reach of her attack.

I grabbed a second staff and tried to follow along as best I could. Ari was clearly a master, every move crisp, deliberate, and uniform. Even if she weren't already a shifter, I was convinced she could defend herself against anything.

"I'm glad you picked a weapon up," Ari said when we'd finished. "You'll have your magic to fight, but if that ever fails you'll want backup."

"You're assuming my magic will work," I said. I had a flashback to the fight against Hayes the day before. To how helpless and useless I'd felt.

"You'll get it," Ari said. "I'd teach you, but Jasper's much better. I'll let him."

"How'd you learn to fight so well?" I asked as Ari took our staffs and returned them to their spots. I threw her a towel from the rack on the wall. I saw a shadow cross her face.

"I learned in prison."

I was taken aback. Whatever I'd expected her to say, it hadn't been that.

Ari noted my expression. "Don't worry, I didn't kill anyone. Just got caught up with the wrong people at the wrong time. So they sent me to Blackveil Paranormal Prison."

"Wow." I wasn't sure what else to say. "That must have sucked."

"It wasn't all bad." Ari turned to show me one of the tattoos crawling across the left side of her ribs. The image of a snarling wolf with a raised paw. *Fang and Claw* was inked around the outside. "I found my own pack of sorts. Then I got mixed up with the wrong people again, got caught up in a prison riot, nearly died, and *poof!* Wound up here."

She gave me a toothy grin. "Personally, I'm not complaining about cutting my sentence short. These guys—the Outcasts— they're more family than any I've ever had."

"They mean a lot to you, don't they?" I said.

Ari fixed me with a hard look. "More than anything. Which is why..." She rubbed the back of her neck. "I'll admit, I overreacted yesterday."

"No, you were right," I said glumly.

Ari smirked. "Okay, we both suck. I was just scared, you know? I can't help thinking about someone killing you—killing any of the Outcasts."

"If someone really is after me, though, then it's probably best I stay put."

"We both know—at least *now* we both know—that's not possible," Ari said. "You need to be out there helping us solve this. I think you might be the only one who can help us solve this. The whole "key" thing, after all."

"I get it, but...I don't want to put any more of you guys in danger."

Ari put her hands on her hips. "Well that's tough, 'cause if someone really wants you gone, being out there or being in here isn't going to make a difference. Best we can do is mold you into a lean, mean, butt-kicking machine."

"Okay, so weapons with you and magic..." I suddenly had a hard time swallowing. "Is Jasper *really* the best one to teach me?"

"He's not a witch, but he gets the fundamentals of magic better than anyone I know," Ari said. "And don't worry. I'll teach you a few moves to use if he gets on your nerves. But while we're doing that, don't leave the Loft unless you have to. And always take one of us with you if you do. Oh, and don't draw any unnecessary attention to yourself."

"You mean like running naked down Birch street?"

Ari laughed. "Sienna told you, did she? Yeah, like that. We'll figure it out."

She punched me on the shoulder. Her eyes widened as I rubbed it. "Whoa, girl. And I thought I had some wicked scars."

I looked down at my right shoulder to see what she was pointing at. Along the top crest of my right shoulder, almost on my back, was a white scar etched into my skin.

"I forgot about that," I said. "I can't even remember where I got it. I might have always had it."

"Pretty sweet," Ari said appreciatively. "I'm sure there's a great story behind it."

I kept staring at it, for the first time looking at it with fresh curiosity. Something about its shape tickled my memory. Something about it looked...

"Holy crap," I gasped, suddenly realizing what it was.

Without another word I sprinted out of the gym, trying my best to remember the way through the maze of hallways. I was already one floor down before I noticed Ari in her cheetah form beside me, easily keeping pace with long, elegant strides.

"Care to fill me in?" she said.

"Living room!" I panted. "Where's the living room?"

"This way." Ari took a sharp right and less than a minute later I was thundering down the steps into the living room and screeching to a halt in front of the obsidian stone above the fireplace. Ari shifted beside me. "You're kind of freaking me out here. What's going on?"

"That." I pointed at the symbol beneath the second line of the prophecy. The one that could have been an ancient-looking Y or a pair of horns on a stick. The same symbol that was scarred on my shoulder.

"Dragon spit," Ari muttered, looking between them. "I never thought that meant anything."

I stepped around the armchair and approached the prophecy. The second my leg brushed the brick mantel a sharp bite of pain stung my shoulder. "Gah!"

"Riley?" Ari said concernedly.

I waved her off, the pain already subsiding. "I'm good. Just surprised me is all."

But Ari's eyes were widening on my arm. I looked down and saw why.

The symbol on my skin had begun multiplying, copying itself a dozen times over as it wound down my bicep and forearm and ended at a single glowing rune in the center of my palm. Each symbol glowed the same red and orange as the words of the prophecy. It took me a moment to realize they were pulsing to the beat of my heart.

I held up my arm and turned it over. "This doesn't hurt either. Though it's going to be a nightmare to explain if it doesn't go away."

"What do you think it's trying to tell us?" Ari said.

I looked up at the lone matching rune on the obsidian, then

down to the single one on my palm. "I'm not sure. But I'm going to find out."

"Riley…" Ari said as I stepped up the mantel and—after a brief hesitation—matched my palm to the glowing rune.

Heat immediately shot through me, flowing all the way to the tips of my toes before receding, leaving through my arms, taking all the new symbols with it until my skin was as clear as before. The rune on the prophecy vanished as fiery veins spread into new lines beneath the first two:

> *The Thirteenth one shall be the key*
> *The remedy to Outcasts' strife*
> *With blood of mortals, blood of old*
> *They ascend the ancients' throne*
> *And from the dark reveal the light*

I stepped down, head spinning. "Have you ever seen this?" I asked Ari.

It took a moment for her to stop gaping. "Never. We've never even come close to finding anything else out about the prophecy." She glanced at the scar on my shoulder. "And now I know why."

"So, the million-dollar question: what the heck does it mean?"

Ari stared at it a while longer before shaking her head. "I wish I knew. I could ask Sawyer or Jasper."

"Ask me what?"

As if summoned, Jasper appeared on the second-floor landing, peering down at us. If possible, he wore an even darker expression than usual. "We've got a problem."

"Jasper, look at the prophecy!" Ari said. "Look at what Riley discovered!"

Jasper's eyes flickered to the new, blazing words, but if Ari had been expecting an exclamation of joy then she'd be sorely disappointed. "We'll deal with it later."

63

"Later?" Ari said furiously. "This is the biggest clue we've had in years! What could possibly be more important?"

Jasper snared me with those unnaturally red eyes of his, and I knew I'd hate whatever he said next.

"The Conclave is more important. They've found out about the attack. They're demanding to see Riley."

CHAPTER EIGHT

Our small group was strangely quiet as we left the Loft and were absorbed into the city. I didn't know much about the Conclave, but if they could make the rest of the Outcasts this worried, well... They weren't anybody I was looking forward to meeting.

"So...any tips?" I asked as we waited at the bus stop.

Ari looked at Jasper, who didn't seem like he wanted to share anything, his arms crossed, staring across the multiple lanes of traffic of Fullerton Ave.

Fine, if I wasn't going to get anything out of them...

"Guys," I said to Sienna and Leon. "What are we dealing with here?"

Jasper had originally wanted it to be just me, Ari, and him, but after Sienna had insisted—nay, commanded—that she come along and I had demanded too, he'd relented. Leon had merely stood to his full, impressive height, and Jasper hadn't argued about him coming.

"You already know that Cliffside is divided into three main factions," Jasper said before either Sienna or Leon could answer.

I nodded. "The vampires, the shifters, and the..."

65

"The Horde," Sienna said, then shuddered.

"There are plenty more beside them," Jasper went on. "But those are the big three. Most of the time they all get along."

"*Mostly* because they stay well away from each other," Ari said.

Jasper glared at all of us. "Am I telling her, or are all of you?"

"Tell it faster," Leon said, giving him a toothy grin.

"The groups have a sort of unspoken rule not to interfere with each other's business," Jasper went on. "If there's a problem, they call a Conclave to resolve it. Most of the time."

"You don't seem too confident in this Conclave thing," I said.

Jasper grunted. "They're...well, you'll see."

I was about to ask more but was cut off as the bus arrived. We all squished into the back, Leon's body creating an impressive barrier between us and everyone else. I found myself pressed up against Jasper. Again I was struck by how surprisingly warm he was. How my skin tingled where we touched.

He was staring out the window, and I made it a point to look at anywhere but his face, choosing instead to examine the other passengers for anyone out of place. Since my first time leaving the Loft, I'd been hyper-vigilant for any other examples of the paranormal world. Thankfully, everyone on the bus seemed normal.

The bus took a sharp turn and I briefly lost my balance and bumped into Jasper.

"Sorry," I mumbled.

His chin brushed my hair as he looked down at me. "Are you nervous?"

"Am I—no, not at all. Why? Do I seem nervous?"

"Your heartbeat's sped up again."

I glanced at where his large arm was squished against my side. I didn't know if it was the upcoming Conclave or our close proximity that was doing that. "What are you, my cardiologist?"

He frowned deeper. "I was just asking."

"I'm fine. Thanks."

"Good."

I gave a jerky nod. "Good."

Behind him, Ari rolled her eyes.

We were at last let off outside one of Cliffside's numerous shoreline parks. Jasper didn't give us time to catch our breath before leading us toward one of the enormous fountains in the center of the large green.

"The Conclave won't actually attack us, will they?" I asked. Now that I assumed we were getting closer, I was in fact getting pretty nervous. Though I'd never tell Jasper that.

In answer, Jasper gave an unconvincing grunt. "Because of the witches' curse, they tolerate us more than they like or respect us—"

"Don't listen to this glum attitude." Leon pushed Jasper ahead and planted himself beside me. "They won't attack us. They'll just want to ask a few questions and try to get a handle on everything that's happened since you arrived."

"What'd they ask when you guys were called?"

Leon's smile wilted. The others shot quick glances at each other and the sinking feeling in my gut grew. "None of you were ever called to the Conclave like this, were you?"

"We've all met the Conclave," Ari said.

"But you weren't, I don't know, summoned or whatever this is."

"Well, no."

None of them were doing a very good job of making me feel any better.

"Riley, *relax*," Ari said, giving my hand a reassuring squeeze. "We'll be there with you. Nothing's going to happen."

"She's right," Sienna said soothingly, sprinkling a bit of the herbs from her pouch atop my head. Instead of making me feel better, it only made me want to sneeze. "Nothing's going to happen." She paused for a breath. "Although...What if Lukas shows up?"

Jasper shot her a look that said he definitely hadn't wanted to bring that up.

"Yeah, Jasper," I said, rounding on him. "What if Lukas shows up?"

Jasper held my gaze for a long moment. "He won't," he finally said. "He'll send Yu or Dana or one of his other sub-alphas like he always does."

"But if he *does*—"

"We're here," Jasper said, cutting me off.

We'd stopped at the other end of the lawn, in front of a fountain nestled between a grove of trees. Though my anxiety was creeping up toward DEFCON 1 levels, I forced myself to focus on where we were.

"The Tax Levy Fountain?" I said incredulously.

That wasn't its real name. It was a decades-old fountain that was *supposed* to have been modeled off the famous Levi Fountain in Rome. Only ours sucked and apparently had cost the city so much to make that locals never called it by whatever actual name it'd been given.

Kids splashed in the fountain's shallows while their parents lazily fanned themselves beside the cool mist of the waterfall cascading down the back. I'd never taken a good look at the worn, misshapen statues before, but I did now. Nymphs bathed under streams of water. Centaurs galloped with bows pulled taut. There was a long, arching man in the back that might have been a vampire beside a dragon and another vaguely human figure, its face so worn I couldn't make it out, with carved sprays of water rising up beside them.

"I'm having a hard time believing this leads to any secret Conclave," I said, looking at all the families and nearby joggers.

"That's the point," Jasper said. "This is just one of the Conclave entrances in the city. Most of them are hidden in plain sight."

He stepped up to the center statue, the one that most looked like a water nymph, with a moderately disturbing man—maybe a vampire, maybe something else—clawing his way up her feet. Not sure what the artist was going for there. Other than creepy.

"We have Conclave business," Jasper said.

At first nothing happened, and I imagined in about ten seconds we were going to start receiving strange looks. But then the statue's eyes glowed blue and tilted down to look at us. The remaining statues around the fountain followed suit, until the dozen or so sculptures looked as though they were possessed.

The curtain of water at the back split apart, sliding away along with part of the wall. Before I could gasp, the pool of water at our feet parted until a narrow walkway ran directly through the center of the fountain and vanished beneath the falls.

I looked at the crowd, certain that *someone* must have noticed, but everyone remained completely oblivious.

"Quickly, before the glamour wears off," Jasper said.

I hesitated a moment before stepping into the fountain's walkway. The water sloshed around my ankles, but I stayed dry. The statues continued staring resolutely at me. Intimidating, but unmoving.

Okay. Weird, but not too bad. I could do this.

We all followed Jasper through the waterfall and into a wider tunnel lit with torchlight. The second we were inside I heard grinding stone as the entryway closed up behind us, ending with a solid *boom*.

Sienna shuddered. "Not a fan of that part."

I had to agree with her.

With only one way to go, our group took the tunnel farther into wherever we were now. Under the city, maybe? A portal to another place? The air smelled faintly of saltwater, but I had no idea if we'd stayed in Cliffside or taken an all-expenses paid trip to another realm.

"Paranormals of the past used these tunnels to move safely, before the Grand Laws were put in place," Leon said.

"That must have been..." I looked down one of the damp, unlit corridors we passed. "Pleasant."

"More pleasant for them than the surface," Ari said.

"Things are better now," Leon agreed.

"Though not everything's perfect," Sienna added.

No one said anything to that.

More tunnels continued splitting off from the main one, so many I was starting to wonder if we'd stumbled into Daedalus' labyrinth. Most looked somewhat maintained, but others...

I jumped as something large scurried into the dark of the next passageway. Something larger than a rat. Sienna quickened her pace behind me.

"Many of the Horde still like using these," Jasper said. "Keep moving."

He didn't need to tell me twice.

At last the tunnel spit us out in a broad hallway, not unlike the kind I'd seen the witches in. At the other end was an arched doorway beckoning us into the chamber beyond.

"Let me do the talking," Jasper said as we approached it. "I know most of those nominated to the Conclave. If anything happens—"

"Don't sound so glum," Jas," Ari said exasperatedly. She patted my shoulder. "They just want to see who you are, and maybe ask a few questions about the attack. Nothing to be worried about. Got it?"

My throat was dry so I swallowed a few times. "Got it."

"We'll be there with you!" Sienna said and Leon nodded.

But before we entered Jasper grabbed my arm, letting the others walk into the chamber ahead of us.

"I don't know what the Conclave actually wants. They've not been known to put the interests of the whole above their own factions, and they might try to draw you into their schemes."

"Comforting," I said. "Want to impart any other encouraging words?"

Jasper's eyes were even more vibrantly intense in the low light of the underground. He seemed to be carefully weighing what to say next. "Whatever happens, I won't let them hurt you. Okay?"

Before my confused brain could begin to come up with a response to that, he brushed past me and joined the others.

I shook myself. That was weird. Jasper had made it clear on no uncertain terms that he was only putting up with me because he had to; because I was important to his—our—end goal of breaking the curse. That was all he'd meant. Protecting me was nothing more than another way to do that.

I sucked in a deep breath, squared my shoulders, and entered the Conclave chamber.

If the hall had been large, then this chamber was immense, a circular rotunda of stone benches rising above a sunken floor in the center. It reminded me of a gladiatorial ring, and not in a good way. In a way that I was a fighter, and a lion was about to come charging out from the entrance on the other side.

There was nobody in the stands except for a single figure I couldn't make out past the enormous torches staked around the edges. Every time I turned my head, the figure vanished from sight.

I hurried to catch up with the others in the center, standing atop some lines gouged deeply into the stone floor. I couldn't make out what they formed, but my attention was stolen by the other people in the chamber with us. We must have been the last to arrive. A group of what I guessed to be shifters milled together, shooting distrustful looks at everyone else. The other group—obviously vampires judging by their pale skin and dark clothing—stood ramrod straight in a perfect circle. I felt the press of their red eyes flicker toward me. My pulse quickened and one of them grinned with all teeth.

"Who's in charge?" I whispered to Sienna.

"Technically nobody is," she said. "Nobody wanted to give

power to anyone else so the Conclave usually just kind of…starts, I guess."

Ari was looking over at the small cluster of shifters. Her shoulders relaxed. I saw one man with a pinched face, and a woman with a Mohawk and a biker's jacket, but it seemed the Lukas guy they feared would come wasn't among them.

"This is stupid," Leon growled.

"What is?" I said.

He continued looking between the three groups. "This. I haven't been to many of these meetings, but each time it's the same. They just stand around, pretending they don't notice the others until someone finally makes the first move."

"Keep your voice down!" Sienna said. "They might hear you!"

"Good," Leon said. I saw one of the shifter's ears swivel.

As I looked around, I couldn't help noticing that something was missing.

"Isn't the Horde the third group? Where are they?"

"They almost never come," Ari said. "No clue why."

I looked again for the shadowed figure watching over all of us, right as Jasper said, "Sienna and Leon take your seats. Riley, Ari, with me. Let's—"

I turned and nearly screamed at finding that a pair of vampires had silently appeared behind me. I bit my tongue until the scream died. One of the vamps grinned.

"You must be the newcomer," she said, her voice rich as velvet. She stood imposingly tall, cheeks sunken and sharp, widow's peak exposed from her slicked-back hair. The other vampire was the total opposite, short and almost round, with hollow eyes and hands that were swallowed by the sleeves of the high-collared robes they wore.

Before I could move, the short one leaned in and sniffed. "You smell…distinctly *human*. Does she not smell human, Valencia?"

"She does, Farrar," the tall woman said. "Very, very human."

"And you look…" I searched for a word. "Gothic."

Valencia's eyes flashed. "We have been around a long time, girl. A long, long time. Tell me, how many centuries have you been alive?"

I crossed my arms. "Number one, I have a name and it's Riley. Vampires seem to have trouble remembering that. Number two, are these the questions the Conclave wanted to ask me?"

"We will get to other questions in due time," Farrar said. "We are simply satisfying morbid curiosity is all."

"Jasper..." Valencia glided over to him, brushing aside a furious-looking Ari. "It's been a long while since you last visited your brothers and sisters of the night."

To his credit, Jasper refused to back down as the pair of them leaned into his personal space. "I've had Outcast business," he said. "You know, that group I'm part of that's not the Deathless?"

"The group you are part of *for now,*" Farrar said, and I didn't miss the glance he shot my way. "We've heard rumors."

"Interesting rumors," Valencia said.

"About your latest addition. Have you given our offer any more careful consideration?"

I started to step forward as the pair drew closer, but Ari stopped me. "They're testing us, looking for a weakness," she whispered. "Let Jasper do this."

I pursed my lips as Jasper broke out in a grin. "Join the Deathless and be automatically ranked as a leader? A tempting offer. Maybe give it to someone who doesn't have a prophecy to fulfill."

This time neither Valencia nor Farrar tried to hide the scathing looks they threw my way. "Perhaps not for much longer. There will come a time when you will have to choose, Jasper. Choose between this false group you've taken residence with, or your true brothers and sisters. You'd better hope then that we're half as gracious..."

"Hey! Watta ya talking about over there?"

The pinched-faced shifter was stalking over, trailed by his cronies. "You talkin' 'bout us?"

"No, Yu," Jasper said.

"Okay…Then we startin' this meetin' or what?"

"Yessss…" Farrar drew out the word.

He began drifting back toward the group of vampires. Valencia did too, but at the last second she swooped in front of me, her red eyes brightening as they bored into mine.

"Tell me what you are. Tell me, key of the prophecy."

I had the sudden, incredible urge to blurt out everything I knew about the Outcasts and what little I knew about what I was. It was an insatiable itch in my throat. I could feel the hands of her compulsion working to move my jaw, trying to get me to speak, even as the free part of my mind screamed that she was forcing me to answer.

"I…I…"

Valencia leaned in closer. "Yessss…?"

The magic had grabbed my jaw. The itch in my throat grew.

Then I felt something else. A pleasant warmth, a burning, stirring deep within my chest. It rose, growing stronger, making my skin tingle as it pushed out through my body. It was the same feeling I'd had when I'd unintentionally unleashed my magic. Maybe I should have been scared, but I knew now this fire wouldn't harm me. I couldn't explain how, but this fire *was* me. It was part of who I was, and so I let it rise.

The fire within filled my veins, burning away the compulsion in my throat, consuming the magic gripping my jaw. My vision went briefly orange as it reached my eyes, and then began to reach out toward Valencia who hissed and backed away.

I blinked and at once the magic within me receded. I could have sworn I heard a low warning growl rumble through me as it did.

Valencia was glaring at me as though I'd just slapped her. "Very well. Keep your secrets for now, but all will be revealed soon."

Her cloak snapped as she swept around and returned to the

other vampires. I put a hand on my chest, still feeling the echoes of heat and the growl reverberating through me.

"What...just happened?" I whispered to Ari.

She looked at me, confused. "You tell me. Valencia stopped for a second to ask you something and then backed off like you'd burned her. Did she say something to you?"

So I hadn't imagined that. "No, she...she just wanted to know what I was."

Ari chuckled. "Don't we all? We'll figure it out, just as soon as we deal with these idiots."

Behind Ari, I noticed Jasper watching me, an unreadable expression on his face. Had he also seen everything I had? Had he felt the same magic that'd coursed through me?

I quickly dropped my hand from my chest. Though I'd tried to use (or failed to use) more of my magic since I'd arrived, I hadn't considered where that magic came from. What I *was*. That seemed to be important. More important than I knew. And until I figured it out, I needed to be careful around the other Outcasts. I didn't need to be accidentally burning any of them. Or unleashing whatever was inside me.

At last Jasper pulled his gaze from me and stepped forward to face the rest of the Conclave. "We're here. What did you want?"

"We wanna talk to the girl, fang face," Yu said, thrusting a grubby finger at me. "She's the special one, in't she?"

"We heard you were recently attacked," Farrar said. "Do you know by whom?"

"We're working on that—" Jasper started.

"Who cares about an attack?" one of the other shifters said. "Attacks happen all the time. We wanna know what she *is*. Where she *belongs*."

"In due time," Valencia said. Her eyes flashed my direction, apparently having gotten over getting her mind seared by my unstable powers. "We'd *all* like to know that."

A muscle in Jasper's jaw twitched. "That's Outcast business. If the Conclave doesn't have any official questions then this is a waste of—"

"Outcast business?" The group of shifters cackled. This time Yu jabbed his finger at Jasper. "Yer only in that fancy house 'cause we allow it. You don't pledge loyalty, you don't help other paranormals—"

"We help plenty!" Ari said furiously, but Jasper cut her off with a quick slice of his hand.

"What about the prophecy?" Farrar said, and the vampires behind him leaned in closer. "Since she's arrived, has it revealed any more of its secrets to you?"

"The prophecy is also Outcast business—"

Yu took a step toward Jasper. "I'm gettin' pretty sick of hearin' that. We're *all* gettin' pretty sick of hearin' that. Your business is our business."

"Not entirely," Valencia said. "We vampires still hold the witch's spell in its proper place of reverence. For now."

Yu's face was growing an uncomfortable shade of red. "Well I—"

"Okay, stop!"

I hadn't expected my outburst to actually put an end to the squabbling, but the chamber went suddenly silent. Seriously, how did anything get done when this supposedly grand Conclave fought as much as kindergartners figuring out whose turn it was to hold the class hamster?

"What are you doing?" Jasper said when I stepped in front of him.

I hoped I knew.

"Just let me handle this," I said. "I'll answer some of their stupid questions and we'll finally get out of here."

That didn't seem to make him happy, but I was confident it was the right choice. I didn't know enough about the paranormal world to reveal any of the Outcasts' secrets, and I *definitely* didn't know enough about what I was to reveal any of mine.

"You wanted to see me?" I said, extending my arms in front of the Conclave. "Here I am. What do you want to know?"

The vampires were silent. This even seemed to throw off Yu. I could practically see the smoke pouring from his ears as he tried to grapple with the new trajectory this entire conversation had taken.

"I want to know something."

The low, gruff voice sent a shiver down every knob of my spine. The man who'd spoken stepped out from the entryway behind the shifters, golden eyes gleaming as they fixed upon me. A predator locking onto his prey. His head was shaved, revealing crisscrossing white scars covering his scalp. A tooth earring dangled from one ear, and a heavy chain with a wolf's head hung right above the folds of his leather jacket.

"Lukas," Jasper growled.

Lukas grinned, his face twisting into a wolffish snarl. "So good to see all of you. Now, I have one important question: How do we know this girl isn't an imposter?"

CHAPTER NINE

Wait, what?

"I'm not an imposter!" I said. "The witches chose me and I became one of the Outcasts."

The shifters scampered to break apart as Lukas stalked through them, that smug grin still on his face.

"Why, that's such a coincidence. The witches also chose *me*." He pointed at the vampires. "And them. And everyone who claims to have died and been picked to become an Outcast."

Lukas' grin grew as he looked around at the rest of the Conclave. "My friends, I'm only saying that she shows up, claiming to be the thirteenth Outcast, claiming that she's due our respect and admiration, and we don't know if she's just using her charm to get the benefits."

I clenched my fists, my anger growing. I'd nearly died, been thrown into a world I had no clue existed, lost any connection to my family, and this smug creep thought I was freeloading to get some benefits I didn't even know about.

"None of us have solid proof that the witches chose us," Jasper said. "Other than that the Loft let us in, and the prophecy states that we're part of thirteen."

"Exactly," Lukas said. "So no proof at all. And yet we here on the Conclave tolerate your failure to give allegiance to your rightful factions."

"Uh, yeah. That's what I was askin' 'em about, boss," Yu said.

Lukas shot a glare at him, and even from here I could feel the pure menace in his gaze. Yu backed down, whimpering. My eyes were drawn past their group, to the shadows where another lone figure stood, nearly out of sight, watching the proceedings.

Hayes.

"*You.*" My anger spilled over, and before I could think about it I was stomping toward him, trying to call up that fire from before so I could turn him extra crispy. "That's the guy right there, the one who attacked us in the Loft!"

A strong hand gripped my wrist, and whatever fire I might have summoned was immediately snuffed out. Lukas squeezed and I felt my bones grind together. I bit back a cry, not willing to give him the satisfaction of knowing he'd hurt me.

"Attacking another group in the neutral zone," Lukas said, loud enough for everyone else to hear. "That goes against the codes of the Conclave."

"You attacked us first!" I yanked my wrist from his grasp and pointed. "That's the guy who attacked us in the Loft. You must have sent him!"

Lukas frowned, but in his eyes I could see gleeful delight. "I have no idea who you're talking about."

"He's right—"

I looked where I was pointing. Hayes was gone, like he'd never been there at all. Both the shifters and vamps were staring into the dark recesses of the tunnel. I imagined the vamps at least had amazing night vision, and it seemed they couldn't see anyone. My spirits sank. Lukas had set me up.

"You," I said, keeping my voice low. "You're the one who got the Conclave to call us in. You sent Hayes. What do you want?"

Lukas smirked. He looked over my shoulder. "You might want

to keep your fake Outcast on a leash, boy. She's got some bite in her."

"Riley, come on," Jasper said, voice brimming with anger.

"That's right," Lukas said, only to me. "Follow your master like a good little pet, because that's all you are to them."

He was baiting me and it was working. I swallowed another surge of rage.

"I won't hold that outburst against her," Lukas said to everyone. "She clearly doesn't know our laws. Which again makes me wonder: who is she? Even the youngest child of a paranormal would know about us, yet she seems ignorant."

Lukas' lazy grin was back. "So if she's going to claim to be one of the chosen, I think she needs to prove she is who she says. Have her show us right here."

A sense of dread overtook me. If it came down to performing magic on command, I wasn't sure I could.

"None of us had to prove it," Ari said. "And neither does she."

"You're right. None of us had to prove what we are." Lukas pulled up one of his sleeves. In an instant, his normal arm shifted to that of an enormous wolf's with terrible, curving claws, then back again. "We just *are*."

The rest of the Conclave was silent. I chewed on the inside of my cheek. I hadn't helped anything, and Lukas was playing them.

"What does he want?" I whispered to Jasper.

"He wants into the Loft," he said, continuing to glare at Lukas. "But I'm not sure why. Regardless, he's doing a good job convincing them."

"Jasper, I won't be able to do magic if they ask."

"I know. And he knows."

"If this girl can't show us any of her powers then we have to assume she has none and has somehow wheedled her way into feeding off our patience and resources. I say we question her further." Lukas' grin grew, though I was sure it was only for me. "I'll question her. I'll find out if she is who she says—"

80

"She revealed the next lines of the prophecy!" Sienna blurted out.

Jasper closed his eyes as if in silent prayer, and I understood why: telling the Conclave about what I'd done with the prophecy would probably prove I belonged. But I had a suspicion it was also exactly what Lukas had wanted to know.

"Is that so?" Lukas said. I could hear the barely contained eagerness in his voice. "And how are we sure you're telling the truth?"

"You'll just have to trust us," I said.

Lukas turned to the vampires. "She wants us to trust them."

"We have always upheld the legitimacy of the Outcasts," Farrar said at last. "Since the witches' curse began, it has been our duty until the prophecy is complete, a duty we have not wavered in."

I nearly smiled. Lukas could try all he liked to worm his way into the Loft, but it seemed reason had still won out.

"However…" Valencia said, and I went cold. "These are unusual circumstances. This girl is supposedly the final Outcast. If she is indeed the catalyst for the prophecy then that changes things."

"I'd like to see the prophecy myself," Lukas said. "I demand the Conclave be allowed inside the Loft to judge its legitimacy ourselves."

I didn't realize I was stepping forward until I felt Jasper's strong arm hold me back. Ari stepped beside him, a truly murderous look on her face.

"Not. Happening," she said.

Lukas' pack spread out behind him. Some bared fangs. Others had already begun to shift, snouts elongating, eyes turning to slits. I heard a warning growl from Leon. Sienna had her hands up, ready to cast a spell. We weren't sending idle threats. Though I hadn't lived there as long as any of them, I knew what'd it'd mean once Lukas was granted access inside the Loft: none of us would truly be safe again.

"Unfortunately the decision isn't only up to you," Lukas said, casually holding up a hand to stop his advancing pack. "If a majority of the Conclave thinks it's necessary—"

"We should give her a chance to prove who she is," Farrar said.

The smile dropped from Lukas' face. "You can't be ser—"

"Two weeks," Valencia said. All the vampires lined up, an imposing wall of black clothes and red eyes that gave me goose-bumps. "We've honored the witches' spell this long. If she can show us her magic and prove her legitimacy in two weeks then we have no need to investigate further." Valencia's eyes flashed. "If not...we will do as you propose, Lukas."

"You've got to be kidding," Jasper snarled. "Two weeks isn't enough time—"

"That's okay," I said.

Jasper turned to me. "What?"

"I'll prove it to you." I stared straight at Lukas. His smile was back, like he knew I was bluffing. "And if I do, you'll leave us alone. Forever."

"That shouldn't be a problem," Lukas said silkily. "In the meantime, I'll keep some of my pack outside your Loft. Just in case the little imposter tries to slip away."

"This is a sound idea," Valencia said. "We shall post watch at night."

"Don't worry," I said. "I won't run."

I could hear Ari sputtering indignantly while Leon glared at each and every member of the Conclave.

"Do you have any idea what you're agreeing to?" Jasper muttered.

I really didn't. But what other choice did I have? It was clear Lukas and the others weren't going to leave us alone until I gave them undeniable proof.

"If we're all in agreement, this Conclave is over," Farrar said.

Nobody moved for a second. Then the vampires filed out, seeming to melt into the shadows. Lukas waved his pack off and they too headed out. I kept my eyes on him as he passed us. I would let him know I wasn't afraid. I wasn't someone he could cower. I wasn't someone he could intimidate.

As he passed me, he grinned, showing me every one of his sharp teeth. "Very brave, girl. You've got some spine to you. I'll enjoy breaking it."

CHAPTER TEN

I let out a breath when we finally re-entered the entrance hall. Jasper, Ari, and Leon stood in a semi-circle, talking in low voices. Part of me felt I should join them, but all I wanted to do was *think*.

"Riley, I am *so* sorry!" Sienna said, immediately drifting to my side. "I thought if they knew about what you did with the prophecy—I didn't think they'd use it against you!"

I gave her a tired smile. Now that everything was over, my limbs were beginning to feel full of sand. "Don't worry about it. Lukas would have found another way to weasel in eventually."

Sienna still looked mortified. I wanted to continue reassuring her, but my thoughts had turned to what I still had to do. Jasper hadn't been wrong: I'd jumped headfirst into this, and now I needed a way to prove I was legit. Fast.

"How hard do you think it'd be for me to learn some magic and show the Conclave?" I asked.

Sienna thought about it, playing with the ends of her hair. "It depends. Ari said you used magic once before, which is good. It means your power has manifested. But it's hard to tell how long it might take to control after that. If it's a more powerful kind of magic it could take longer, and if you haven't had any magical training whatsoever it could take even longer than that."

Crap. I was down two for two.

"I'm sure you'll get it," Sienna said, giving me a warm smile.

"In a couple weeks?" I said.

I was grateful when Sienna's smile didn't waver. "I'll help as much as I can. We'll kill it, I promise."

"Ari said Jasper was one of the best teachers for magic."

Sienna looked over at him, his arms crossed and face sullen among the others. "That is true, which is weird since he doesn't have any magic of his own. He's even helped me with some of my more advanced spells. But…"

"What?" I said when she hesitated.

"Well he's *Jasper*. The guy isn't exactly a buttload of rainbows and sunshine. Definitely not sunshine."

That he was not. But if he was the best the Outcasts had, I'd suck it up and deal with it.

I caught myself staring at his face; at the way his full lashes rose and fell with every blink. At his sharp jaw and how it looked—

Snap out of it!

I pulled my eyes away and as I did I caught the shape of another figure, nearly out of sight in the shadows at the side of the hall. They raised a hand and beckoned me over.

"Give me a sec," I told Sienna.

I warily approached the figure, making sure to stay well in sight of the others. "Can I help you?"

The man at last stepped into the light, and I realized I'd seen him before. "You were the guy on the street!" I said. "The one with the…"

I swallowed the rest of my words as his peeling skin came into stark view beneath his hood. The shock white of his teeth peeked out from a ragged gap of missing flesh in his cheek.

I realized my mouth was hanging open and shut it. "Sorry, it's just I've never seen anyone like you."

"Yesss...we ghouls are quite unmistakable," he said.

His voice sounded like the rattle of air over wet leaves. His long tongue darted out to wet his lips every so often, like a lizard. "I was watching that...interesting display our Conclave put on."

He paused, then looked over his shoulder. "Kaia."

I was about to ask him what he was talking about when a girl materialized beside him. Her black skin appeared almost semi-transparent, like I was catching glimpses of her through a fog machine. Her hair had been done in multiple braids and draped down to her shoulders.

"So you're the new girl," she said.

I stiffened. The girl smiled, her face briefly flickering transparent.

"I'm Kaia. I'm one of the Outcasts too."

"Oh, good." I took her offered hand. It felt solid beneath mine, and yet...not. Like I was holding onto a pile of sand that could sift through my fingers at any moment. "Sorry, it's just...I haven't been getting the warmest reception from some people."

Kaia nodded like she totally understood. Which I suppose she did. "I don't blame you after that horrendous display in there."

"You were watching, too? I thought..." My eyes moved to the ghoul, who continued looking at me with his sunken eyes.

"We have ways of staying out of sight," he said. "Most can't see us when we so choose. Other are more *perceptive*."

Kaia rolled her eyes like she dealt with this stuff all the time, and I was strongly reminded of Ari. "Try speaking a little more cryptically, Uko," she said. "Yeah, girl, the way they treated you sucked. They never had any of us confirm who we were."

"In times past, we of the Horde were also part of the Conclave," Uko said. "It was us, the ones closest to death, who would confirm the Outcasts were legitimate."

His ice-blue eyes flared briefly and my skin tingled with the aftereffect of whatever small magic he'd just performed. "It is as I thought. You are as you say you are. You are the thirteenth."

"That's great!" I said. "We just have to tell the rest of the Conclave..."

Kaia was shaking her head. "There's a reason the Horde wasn't there today. The rest of the Conclave doesn't trust them anymore." She scowled. "That creep Lukas has been spreading lies about them for the last couple years. Now they're not even invited to the meetings."

I curled my fists in frustration. It would have been so easy to clear this up if the Horde had been there. It seemed Lukas had been planning for this moment for longer than I realized.

"It's okay, I guess," I said. "I'll just have to learn some magic in time and prove them wrong."

"That won't work either," Kaia said.

I looked sharply at her. "Why not?"

"Just using magic won't be enough. Anything you do Lukas will argue is just another trick. The Conclave will happily agree, and Lukas will get access to the Loft and to you and your powers."

I stared at them, mouth agape. "Then there's literally no way I can prove anything!"

"There isss a way," Uko said, and the way he did I knew I wouldn't like what came out of his mouth next. "You have to fulfill the prophecy."

I let out a small growl of frustration. "*How*? I can't even do magic. Fulfilling prophecies is kind of endgame stuff."

"I've been working with the Horde a lot so I haven't been to the Loft lately," Kaia said. "But I overheard Sienna say there were a couple new lines to the prophecy."

"There are, but..." Like I had any clue what they meant. What any of the lines meant. How was I supposed to fulfill some prophecy that had been around for years? I really hoped it was right and I was this "key", otherwise I doubted there was any chance at all of figuring it out.

"I'll ask around the Horde," Kaia said. "Maybe there's something there that will help you out."

"I just don't get it," I seethed. "I thought the Conclave was supposed to help us. They just stood around and let Lukas do whatever he wanted."

Uko and Kaia shared a look.

I sighed, getting it. "They purposefully let it happen, didn't they?"

"The Deathless aren't stupid," Kaia said. "They knew what Lukas was up to."

"Then why didn't they stop it?"

"There isss still much superstition around the witches' curse," Uko said. "That isss why they will not attack you outright; they believe if they do so, the curse will punish them. The witches' magic is your curse, but it is also your sssalvation. But that belief in punishment isss changing. It is likely the Deathless think if they 'legitimately' disprove you, they can have access to the Outcasts' secrets without any adverse consequences."

Uko leaned in, and his warm breath, tinged with a hint of rot, brushed over my face. "You cannot trust anyone but those in the Outcasts. And even then, take care."

Kaia shot him an annoyed look. "Hey."

Uko didn't break my gaze. "I don't know what Lukas' plans are for you, but if he gets what he most desires, all paranormals are in trouble. Stay wary, stay alert."

And with that he backed away, blending into the darkness just like the vampires.

Kaia watched him go, a troubled look on her face. "Tell Jasper I'll stop by the Loft soon. And..." she bit her lip. "Uko sounds ominous, but he's right. Watch your back."

Then she faded away until I was left standing alone in the shadows.

This was getting out of hand. Learning enough magic to impress a few heavily fanged individuals was one thing. I had no idea how I'd even go about solving a prophecy I supposedly had a major part in. And if Uko was right and Lukas' entire plan was to gain access to the Loft and to my powers, even doing that might not be enough to stop him.

I sighed. There was no helping it. I was in this totally and completely, one way or another. It was time to suck it up and shut up, buttercup.

I was about to return to the others when I felt a cool brush of air stir the hair on my arms, making me shiver. I looked back at where Kaia and Uko had stood.

There was a new passageway.

I blinked, making sure my eyes were working properly. I was sure the hall only had columns on either side; I hadn't seen any other tunnels splitting off from them, yet here was one, feeling as though it were…calling to me.

I walked toward it, unable to explain the strange sensation that drew me to it. It was like the world's biggest case of déjà vu, like returning to a childhood home after being gone for years. A siren song sung directly to the deepest parts of my soul. The realistic part of my mind knew with certainty that I'd never seen this passage before, but a deeper part of myself, the part where my fiery magic sprang from, knew better.

Whatever was at the end of this tunnel, I wanted to reach it.

I walked almost in a trance, barely feeling the cold of the damp tunnel anymore, barely feeling my feet as they touched the stone.

I began making out markings on the wall; strange, almost runic symbols that ducked and wove in and out of the pock-marked stone, seeming to lead me. There were no torches down here, and yet I could see. I realized it was the symbols on the wall that were beginning to glow brighter and brighter with each step I took.

I turned the corner and the runes flared brighter still. The feeling of longing in my gut grew. At the far end of the tunnel was an immense stone door. Whatever I was searching for, it had to be beyond that.

I took a step toward it. For the first time since I'd walked into the tunnel I felt a seed of doubt. Whatever lay beyond it, I was certain it would change everything, I just wasn't sure how. Part of me wasn't sure I wanted to know.

Another step. I was hearing voices now. Whispers in the air. Crooning. Calling.

Another. I reached for the door and as I did it seemed to bend away from my touch—

"Riley!"

I blinked and the entire glowing tunnel vanished, replaced by a smaller, nearly dark one. I stood frozen in place, letting my eyes adjust, before turning to find Jasper's red eyes peering at me. I'm not ashamed to admit I nearly jumped.

"What are you doing here?" I said.

"What am I doing here?" he said. "I should ask you the same thing. You wandered off without anyone around, right after what happened with Lukas. Are you stupid?"

His tone was biting, but there was a note of something else in it.

"I..."

I looked around the tunnel now that I could see a little better. There was no sign of the original passage I'd walked down. No glowing symbols or door. Certainly no voices. If those had ever been real at all.

"I thought I saw something," I said at last, unable to come up with a better answer.

Jasper also looked around, then back at me. "Sure."

"I *did*," I insisted. "There was a tunnel with glowing runes and someone—well *many* someones—were speaking to me, and...

and…" I trailed off, realizing how stupid I sounded. "Never mind. Forget it."

"Gladly. I have enough things to worry about without playing fetch—"

Jasper turned around, only to find that the way I was sure we'd come in was now a dead end.

"What the…" Jasper muttered.

"Believe me now?" I said, smirking.

Jasper ran his fingers against the wall before brushing past me, heading the opposite direction. "I believe you got us even more lost than I thought. Hurry up. And stay close to me. No doubt your human eyesight is terrible down here."

I kicked him in the back of the leg. "Whoops. Excuse my human eyesight."

Jasper grumbled something I couldn't make out but I'm sure wasn't flattering.

The tunnels twisted and turned, sometimes seeming to dip lower, other times dead-ending and forcing us to backtrack. They looked older than even the ones we'd traversed when heading to the Conclave. I wondered just how lost we were, and how many turns it'd be before we came across the first skeleton.

Jasper let out a growl as we hit another dead end. "Just where did you take us?"

"Me? You're the one leading. And nobody asked you to follow me."

"You think I'd just let you wander off on your own?" Jasper scoffed. "Not likely."

We backtracked until we found the last tunnel we'd been in and kept following it. I felt the press of the rock walls on all sides. It was beginning to feel a little claustrophobic. A small, dark voice in the back of my mind began whispering that we were truly screwed.

I picked up the pace to stay next to Jasper. Despite what I'd said, I was grateful someone else was down here with me. Even if

91

he was an undead. Even if he didn't seem to *like* me that much. Or at all.

"Thanks, by the way," I said, breaking through the sound of our footsteps.

Jasper glanced back. "For what?"

"For sticking up for me at the Conclave. You said you'd protect me. And you did. So…thanks."

Jasper was quiet so long I thought I'd offended him somehow. Maybe that was another vampire weakness: niceties.

"You're welcome," he finally said. "But you don't have to thank me. I'll always protect the Outcasts. Watch it."

He pointed out a puddle of standing water for me to jump. "Though my job would be a lot easier if you kept that fiery temper in check."

I rolled a strand of my hair between my fingers. "What can I say? Comes with the whole package."

I could have been wrong, but I thought I saw him grin.

"So you admit it, then," I said.

"Admit what?"

"That I'm actually one of the Outcasts."

The look Jasper gave me was so sharp you'd have thought I'd just insulted his mother. "I never said you weren't."

Now it was my turn to scoff. "You can't be serious. You practically interrogated me when I arrived and have pretty much avoided me ever since."

"I was…surprised is all. And I haven't avoided you."

"Sure. Whatever you say."

I nearly ran into Jasper as he abruptly stopped. This close, I'd forgotten how much bigger than me he was. "Let's get something straight: I know you're one of us, and nobody can say otherwise. I was a bit of a jerk before, and for that I'm sorry."

I swallowed, temporarily unable to speak thanks to his nearness. "Apology accepted."

"Now that that's out of the way, don't expect to get any special treatment, princess."

I smirked. "Don't worry, I'd never get that idea from you."

Jasper's lips didn't even twitch. He turned and kept walking. "Good. Because you're not the only one who has a lot to lose if we don't figure this prophecy out."

There was a note of pain in his voice. I remembered what Ari had said about Jasper's family. Mainly, nothing at all.

"Do you have anyone you're hoping to see?" I said.

Jasper stumbled, then continued walking as though nothing had happened. "Yes."

"Who—"

"We're not talking about this." Jasper suddenly increased his stride, briefly leaving me behind. I'd clearly hit a tender subject. I hadn't meant to pry, but the guy was an enigma. How was I supposed to learn anything from him if he wouldn't talk?

I shook my head and hurried to catch up. Jasper waited for me at the first four-way junction we'd come across. He pointed down the left tunnel. "Air's coming from that way. And..." he sniffed. "Saltwater. Probably the park."

"It sounded like Valencia and Farrar have asked you to join them a couple times," I said when I started walking toward where he'd pointed.

"Has anyone ever told you that you talk too much?" Jasper said.

"Has anyone ever told you that being a brooding bad boy is overrated?"

He grinned. "No."

"Good. Let me be the first."

Jasper let out a sigh like he was suffering a fate worse than death. Or was it un-death? "They've offered a few times, each one more insistent."

"You ever considered actually joining them?"

Jasper cast me a surprised look. "Like I said, the Outcasts are my family. I'll do whatever I have to in order to keep them safe. The Deathless and the Pack have a lot of power and they don't give idle threats. I think it's only a matter of time before they stop asking me nicely."

I shuddered. Lukas was bad enough. Valencia and Farrar at least gave the impression of being the more levelheaded ones of the Conclave. But as Kaia had said, they weren't above trying to use the Outcasts for their own purposes. If both of them stopped pretending to be nice, we'd all be screwed.

At last the tunnel came out at another chamber like the Conclave's, though much smaller. Crumbling walls and rocky seats ringed the outside. I could see blinding sunshine through the tunnel's archway on the other side. Seagulls cawed and I felt my spirits lift. Guess we weren't starving down here after all.

"I'll have to bring a compass next time," I said, starting across to the exit. "Maybe then—"

Jasper grabbed my arm.

"Hey, what—"

"Quiet."

His narrowed eyes scanned the room. My senses went on immediate alert as he stepped in front of me. "Go back to the tunnel, now—"

"Too late for that, fang face," a deep voice said from behind us.

I spun to find a man emerging from the tunnel we'd just left, grinning maliciously at me. Another man and woman appeared from the other side of the chamber, all three of them closing us in.

"Took us a while to sniff you out," the woman with the mohawk said. I recognized her from Lukas' group at the Conclave. "Where'd you scamper off to?"

"Doesn't matter now, does it?" the third shifter said. "This is better. No witnesses."

"Lukas is a patient man," the first shifter said. "But not that patient. Hand over the girl and we'll only hurt you a little, vamp.

Heard you heal back extra fast like we do. How about we break a few bones and see how long it takes?"

I picked up a rock, frantically calling on my magic. *Now* would be an excellent time for it to make an appearance.

Jasper smirked, not looking the least bit scared. "That's cute you think you stand a chance against me. And you didn't even try hiding who sent you. Guess they don't make brainless henchmen like they used to."

"The Conclave won't do anything!" the woman snarled. "We're just making a move before those stupid Deathless do it first."

My magic was pulling a no-show. Looked like this was coming down to old-fashioned brawling. I raised the rock higher. "Sorry to disappoint, but I'm taken."

The first shifter grinned. "I was hoping you'd say that."

He began to grow, thick brown fur encasing his body, claws splitting the earth as an enormous bear took his place.

Then he roared and charged straight at me.

CHAPTER ELEVEN

I dove aside, smelling the stench of the bear shifter's breath as his jaws snapped for my legs. Jasper had been surrounded by the two others—wolf shifters, bigger than any normal wolves I'd ever seen. I really hoped he'd be okay dealing with them. I'd try to occupy Yogi for as long as I could.

"Come on, little girl," the bear shifter taunted. He flexed his claws, each one as long as my foot. *"I'm not supposed to kill you, but that doesn't mean I can't leave a few puncture marks."*

Pretty sure that *would* kill me, but I didn't point that out. He didn't look like he was in the mood to have an intelligent conversation. Or be intelligent at all.

The bear shifter swiped at my head and I ducked, bringing the rock I held down where I guessed his kneecap should have been. My blow was softened by thick fur and muscle. I was sure he didn't feel it at all. But I certainly felt something when he rapidly turned: his arm knocking me across the ground.

"Riley!" Jasper yelled.

The bear shifter loomed over me, both paws up. *"So weak!"*

I kicked my legs back over my head and rolled right as the paws came down, spraying me with bits of the floor. A small crater now occupied the spot I'd just been and my heart thudded harder in my throat. Did this guy even know the concept of alive versus dead?

"I'm okay!" I yelled back to Jasper. "You focus on dumb and dumber!"

I heard a wolf squeal in pain as an answer. I couldn't resist grinning. Sounded like Jasper had things under control, which was good for me. If he went down and it was three against one then I might as well hang a "Dinner" sign around my neck and call it done. If only I could use my stupid magic, but it remained as dormant and useless as ever.

"You're fast, for a human," the bear rumbled.

"I'll take that as a compliment," I said, circling him. "Especially if being human means I don't smell like you."

He roared and nearly ran me down again. Now that I was starting to read his movements, he wasn't too hard to dodge. The guy telegraphed more than they did in the 1800s. But he didn't need to be fast. One good hit was all it'd take to put me out of commission. Every minute I spent dancing around was a risk.

"What does Lukas need me for?" I said, trying to stall for time while I thought up a way to get out of this.

"Boss doesn't tell me nothing," the bear said. *"Just said he wants you alive and that you're special."*

"Tell you anything," I corrected. "And a smart guy like you? I can't imagine why not."

The bear shifter's face crumpled in confusion, but I plunged ahead before he could puzzle out what I'd said, "You really think attacking me here was a good idea? We know Lukas sent you. As soon as we tell the Conclave—"

The bear gave a roaring laugh. *"We told you, girlie, the Conclave won't protect you. They don't care about anyone but themselves."*

He moved, faster than I'd expected. I managed to spin out of the way, but not before one of his claws scored a hit on my back, sending a string of fire down my spine. I felt the magic inside me stir.

Yes, I thought. *Anytime now would be wonderful...*

It rose, rolled over, then remained stubbornly in place.

What had Ari said? Dragon spit? Yeah, that sounded about right.

I grimaced as I backed away from the bear shifter's advancing claws. "Now what would Lukas find special about little ol' me?"

Another swipe. I easily sidestepped it, but he was getting closer.

"He needs you to find something. Something valuable."

Another dodge. I was running out of room. Behind the bear, Jasper was still fending off the wolves, his movements so fast they were almost a blur.

"Hate to break it to you, but I'm not a GPS. I won't help him."

The bear shifter nearly grabbed me this time. I was almost out of space and way out of time. I couldn't risk trying to milk any more info from him if it meant dancing with possible dismemberment.

My eyes fell on a part of the chamber's crumbling inner wall beneath the bear's massive arms, and at last my frantic mind settled on a plan. I had to time it perfectly. If not...

Nope, I had to time it perfectly.

"You've got quite the mouth." The bear raised his arms, blocking any path of escape. *"I'll be sure to rip it off before I deliver you."*

I hefted my rock, lined up my shot, gave a little prayer, then threw.

It flew straight and true, smashing into the bear's face with a satisfying squelching sound. Thick droplets of blood watered the dry ground. Bullseye. Or bearseye.

The bear roared in agony. I was already sprinting straight at him, sliding beneath his stumbling legs and taking off toward the opposite wall the moment I regained my footing. I spied a portion of the crumbling stones I could climb up and zeroed in on that. Already I could hear the ground shake as the bear came after me, murder undoubtedly on his mind.

I hit the wall and immediately began to climb, hands scraping across the jagged bits of stone, shoulder muscles screaming as I wrenched myself up. Just a little higher and I'd be safe—

My foot got stuck. I looked down, frantically trying to pull it out, but it'd wedged itself firmly between two slabs of the collapsed rock.

The bear was nearly on me, close enough now that I could see his enraged, bloody face, practically feel those immense teeth close around my body and shred me apart.

I tugged my leg hard, panicking now.

"I'll rip you limb from limb!" The bear roared. *"I'll chew you into little pieces!"*

He leapt for me, all his gargantuan momentum careening forward with a single-minded purpose.

A millisecond before he hit, I threw myself to the side, easily freeing the foot I'd pretended was stuck.

The bear collided with the wall at such force I swear the entire chamber rumbled. The already weakened wall swayed, tilted over, held in stasis while I pleaded for it to *freaking fall.*

And at last it did, hundreds of pounds of stones collapsing atop the bear shifter and pinning him so completely that only his unconscious, stupid face poked out.

I stood, shaking now that the realization of how close I'd gotten to becoming mincemeat could register. When he woke up, it'd take a while to free himself. By then, Jasper and I—

Jasper!

I whirled in time to see one of the wolves leap for Jasper's exposed back.

"Jas—!"

Jasper spun before I'd finished yelling, the afterimage of his angry red eyes trailing in his wake. He caught the wolf midair by the throat as though it weighed nothing.

I watched, fascinated and horrified, as Jasper bared his fangs. The wolf whimpered as something not unlike fine dust—shimmering where it caught the light—drifted off its body and flowed into Jasper's mouth. His eyes grew brighter. He hurled the wolf to the side where it lay still.

Jasper blinked a few times, seemingly overwhelmed by the effects of whatever he'd just done.

That was when the other wolf struck.

Snarling, snapping jaws slammed into Jasper and the pair of them rolled. The wolf's teeth cut into his shoulder, raking open a trail of ragged, bloody flesh. Jasper let out a cry of pain that twisted my heart. I didn't think, didn't even consider the consequences, but charged straight at them, wanting nothing more than to rip that stupid wolf off him.

The wolf saw me coming. It unclamped its jaws from Jasper and leapt. I had no time to move, no time to react except to throw my hands up on instinct. Sharp incisors wrapped around my arm and *bit*. Hard enough at first to make my eyes water. Then harder still until I screamed, arm on fire, blood running hot down my elbow.

I was slammed against the ground as the wolf continued to shake my arm like a chew toy. Droplets of blood speckled its teeth. In its eyes I saw the animalistic fury of a shifter who wanted nothing more than to see me dead.

That's when I snapped.

The magic that'd stayed safely coiled deep inside came to full, blazing life. My skin grew hot with a feeling of power, not of pain. Orange fire leaked from my center, tracing the lines of my veins until the wolf gave a yip of pain and released me.

The magic pushed to the edge of my hands and then out, coiling in midair and taking shape. In moments, a tiger made entirely of flames stood between me and the wolf. Its body was the red-orange color of an overheated furnace. Its face was a snarling mass of flames, ropy tail flicking back and forth like a whip. But its eyes…its eyes were embers, smoldering a white, blazing heat like the sun.

"What is this?" The wolf shifter snarled, taking a step back. *"What have you summoned, witch?"*

I could only gape at it, overwhelmed with horror and fascination. "I didn't…"

But I had. This was part of my magic. The same thing, I was sure now, that'd awakened when I'd been attacked at the fair. The firelight dancing off the bathroom tile and the rough, warm tongue licking my cheek. Those hadn't been pre-death delusions.

The flaming tiger—*my* flaming tiger—let out a roar that seared my bones with fear.

No, definitely not delusions.

"Fenrir's teeth…" The wolf took a step back. *"You wait 'till Lukas hears about this—"*

The tiger pounced, bringing a paw across the wolf's snout in a blow I could almost feel.

The wolf flopped to the ground ten feet away, motionless but still breathing. The tiger stalked toward it. I could see it working its jaw, thinking perhaps of how cooked wolf would taste.

"Stop!" I yelled.

The tiger paused. It turned those searing eyes on me. My mind went temporarily blank, body seizing. This thing was so powerful it could finish me off easily if it wanted to.

Yet it was *me*. It was part of me. If I couldn't control, it then nobody could.

I swallowed, throat dry. "You can't kill them. Bad, uh, kitty."

The tiger growled. I could feel the rumble through my feet. I held my ground, determined not to give an inch.

"That's enough. I'm safe. You've done your job. Now, uh, return to where you came from."

The tiger's gaze didn't waver. For a horrible moment I imagined it coming for me next, those powerful, fiery jaws around my throat…

I held up my arm, veins still glowing with that orange magic.

"I said *return*. Now."

I held my breath until the tiger gave a sort of tiger-ish shrug, then padded back over to me. I stood frozen as it rubbed against my leg, its fur warm and soft. It gave another low growl and broke apart, pieces of flame flowing back into me, the orange lines receding along with them until I was alone.

My legs gave out and I fell on my butt, suddenly overcome with fatigue. What the heck had just happened? I show zero signs of having any magic and then *bam!* That creature appears. Was I hiding a whole circus-full of fiery animals inside me?

I looked over at Jasper and went still. He was staring at me like I'd sprouted three heads. Or, I don't know, a tiger made of flames. His look was that of someone stricken. Of someone...

Hungry.

I realized at once what it was I'd seen him do to that wolf shifter. Jasper was a Forsworn vampire. He'd fed off a little of that shifter's magic. And I'd just showed him an entire buffet.

"Jasper?" My voice came out hoarse. "Are you okay?"

He began to walk toward me. I started shrinking back, trying to reason with myself. Jasper couldn't—wouldn't—hurt me. He'd promised to protect me from anyone who tried.

I wondered if that included himself.

"Riley..."

His voice was rough. He was close now, close enough that I could see the tension in his sharp jaw; could see the muscles beneath his shirt bunch and tense as though he were physically fighting against something holding him back. "You have...so much power."

I took a shuddering breath, forcing myself to hold his gaze. If he decided to attack me I wasn't sure I had enough strength to fight him off.

"Get control, Jasper," I said. "I'm not someone to feed off of."

Jasper let out a ragged breath. His eyes fluttered closed for a long second before snapping open again. He took another step closer until he was looming over me.

"Jasper...?" I whispered.

"You..." He growled. He leaned down and I prepared to push him back as his arms wrapped around me—

He easily lifted me, cradling me against his chest like I weighed nothing more than a packing peanut. "...need to be more careful. What were you thinking, attacking that bear shifter?"

It took a moment for my brain to register that he was back to normal. All traces of his earlier struggle were gone as though it'd never happened at all.

And he was *reprimanding* me.

"Um, you're welcome?" I scoffed. "If I hadn't done something, you would have been wolf chow."

"I would have been fine," Jasper said.

Anger started to replace my earlier concern. Of all the ungrateful, narcissistic—

Jasper's eyes flicked down to where blood still ran freely down my injured arm. Now that the adrenaline rush was draining out of me, I was starting to feel it. A lot.

"Can you stand?" Jasper asked.

"Of course I can," I said.

But I still wobbled when he put my legs down, steadying me against his side. With one easy movement he tore off the sleeve of his shirt with his teeth and began tightly wrapping the injured part of my arm. I noticed the sight and smell of my blood didn't seem to affect him at all. There was no hungry look in his eye like there had been for my magic.

"There." Jasper finished wrapping, but he didn't let me go from his side.

"Lukas sent them," I said. "And apparently the Conclave won't do anything, even if we tell them."

"They won't." A muscle was feathering in Jasper's jaw again.

He glared at the nearest fallen shifter. "Go on ahead. I need to… make sure they won't tell Lukas anything."

I gripped his shirt to stop him. "You can't kill them. Not if we don't have to."

"If I don't, they'll go straight back to Lukas and tell him everything, Riley."

"Still. I can't…Not unless we have to. I don't want anyone else dying."

"Don't you understand what you did?" Jasper furiously returned my glare, but in his expression I saw something that shocked me: fear. "If you just did what I think you did, this is… this is a big deal. Don't you get that?"

"No, I don't," I said. "I don't understand anything that just happened. We'll figure it out, but they don't have to die to do that."

Jasper turned away with a huff, but I could tell I'd gotten to him. He didn't want to kill anyone any more than I did. But it seemed whatever I'd done was important enough to try.

"Lukas probably already knows way more about me and whatever's happening than we realize," I said, suddenly weary. "One more bit of information isn't going to hurt. If they even remember anything."

I jerked my head over to the bear shifter. I figured those few rocks to the head would give him a brutal headache when he woke. And if we were lucky, a case of amnesia.

"Fine," Jasper said tightly.

"What *did* I do?" I asked.

Jasper pulled me tight against him, helping to support my wobbling steps as we limped outside.

"I'll tell you later. I'm not sure if I'm right yet."

And I wasn't sure I wanted to know, but I kept my chin up as we stepped into the sunlight.

CHAPTER TWELVE

The Loft didn't feel safe anymore.

Though to me it hadn't been the bastion of security and comfort it had been to everyone else, there was a tension throughout the next few days I could practically taste.

After we'd returned, Sienna had freaked. Ari and Leon had both pledged to personally smash whoever it was who'd attacked us. Collette had shot me scathing glares the entire time she'd used her magic to heal my arm as best she could before re-wrapping it painfully tight.

"Now we can't even leave without some smelly shifter freaks watching us," she'd complained before stomping back to her room.

"Not all of us are smelly," Leon had grumbled.

Collette wasn't wrong, unfortunately. The very next day after the attack, I'd looked out the first-floor window to see a pair of men loitering beneath the awning of the convenience store across the street. One had flashed me a fanged grin before I'd pulled the curtain.

Night was worse. Though none of us went anywhere after dark if we could help it, just the knowledge that there were vampires somewhere outside, watching any move we made, was enough to make my skin crawl. The worst moment came the second night when I awoke in my bedroom to find a vampire pressed up against my window, red eyes watching me.

I left the blinds closed after that.

But the worst thing about this wasn't the scrutiny or the invasion of privacy; it was that I couldn't help feeling Collette was right. It *was* all my fault. I'd set the Conclave off. And it was my job to solve the prophecy before time ran out. If not...If not...

I didn't want to think about that.

꙳

I SAT in the living room, staring up at the glowing prophecy, just as I had three times since coming back from the Conclave meeting. So far I hadn't gained any new insights. Even after staring at the words long enough to make my eyes sore, the meaning still wasn't clear, and I had no better ideas on how to move forward. I wasn't sure what I'd expected; that if I squinted hard enough at it some knowledge I didn't know I possessed would suddenly reveal itself to me? I was ignorant about a lot of the paranormal world. I knew that much. Although, the couple times Ari had sat with me to try to help, she hadn't come up with anything either. I hadn't asked any of the other Outcasts, mostly because many of them were out doing...whatever it was they did during the day. Leon still left early with his helmet to do deliveries. Ari and Jasper had also been out a lot, running errands of one kind or another.

I leaned back into the bean bag chair and let out a groan of frustration. I had less than two weeks to figure this out and I wasn't getting any closer. At this point, mastering whatever fiery, cat-based magic I possessed sounded a whole lot easier. At least then I'd have a chance against those in the Conclave when they decided to try taking the Loft by force.

"What seems to be the problem, *compadre*?"

I craned my head to see a new face looking down at me. I immediately scrambled up, looking at the boy warily. "Sorry, but...who are you?"

The boy sleepily scratched the back of his head, not failing to stifle an enormous yawn. "I'm Rodge. An Outcast? Though I guess we're all outcasts in one way or another, aren't we? I think I'm...the seventh one?"

He gave another yawn, this one so large even I started to feel sleepy. This guy was like a walking Ambien.

I wracked my brain. The name Rodge sounded familiar. Had Ari mentioned him? Regardless, I slowly let myself relax. This guy didn't look like a shifter or a vamp who'd gotten past the charms. Certainly nobody like Hayes that Lukas would have sent unless he wanted to kill us via sleep deprivation.

"Sorry, didn't mean to be so nosy," I said. "We just had a little...incident with someone who wasn't an Outcast."

"I think I heard about that," Rodge said. "Sounds like a lot's been happening around here lately."

"Uh, that's kind of an understatement. Where have you been?"

"Sleeping. I do that a lot."

Rodge cocked his head to one side when he smiled. He had boyish good looks, with the kind of face that often had one of two expressions: mischievous or sly. A blonde mullet swooped off his neck and sideburns flared out on either side of his head, giving me the impression of a love-able golden retriever. He let off another long yawn that I'm sure could have KO'd a bull.

Maybe not a golden retriever. Maybe a sloth.

"You're Riley," he said. He looked up at the prophecy, eyes lazily scanning it line by line. "The thirteenth one of us. I'm guessing you're trying to figure this thing out?"

"And having no luck," I said.

"Ah, well, I'm sure you'll get it." He gave a sluggish wink. "I don't know you very well, but I can tell you've got a driving fire inside you. Wish I had some of that. But, alas we are all burdened by our given mortal confines...Anyway, I'm missing my second nap. Maybe we'll see each other soon."

He slouched back to the stairs but paused on the first step.

"That's strange..." he muttered.

"What's strange?"

He turned back to the prophecy, looking more awake than he had moments before. "That fourth line, *the ancients' throne*. There isn't any paranormal royalty, at least not that I know of unless you count the Fae. Them or...or..."

He rapped his forehead with his knuckles, but it seemed his brain had reached its maximum usage for the day. He flashed me another adorable grin. "But I don't know that much. Maybe Sawyer would, if you can get him to talk to you. Aaannnyway..."

He continued up the stairs. I turned back to the prophecy, now more confused than ever.

I SPENT the better part of ten minutes uselessly pounding on Sawyer's door.

But after waiting for an answer, I concluded the guy was either out somewhere or ignoring me. I really hoped he was some sort of arachnid paranormal 'cause the guy was a recluse.

Until I could talk to him I was up against a dead end and more frustrated than ever. I spent the next hour aimlessly stalking up and down the halls, mind spinning, before realizing my frustration wasn't anything beating a practice dummy with a stick couldn't fix.

I threw on some workout clothes and booked it up to the gym—

Jasper was in the center of the sparring mat, surrounded by various fighting dummies I'd never seen before. There was one the size of a mail truck with far too many legs to make me feel comfortable; another that looked not unlike the bear shifter I'd faced the other day, minus the ugly, snarling face.

Every time he hit a dummy, some kind of spring mechanism inside it would fire back, forcing him to block or evade. He looked like he'd been going at it for a while, judging by the light sheen of sweat coating his face and dampening the tight workout shirt he wore. Not that I was staring. Nope. Definitely not.

Jasper leapt and delivered a snapping kick to the dummy with too many legs. The second he connected, the dummy's opposite arm snapped across and Jasper was forced to dodge in midair, flipping over it and chopping it in the head as he fell. He landed elegantly on the ground, staring right at me. Heat flushed through my face. Crap. He'd known I was watching.

"I'll go," I mumbled, starting to back out. "I didn't realize the gym was occupied."

"I was about to come get you."

I paused, surprised, but waiting for the reprimand. "Yeah…?"

Jasper started unwrapping the worn fabric he'd woven around his hands. I noticed the wounds on his arm the wolf shifter had given him were totally gone. "You did well the other day. For someone who's barely ever been in a real fight or used magic, you adapted well." His teeth flashed as he grinned. "For a human."

Despite the jab, I hadn't expected to hear praise. Especially not from Jasper. He'd been gone most of the last few days and I'd been left with the distinct impression he was still annoyed at me for, you know, saving his life.

"That's…thank you, I guess?"

"You sound surprised. You expected me to say something different?"

"Honestly? Yeah. Very much yeah."

He shrugged as he removed the last of the wrappings. "Okay, here you go: You screwed up a lot. You misread your opponent's strength and tried to engage without properly knowing both your limitations and theirs. You also stalled to buy time that could have proven your downfall if your opponent had been halfway competent."

The last of the wrapping came off and he tossed it aside. "I could say more, but with you I'm learning any criticism I give will be dished back ten-fold. You'd make a terrible student."

I crossed my arms, frowning. "And I'm sure you'd make a terrible teacher."

I could have sworn he chuckled. "Guess we'll find out."

Jasper easily lifted the nearest dummy and moved it off the mat.

"Why do you need to train?" I asked. "Aren't vamps eternally young and strong?" *And gorgeous?* My brain offered. But I kept that particular thought carefully sealed behind my lips.

"We are, yeah. But even so we have to practice." He set the last dummy down and leaned against it. "It's like having a Ferrari but not knowing how to drive it. Doesn't do you any good, even if it's nice."

"Conceited, but I get the picture."

"You've been spending a lot of time in front of that prophecy. Figure anything out yet?"

I shook my head with a sigh. "Nothing. The more I try, the more I feel like beating my head against a wall. Figured I'd try to come up here and actually beat something. Maybe attempt to control that...well, whatever magic I used."

Jasper motioned me onto the mat. After a moment's hesitation I joined him, taking a spot across from him like we were about to dance. Or fight.

"Without your magic you'll be next to useless," he said.

"Excuse me?" I sputtered. "Remind me who just saved your butt?"

"You got lucky," Jasper said. "We both did. But when facing off against paranormals—those even more trained in magic than those idiots we faced—getting lucky won't cut it."

I glared at him, but couldn't fault him for what he said, only how he said it. I needed to learn magic. I couldn't be stuck at a disadvantage like that again.

"You've clearly got a little fighting experience," Jasper said. "What else have you learned?"

"Ari's been teaching me how to use some of the weapons." I gestured to the rack of sparring equipment. "And...that's about it."

Jasper's frown deepened. "Not enough. Ari's an excellent fighter in both her human and shifter forms, but she's soft. Like a mother hen."

The corner of my mouth quirked up. "Oh really? Does she know you call her that?"

"If she did, I wouldn't still have all my limbs attached," Jasper said. He stepped close to me and a breath caught in my throat. "I won't be soft. You want to learn magic from me, you'll listen to what I say, no matter how difficult it is. Do you understand? I will break you down in order to build you back up."

I met his hard gaze with one of my own. "You'll try."

"Then we understand each other. Let's begin."

※

JASPER WASTED no time in having me show him everything I'd learned in the self-defense classes I'd taken. He then wasted no time informing me that pretty much all of the techniques wouldn't work when fighting against paranormals.

"Most of them are trained and will be faster and stronger than you," he said. "You might have magic, but it's unskilled. And as a human you're slow, way too slow."

Sweat burned my eyes. I was in the middle of going through a new sequence of strikes for what had to be the tenth time. "You think I don't already know that?"

"You should. And you better remember it. You can't stop someone—"

In a blink he was beside me. I stumbled back with a surprised cry. "—that will be physically superior to you in every way. You have to be smarter. Cunning. Better trained. You can't just be good enough. You have to be better. Do it again."

I swallowed the lump in my throat and started the sequence once more. I longed to smart back, to take him down a couple notches from the Mount Olympus where his ego lived, but he made good points. I'd seen firsthand just a taste of what I'd be up against. And Jasper knew better than most what other threats existed for me out there. If he said I had a reason to worry, then I knew I did.

After another hour of more new fighting sequences, Jasper at last let me rest. I leaned against the nearest dummy, entire body practically shaking with strain. Jasper was staring at the sparring mat, looking as though he was concocting more brutal training to put my poor body through. My bones hurt just thinking about it.

"I get why the fighting part is important," I said. "But if I need to even the playing field then I'll just use my magic. That's why I have it, right?"

Jasper at last looked up at me. He went over to the fridge near the towel rack and threw me a bottle of water from inside. It took a couple tries for my sore wrists to screw the lid off before I greedily gulped it down.

"If you don't have a strong body then magic doesn't do anything for you," Jasper said. "A shifter might know how to shift, but if they can't fight in their new form then there's no point. Same with me. I might have speed and strength, but if I don't have the technique to use it properly—"

"Then it's useless," I finished. I nodded wearily. "I get it."

"Your body is a tool for the magic to use. If it's a good tool, it won't let you down."

I finished the water and tossed the bottle to the side. I pushed off the dummy and forced my tired body back onto the mat. "Would be nice to learn a *little* magic, though. Just sayin'."

I thought for sure Jasper was going to shut me down, but he actually nodded. "There is something I want to test."

That sounded ominous, but if it was a chance for me to try using magic I didn't care. "Sweet! What do I need to do?"

"Close your eyes."

Okay…Less sweet. But he was the one who knew what to do. I straightened up and closed my eyes.

"No peeking," Jasper said. "Center your breathing and deepen it. Focus on your core."

"You mean the place I feel the magic coming from?"

"That's it. Concentrate on that."

I breathed in deeply, feeling a slight stirring where the magic had risen up before. Maybe I could coax it to help me. Maybe the tiger was in there, waiting for me to command it.

Jasper was being awfully quiet.

"What should I do now?"

He didn't answer.

"Jasper?" If he'd ditched me, I swear—

I opened my eyes to find him standing mere inches from my face, close enough to kiss. Close enough to bite.

The magic in my core surged as I threw my hands up in surprise. "Jasp—"

Jasper lunged at me. I managed to backpedal and dive behind the nearest dummy, heart thudding, muscles screaming. *"What are you doing?"*

He tossed the dummy aside as though it were light as a ball of paper. It smashed against the weights, scattering dumbbells and practice weapons everywhere. I lashed out as Jasper approached but he easily caught my arm and threw me. I swear my bones rattled as they hit the mat. I saw Jasper jump again, driving his claws right at my throat. My mind seized, all thoughts of defensive moves and counterattacks fleeing.

SEAN FLETCHER

The magic inside me surged to the surface. Bursts of fire spurted from my fingertips. I felt the low growl of the tiger trying to emerge.

No.

I pushed it back, squeezing my eyes shut in the process. I couldn't let it free. Not now. This wasn't an enemy, this was Jasper. He would never hurt me...He would never....

I opened my eyes to find Jasper standing over me. All traces of his brief bout of violent madness were gone. "I was right. That tiger magic is a defensive mechanism."

I gaped at him. "You *jerk!*" I batted away his offered hand and pushed myself up. "Were you trying to scare me to death?"

"No. Just scare you enough to force your magic to take over."

I couldn't think of anything to say to that, except, "And what if it had? What if the tiger had come out and roasted you?"

Jasper didn't look the least bit concerned at the possibility. "You wouldn't have let it."

"Oh, great. Glad you have so much confidence in me," I grumbled, but Jasper was quietly thinking again, not paying the least bit of attention to me or my fury. Figured.

"It comes out when you're most in danger," he mused. "It's powerful, but it's not reliable. Although it did listen to you. Like it was almost...thinking. That means it's sentient."

"So what?" I said, still fuming. "What does it matter if it's sentient?"

Jasper crossed his arms. "Only very, very high-level magic or spells can have minds of their own like that. And that means you'd have to be a high magic user like the Fae or a master spell caster."

I looked down at myself. "I...don't think I'm either of those things. Aren't the Fae, like, perfect-looking?"

"No, you're definitely not Fae," Jasper agreed.

That was it, I was going to kill him.

114

"I don't know what it means, exactly," Jasper went on. "Only that you'll need a lot more training to figure this magic out."

He frowned when he saw my still-furious expression. "Don't look at me like that. This was the only way I could think to trigger your magic, Riley."

"Sure. I get it."

I turned to get a towel, so done with this stupid training session, but Jasper spun me back around to face him. "Riley, I promised it once and I'll say it again: I'd never let anyone hurt you. That includes myself."

I didn't mention that there wasn't much he could do when other paranormals went after me. He was just one guy. I didn't mention the look he'd given me back in the chamber; the hunger in his eyes. The way I'd felt that, for a brief moment, he'd been more dangerous to me than any of the shifters who'd attacked us.

"Yeah, I know," I said, gently removing my arm and immediately missing his touch. "Break me down to build me up, right?"

Jasper looked like he wanted to say more, but at that moment Leon walked in, dressed like he was ready to go for a jog. His eyes widened on the training dummy Jasper had thrown into the weights.

"Whoa. What's going on in here?"

Jasper threw me a grin. "Training. Just training."

CHAPTER THIRTEEN

The next morning, my body felt like it'd been thrown into a dryer set to "Bruise Evenly.". I regretted every movement I was forced to make, yet I still felt happy. There was a pride along with the pain. I was growing stronger. I was learning to fight back. That, and I'd awakened with an idea. It was a burst of 2:00 a.m. inspiration so it probably wasn't a brilliant one, but it was something, which was more than I'd come up with the day before.

I needed to find Sienna.

I was on my way to her room when I ran into her in the hallway. She was soaking wet like she'd been the first time I'd met her.

"Riley!" She quickly wrung out some strands of her hair, creating a neat little puddle on the floor. "What are you..." She studied my face. "You look like you're up to something."

"I could say the same about you." I nodded to her sopping clothes. "More fully clothed water aerobics? Or was it underwater basket weaving this time?"

Sienna smiled sheepishly, and with a wave of her hand she and the floor were dry again. Soon I'd pry out of her where the

116

pool actually was and what she was doing there, but I needed her for a different reason today.

"I'm going back to the tunnels," I said, being sure to keep my voice low.

"The tunnels?" Sienna looked confused. "Wait, you mean where the Conclave chamber is? Riley!"

"Shh!" I shuffled us back into a corner of the hallway, where I hoped it'd be a little less likely for someone to overhear us. "I know it's not the best idea..."

"No, it's really not," Sienna said firmly. "That's the same place you just got attacked, and now you want to go back? What do Jasper and Ari think?"

"They don't know," I admitted. "And I'd prefer it stay that way, Sienna." I tried not to plead. I knew leaving the Loft without a super good reason was dangerous, but I wasn't coming up with anything else, stuck as I was in here. I needed to get out— dangerous as it might be—and try to find clues to the prophecy elsewhere.

"Last time I was there I saw a new tunnel. It had to be magic. I think it had to do with the prophecy and I want to find it again."

Sienna crossed her arms, staring hard at me. I realized that, for how colorful and mostly cheerful she was, she could put on a mean serious face when she wanted to.

"You really think searching them is your best option?"

"Until I can think of some other dumb idea, yeah."

Sienna didn't crack a smile. "And you're going to go whether I agree to join you or not."

"Uh...Probably. Yeah."

Sienna let out an airy sigh. "Allll right..."

"*Thank* you, Sienna!" I squeezed her tight. "We'll pop down there and be back before anyone—"

Sienna grabbed my hand and tugged me along behind her. "Yeah, yeah, sure. But before we go, I need to try something first."

❧

EVERY SQUARE INCH of Sienna's room screamed *SIENNA LIVES HERE!!!*

"I've been meaning to clean up," Sienna admitted as she led the way inside. "Just...try to stay near the middle where it's cleanest."

I wanted to point out that *nothing* in here could be considered the cleanest, but I think she already knew that.

Colorful scarves and sweaters were thrown over clear tubs filled with what I guessed were witch spell materials: chalks, roots, powders, and bits of metal. Crystals had been carefully placed at each corner of the room, all pointing to a kaleidoscopic mobile hanging from her fan. The drawn curtains were painted with an ethereal landscape of rust-red dirt and an endless sky that was strangely calming to look at. The air hung heavy with incense.

Sienna picked her way over to one of the clear tubs and began digging through it. I removed a half-eaten pack of chickpeas from the bed and sat down, waiting.

"Wormroot, ginseng, magnesium...ah!"

She emerged triumphant with a small vial of clear liquid between her fingers. "Ketrim extract."

"What exactly are we doing?" I finally asked.

Sienna kicked aside a pile of scarves on her way over to me. "Disguising you. Kind of. You can't expect to walk out the front door and *not* have the shifters freak and tell Lukas."

She had a point. I eyed the liquid in her hand. "And that is?"

"Hold it."

The vial was cool against my palm. Sienna had me face her. "I'm going to turn you temporarily invisible. It's kind of an advanced spell and I'm still learning it..."

I leaned a little farther back. "This isn't going to explode in my face or anything, is it?"

"Of course not!" Sienna said indignantly. "Probably."

"Strangely enough, that's not calming."

"I'm still learning that some of the more advanced spells have the potential to go wrong," Sienna said. "But that's why I use items to channel and assist my magic until I can get it on my own. Think of them as magical training wheels."

She patted my leg. "I promise I won't blow us up, Riley."

"Okay...I believe you." I leaned toward her again, clutching the vial tightly in my hands as though my life depended on it. Which it might.

Sienna closed her eyes. I watched her soundlessly mouth the words to the spell, her hands moving in a bizarre pattern. The vial grew even colder in my hand, and then that cold began spreading up the rest of my skin until I felt as though I'd taken part in an ice-water dunk booth at the fair.

Sienna opened her eyes and let out a delighted squeal.

"It worked! Kinda. Take a look."

I looked down and gasped. Where my body should have been was nothing but a butt-shaped indentation on the bed. That and...

"It's not perfect," Sienna admitted. She brushed her fingers along the outer fringes of my shoulder, where I could see there was still a visible fuzziness in the air. "I'm not sure how long it'll last. And it won't stop an adept magic user from sensing you." She looked unsure. "Or maybe a shifter from smelling you."

I stood, feeling confident in spite of her uncertainty. "It'll work great. So what do you say we do a little investigating?"

※

I HELD my breath as we stepped outside the front door of the Loft. Not just because there were two burly shifter lookouts hanging around on the street, but because Sienna had put so much *Essence of Aura* perfume to mask my scent that I was sure I was going to die by blissful asphyxiation.

"Hey, sweetheart." One of the shifters pushed off the wall and blocked Sienna's way. He didn't even glance at where I stood. "Where do you think you're going?"

"To the vet to get my dog neutered," Sienna made a show of looking him up and down. "You could come too. I'm sure you could empathize with it."

The shifter snarled. "Cute. Where's that red head? The one who duked Jocko's crew? I'd like to tear her apart piece by—"

A thick hand gripped his shoulder and pulled him back. This other shifter was huge. Buzzed head, scars along his chin. Had to be a bear. Or something bigger, if that was possible.

He inclined his head politely to Sienna. "Have a good day, miss."

"Why'd you let 'er leave?" the first one complained as we hurried off.

"Creep," Sienna muttered.

"Glad to see not all of Lukas' pack are total monsters," I said.

Sienna shook her head as we waited to cross to the train. "No, they're not. Most shifters are good. Obviously. You've met Ari and Leon. You'll meet Daniel later. But the kind Lukas attracts are usually the worst. Just a bunch of thugs."

She was shaking. I took her hand and gave it a comforting squeeze. She returned a grateful smile. Which must have looked really weird to anyone watching.

Getting the rest of the way to the tunnels was interesting. Sienna had to block off a corner of the L train so I could stand without hitting someone, and we walked practically atop each other to avoid anyone running into me. I was glad we'd taken precautions, but I didn't think we were being followed. The lookout had made it clear they were mainly interested in me.

Whoopee.

"What are we looking for?" Sienna asked when we at last arrived at the hall before the Conclave chamber.

I looked around, hoping another new tunnel would appear and call to me like the first one had. Maybe Kaia and Uko were somewhere nearby and I could ask them for help.

"Not sure," I said. I headed into the main Conclave chamber and toward one of the tunnels branching off from it. That looked like a good place to start. "Wait here. I'll be right—"

"Like hell." Sienna pinched her fingers together and pulled, producing a luminescent string she wedged tightly into a crack in the chamber's wall. "You're not leaving me in some smelly dark place all alone. Lead the way."

⚜

I wish I could say I found what I was looking for. I wish I'd stumbled across a new tunnel, or heard the haunting voices call to me; felt a stirring in my chest that told me I was growing closer, or a growing sense of connection to my magic.

What actually happened: we got lost. A lot. And hungry. And thirsty. If not for Sienna's magical string to guide us back, we might have wandered around for hours more.

"It's not the end of the world," Sienna consoled me. We'd left the chamber and had returned to ground level, on the corner of a busy street. "At least you didn't run into more shifters. Or the minotaur."

I smiled weakly at her joke, but I was distracted. I'd done the exact same thing as I had before and yet still no tunnel. I wasn't even sure what it led to, only that deep down, somehow, I knew it tied into fulfilling the prophecy. Or at least fulfilling an untapped part of me.

I looked over at Sienna, peering eagerly into each of the windows of the shops we passed. Then I looked at myself in the reflection. Sienna's invisibility spell had worn off sometime in the tunnel, and a frustrated, tired, frizzy-haired girl looked back. A girl that something was eating at; something I couldn't put into words that had begun gnawing at me somewhere in the dark recesses of the underground. It was a sudden realization, one as jarring as the voices I'd heard.

Sienna turned and saw me being all introspective.

"Okay, someone needs a pick-me-up."

Before I could wonder what that meant, she pulled me around the corner and into the French Kiss Creperie.

I remembered when the small shop had first opened. Iris and I had been so excited we'd waited in line outside for a stupidly long time just to be one of the first to get a taste. It had been cold that day, so Iris had brought a portable space heater and blankets and we'd played Go Fish on the sidewalk until they'd finally let us in.

I found myself smiling as Sienna planted me in front of the menu. "Get whatever you want. On me."

"I can pay for my own, Sienna."

She pulled out a few crumpled bills from her wallet, and my eyes widened on the Benjamins peeking up at me.

"Do you get paid for performing cleaning spells and energy manipulation?" Sienna said. "Didn't think so. Choose, girl."

I didn't comment that she may want to use a cleaning spell for her room, and chose a Nutella and banana crepe (basic, but classic). Sienna had them load hers up with a rainbow's assortment of sprinkles. I almost immediately felt better the moment I bit into mine. The crepe was warm and delicious and pretty much everything I needed right then.

"This was a good idea," I said as we left the counter. "Thank you."

"You're welcome. Being an Outcast can get lonely," Sienna said. "You're disconnected from your old life, and you're kind of disconnected from those in your new one. Makes you forget the simple joys, you know? What it's like to be alive."

She held up her crepe and took a big bite. "But there are few things sugar can't fix. I'm sorry this little jaunt didn't work out. Just remember to include me in any of your other schemes in the future. I know you'll have some."

She was right. I was already thinking of our next move.

I was about to tell her when I spotted someone familiar sitting at a lone table in the back. I froze, crepe halfway to my mouth.

"Iris."

Sienna saw where I was looking. Her face softened. "Is that your friend? The one who was at the fair with you?"

I could only nod. Though it'd only been a short time, I felt as if I hadn't seen her in an eternity. She sat with a drink and a notebook, her pen moving furiously across the page. Every so often she'd look out the window as though searching the passing crowd for someone.

I took a step toward her. Sienna put a gentle hand on my arm. "Riley, you know she can't…"

"I know. I just…" An idea hit me. "Maybe you could—"

Sienna shook her head. "I know what you're going to ask, and I wish I could. The curse cuts off all, and I mean all, contact. That means you can't talk to them, and neither can anyone else on your behalf. Believe me, I've tried."

I mutely nodded. Of course the Outcasts had tried that. It should have been the first thing I did.

Sienna removed her hand. "I'll wait outside. Take as long as you need."

I approached Iris and slowly sat across from her. Though she was my best friend, though I'd seen her pretty much every day for as long as I could remember, sitting across from her now felt like sitting across from a stranger. She looked well, I guess. Her drink was mostly unfinished beside her scribbled collection of notes. I wondered briefly how we looked to the people around us. Could they see the both of us together? That would be an unnecessarily cruel thing for the curse to do: others could see us together, yet we couldn't see each other.

Iris looked up at me and my heart nearly stopped. "Iris?"

I realized only after I'd spoken that she wasn't looking at me, but *through* me. She stared for a long time, probably at the group of girls giggling at the table behind us. Then she sighed and took a long sip.

"I feel that," I said, giving a sad laugh. "This is crazy, right?"

Iris must have thought of something else because she craned over her notebook and scribbled it down. I tried to glimpse what she was working on, but her writing was as cramped and impossible to read as always. It didn't help that she threw her arm over the pages like someone around us was going to cheat off her.

"I've been trying to figure this whole thing out," I said. "Trying to get back to you and my mom and dad and...well, *everything*. I'm not sure how much longer it's going to take. I'm not sure..."

The new feeling that'd begun in the darkness of the tunnel hit me again. The one I'd felt again outside on the street, eating away at me. The one I hadn't been able to put into words then but burst from me now, "I don't think I can ever go back to the way things were. Even if I solve this prophecy, I..."

Iris shook around the ice in her drink while I tried to find the right words to explain to her what I couldn't properly explain to myself.

"This is so much bigger than I knew. I thought I'd be able to solve everything and come back but I can't, this world won't *let* me." I stared down at my hands, the ones that had been covered in strange symbols and cast tigers made of fire. Things that once would've seemed unimaginable. Things that had shattered my reality forever. "There are people who want me and that's never going to stop even if I solve the prophecy."

A single tear fell between my fingers and splattered on the

table. I wished Iris could see it. I wanted her to hear *something*. To know that I was trying to reach her.

I furiously wiped at my eyes before any more tears could fall. "Anyway, I wanted you to know that. I'm not going to stop fighting. I'll see you all again soon. No matter how much things change. Everything may be different but I'll see you again."

I stood. Iris looked up. I waited, holding my breath, as her eyes searched the rest of the shop, passing right over me.

I turned and left.

Sienna was waiting outside as promised. She took one look at my probably splotchy face and said, "Oh, honey..."

Now I burst out crying. I couldn't help it. I probably looked like a crazy person crying outside a creperie, but it felt as though I had cut off the last parts of my old life and left them back there with Iris. An aching, longing pain had settled in my chest.

Sienna pulled me into a tight hug. Her *Essence of Aura* perfume wasn't so bad anymore, though it did choke me up a little when I started sniffling.

"That had to have been hard," Sienna said when she released me. She dug into her pocket and produced a colorful handkerchief. I gratefully took it and messily wiped at my eyes.

"I'm impressed you even had the courage to see her again. A lot of the Outcasts..." Sienna twisted her fingers together. "A lot of us don't even try seeing our loved ones. Even after the curse is broken, I wonder..."

"Would you? If you could?" I said.

Sienna tilted her head, thinking. "I'm not sure. It'd be nice. But..." She beamed at me. "We'll just have to beat this stupid prophecy and talk to them for real, won't we?"

I nodded. "Thanks for the handkerchief."

"Oh, ah...you can keep it," Sienna said politely.

"Oh, yeah. Thanks."

"So what's next?" Sienna said. She winked, a twinkle in her

eye. "I know you well enough now to know you've always got something in mind. What's it going to be?"

She seemed to have way more confidence in my idea-planning and decision-making than I did. But this time she was right. I did have another idea.

"It's time to meet Sawyer," I said. "Whether he wants to meet us or not."

CHAPTER FOURTEEN

We arrived back at the Loft as the sun was setting and our vampire watchers were about to start slinking in from the shadows. Sienna had just enough magic left to cloak me long enough for us to slip back inside. I immediately stomped up to Sawyer's room, filled with new determination, Sienna frantically tried to keep up with me.

"Riley, Sawyer doesn't really like to see anyone that much!"

"He'll see me."

"You can't just barge in and expect—"

I reached Sawyer's door, raised my hand to pound it, then paused. I'd tried the brute force method once before. If I was going to get anywhere, I'd have to go against my natural inclination and coax him out.

I lowered my hand and gently knocked.

"Sawyer? This is Riley. I know we haven't talked much. At all, actually. You've been a bit...hard to reach, I guess. But I have some questions and I think you have the answers. Can we talk, just for a bit?"

I waited with bated breath. I didn't hear a sound from the other side. No sign that anyone else was even alive in there.

"I told you," Sienna said regretfully. "Maybe Ari or Jasper could ask him?"

I rested my forehead against the door. "I don't have any other ideas, Sawyer. And I'm running out of time. Please."

My voice hitched on the last word. Maybe it was my fatigue, or desperation, or the fact that I'd sat across from my best friend and been able to do *nothing* to change that she couldn't see me, but I hoped my feelings were getting through.

I felt the slightest tremor against the other side of the door. Like someone leaning against it.

"Sawyer?" I said, not daring to believe it.

"Do you...really need my help?" Sawyer's muffled voice—far younger than I expected—came from the other side.

Sienna gave me a flabbergasted look.

"Yes. Yes!" I said quickly before Sawyer thought I was reconsidering. "All the other Outcasts say you know pretty much everything."

I stepped back from the door as it opened just a fraction. I was reminded of my first day in the Loft as large eyes, framed by a glowing backdrop, peered out at me.

"I don't know *everything*," Sawyer said.

"That's fine," I said. "I'm sure you know more than me, and that's all that matters."

There was another long moment—the sound of a deep breath, as though Sawyer was bracing himself—then the eyes moved away from the door. "Hurry up."

If it was possible, Sienna looked even more shocked. She quickly motioned for me to push my way inside. I did so, my eyes struggling to adjust to the dimness.

"Sawyer?" Sienna said, clearly struggling to see as much as I was.

"Over here."

Sawyer *was* much younger than I'd thought. Probably no more than late middle school. He sat with his knees tucked to

128

his chest in a chair, wearing a baggy hoody and sweatpants. His hair was as long as Rodge's, but shaggy, the bags beneath his eyes a touch dark. I wasn't sure how he was hearing us because he wore an enormous pair of headphones with cat ears on the top.

The background glow I'd seen earlier became obvious now: computer screens. A dozen of them. Sawyer was clicking away at at least three, but more lined the back of his room, running through lines of text I couldn't begin to decipher.

"Tell me you're not a bat shifter," I said. "'Cause this sure looks like the bat cave."

"Witch," Sawyer said, never taking his eyes off the screen.

Sienna immediately walked over and clucked at the long strands of Sawyer's hair. "When's the last time you got this cut?"

"Dunno."

"And have you been eating enough? You know how worried Ari—how worried we *all* get— when you don't eat enough."

Sawyer gestured to the pile of bowls on the end table, mostly crusted over with old oatmeal, as though this was a perfectly adequate answer to the problem of malnourishment.

"You said you have some questions," Sawyer said.

The computer screens were mesmerizing. The rest of the room was like mine, totally devoid of anything sentimental. That was a little strange. According to Sienna, Sawyer had been there quite a bit longer than I had.

"Do you?" Sawyer asked again.

"Yeah, I did—I do. Uh...How do you get these to work?" I rapped on the top of the nearest monitor. "I know some electronics still work, but my phone fritzed out the second I got here. Ari said magic causes most electronics with any sort of signal to stop working."

"I designed my own magic-proof electronics. They work well enough. Can you please not do that?"

I abruptly stopped tapping the top of the computer like a

grandma trying to figure out the newfangled device her grandson had brought home. "Sorry."

"What did you want to know?" Sawyer swiveled around to face both of us. Even from here I could almost make out what his headphones were playing, some kind of ambient noise without any tune or rhythm. Sawyer reached out, still looking at me, and made a couple clicks on his computer. The noise lessened.

"I'm trying to solve the prophecy," I began.

"I know."

"I only have a little over a week before the Conclave is going to try to take the Loft."

"I know."

"Sawyer," Sienna said gently. "Be polite."

Sawyer appeared to mull over this concept of "politeness" before nodding. "Please, continue telling me things. I'll pretend I don't already know them."

Sienna sighed and went over to start magically cleaning the crusted oatmeal off the bowls.

I plunged ahead and told Sawyer about what I'd found about the tunnel, and how we'd gone back to search for it. That was really the only solid lead we had, not counting the Riddle Me This fun of the prophecy.

"And you believe this tunnel has to do with your connection to the prophecy?" Sawyer said when I'd finished.

"I'm almost positive. Though I'm not sure how."

"The tunnel won't show up in the exact same place again." Sawyer turned to his computer, talking as he typed, "It could be you found one component of the prophecy's answer, some sort of ley line, a line of powerful magic that crisscrosses the world. It's likely *your* magic was what the tunnel was reacting to. I heard you have a very rare, sentient kind."

"Yeah, that's true I guess."

"I didn't know that!" Sienna said, jaw dropping.

That was because I hadn't told her, or anyone outside of Jasper. I wondered how Sawyer knew.

"So you think whatever I am has something to do with triggering the tunnel to appear? But now it won't appear in the same place again."

"It'll appear when it thinks it's needed most," Sawyer said. "It might be semi-sentient, just like your magic, appearing at the best time."

"But *now's* the best time," I insisted. "I felt...I can't really explain it, but that tunnel is the answer to the prophecy. I have to find it."

"You won't," Sawyer said bluntly. "You probably won't find it until you're ready. Something similar to this happened in a town called Scarsdale on the east coast. A magical path appearing and reappearing at random. The dragon-kin there reported they were only able to go through when they were deemed ready."

I gritted my teeth, almost wanting to knock over the nearest flickering screen. "So I can't do anything."

Sawyer played with the strings of his hoodie. "You can keep trying to search for it, but I don't think you'll find it. And the more you search, the more someone else might find out what you're up to and figure out a way to exploit it without your magic."

Lukas. I had no doubt in my mind that given half the chance he'd try to use me to get to the prophecy's end.

"Okay, let me think," I said, knuckling my forehead while Sawyer clicked away. "No tunnel, so what about the prophecy? Have you seen the new lines?"

Sawyer made a couple more clicks and soon every screen in front of him held a high-res photo of the prophecy. Complete with the top part of my head at the bottom, frizzy red strands and everything.

I choked. "*When* did you take this?"

"Sawyer, sweetie, you know that looks super creepy, right?"

Sienna said. "Maybe next time take a picture when nobody's in front of it."

"...Okay," Sawyer said, sounding like he'd never thought of that before. "But yeah, I've seen it."

I took a deep breath. He's just a kid...Just let it go... "Great. What do you think?"

Sawyer leaned toward the nearest screen so that his nose nearly touched it. Sienna tugged his head back as she passed, carrying the now clean bowls to the door.

"The first two lines are obvious," Sawyer said. "You're the thirteenth Outcast and you're the key. You'll remedy our strife, which is the witches' curse we're all under."

"What about the blood of mortals, blood of old line? I was hoping that'd be some sort of clue to what kind of paranormal I was."

"Not really," Sawyer said. "There are plenty of paranormals that'd apply to. Most vampires are fully human before they're turned. Less with shifters, but it's possible. And many of the paranormal races can be considered old. That doesn't narrow it down at all."

"Oh." I tried not to let my shoulders sag. "Pretty sure I'm not any one of them. And Rodge told me there are no paranormal royalty."

When Sawyer didn't immediately answer I perked up. "Right?"

"Technically right," Sawyer said.

"The word 'technically' is in there."

"In the old days, in the time of dragons and demons, there might have been royalty, but probably not."

"Sawyer, if you're implying Riley might be a demon then I'd have to disagree," Sienna said.

I swallowed, throat dry. "Uh, yeah, me too." Not that I had any clue what it would look like if I *was* a demon. Would demons have the ability to, I don't know, summon bursts of flame?

"There is one royalty still around today, and that's the Fae," Sawyer said.

"There's no way this girl is a Fae."

I whipped around as Collette entered the room. She looked at all of us, arms crossed, eyebrows cocked. "Have you *seen* her?"

"The name's Riley," I said through gritted teeth.

"What are you doing here, Collette?" Sienna said.

Collette jerked her perfect head back to the door. "You left it open. And all of you talk so loud it's impossible to ignore."

I watched her eyes flicker around the room, taking in everything in a flash before settling once more on me. "But yeah, definitely not a Fae."

"And how do you know?" I challenged. "Nobody knows what I am."

"First off, no. Just...no. Second, you don't have any glamour. And third," she ticked the points off one by one on her long fingers, "don't you think that if the Fae had some sort of long-lost Fae princess they'd seek her out the second there's any sign of her?"

"That is a good point..." Sienna said, and as much as I hated to admit it, Collette was kind of right. Not that'd I'd actually believed I was Fae.

"Of course it's a good point," Collette said smugly.

"I don't know any more than that," Sawyer said. He'd minimized the prophecy picture and returned to his screens filled with numbers. "Maybe something will show up given enough time. After all, we've waited this long."

"We don't have time," I said. "There has to be something else. Some*where* else."

"Maybe we can stall," Sienna offered. "Lukas was able to convince the Conclave, but I don't think everyone there was on board with it. We could appeal..."

But I wasn't thinking about appealing. I was thinking about Lukas, my mind taking off with new possibilities. Collette was watching me shrewdly, her perfect nose already wrinkling in distaste before I'd even spoken. "You look like you've thought of something stupid."

"Sawyer, do you know where Lukas' hideout—den—whatever is?"

"Riley." Sienna's face had drained of color. "No."

"Yes," Sawyer said.

Sienna whirled on him. "*No.*"

"He has multiple smaller dens all over Cliffside," Sawyer said, clicking around the screen. "Plus some night clubs, liquor stores, and other establishments the Northern Pack technically owns."

"Which one of those places would it be most likely he'd keep important information he didn't want anyone else to know?"

"Told you it was a stupid idea," Collette said as Sawyer clicked away. A few seconds later an enlarged map of Cliffside appeared up on the screens for all of us to see. A single red dot blinked on the western part of the city, in some suburbs right outside downtown, a place called The Heights. I knew it was a more high-end residential neighborhood. A pretty classy place for such a classless shifter.

"This location is the most central to the rest of his dens. Anything important or valuable would most likely be kept there."

"How do you even get all this information?" Sienna said exasperatedly. She seemed to reconsider. "Never mind, I don't want to know."

"I watch and I listen," Sawyer said simply.

"That is soooo creepy," Collette said. I decided not to mention the picture of the back of my head Sawyer had pulled up earlier.

Sawyer merely shrugged. "Every paranormal in Cliffside knows where we are. I figured it was only fair we know where they are too. I don't want to be at a disadvantage if any of them decide to try hurting one of you."

We were silent. Collette actually looked sheepish now. She

clearly hadn't thought of the "why" behind Sawyer's Cold War level of surveillance.

"Well, thanks, Sawyer," Sienna said quietly. "Riley, you can't seriously be thinking what I think you're thinking?"

"I am seriously," I said, growing surer of the idea. "Look, we need answers and Lukas knows something. He was the one pushing to have me discredited and it looks like he's been planning to get his hands on the Loft and whatever power he thinks we have for a while. He's power obsessed and a brute, but he doesn't strike me as the kind of guy who'd go for something without knowing exactly what he's getting."

"So you're a psychologist now?" Collette drawled.

I glared at her. "No offense, but why are you even here?"

Collette shifted uncomfortably as the other two looked at her. "I'm making sure you don't screw anything else up, that's what! Which is exactly what *this* sounds like."

"You can leave anytime," I said.

"Maybe I will!" Collette shot back. But she didn't move, and after a bit I rolled my eyes and continued laying out what I'd come up with.

"Lukas knows about the prophecy," I said. "Hayes, the guy who I...er, let in the Loft..."

"Oh..." Sienna said, and in the glow of the computer screen, I saw her face begin to redden.

I couldn't help grinning. "Yes, the cute one."

"*Gross!*" Collette whispered.

"I saw him at the Conclave meeting," I went on. "He works for Lukas."

"Oh..." Sienna deflated a bit. "Still...bad boys are kind of hot, right?"

Collette made a disgusted face.

"Lukas didn't just send him here to try to disband us," I said. "I'm sure he told Lukas about whatever part of the prophecy he could see and anything else interesting. He's scouting. I bet Lukas has even more info like that. Info on us and other things we might not even know about."

Sienna pinched the bridge of her nose. "Riley, this is so…"

"I'll say it," Collette said. "This is stupid, and it's gonna get us all in even more trouble."

"I was going to say it kind of makes sense," Sienna said.

Collette turned on her, aghast. "*What?*"

"My only fear is, obviously, that Lukas wants you, Riley. Badly," Sienna said. "You'll be walking right into his furry arms."

"That actually might not be true." Sawyer clicked a few times and the single red dot on the map was joined by two dozen more, mostly concentrated on the west and north ends of Cliffside's downtown and the surrounding areas. "I'm sure Lukas moves between a lot of his dens. Though this is his central one, statistically there's a low chance he'll be there."

He swiveled in his chair to face us. "And if you decide to go through with this your different skillsets would be advantageous. Sienna is good at dismantling any defensive charms you might find. I assume Riley has some offensive magic."

"Well…" I said.

"And Collette can use a little glamour to keep everyone out of sight."

"Wait, glamour as in the Fae?" I said.

"W-what?" Collette sputtered. "I am *not* part of this crazy plan. In fact…" she drew herself up. "I think Jasper and Ari would love to know about it."

She stalked toward the door.

"If you tell them, I might let slip who it was that tore Maxime's favorite scarf trying to shrink it down to fit you," Sienna said.

Collette stopped dead.

"And who it was that let the Cornish pixies loose inside last month."

"You wouldn't," Collette said, eyes narrowing.

Sienna pretended to think some more. "And who broke Ari's favorite sword. I distinctly remember she was *pissed* about that."

"I don't want to imagine how she'll react when she finds that out," I said, playing along.

Collette gave Sienna a scowl so intense it almost hurt. She looked at me. "If you think this...this...*crazy* idea is worth it—"

"I do," I said. "But I don't expect any of you to put yourselves in danger."

Sienna scoffed at that. "Riley, you've got a lot of fight, but I know magic isn't your strong suit. Of course I'm coming. But just so we're absolutely clear, are you sure this is the best way?"

I wasn't, but I couldn't let my confidence waver. Lukas had to be hiding something we could use. "He'll never expect us to break in."

"Because it's *insane*," Collette snarled.

I grinned. "Exactly."

❧

"THAT'S PATHETIC. You're not focusing."

And Jasper's nagging wasn't helping. Normally I looked forward to our lessons—just the lessons, not the instructor or anything—but since deciding that we were going for Lukas' place tonight, I had a lot on my mind.

I brought my attention back to the condensed column of fire swirling in front of us. It sputtered weakly, even as I tried to feed it more magic, siphoning it from that great power reserve inside me.

After my magical outburst during our first lesson, using magic did actually seem to get easier. And Jasper hadn't lied: he was a tough teacher, sparse with praise and lavish with critiques. But it was like I'd pushed past a block holding me back. I'd progressed to throwing small fireballs, heating up the floor beneath my feet, even coating my arms in flames without burning my clothes or skin. I was slowly, ever so slowly, mastering control of it.

The pathetic column of fire sputtered one last time and died. I sighed.

Not today, though.

I turned to Jasper. He'd remained strangely silent, but I had no doubt he was getting ready to deliver a few choice words.

"Take a break," he said. "You've done enough for now."

"I haven't done anything," I protested, thrown by his mild response. "I've learned a few party tricks, great. But if I don't learn more—"

The rest of my protests were cut off as he threw a towel at my face. "You won't learn anything if you're exhausted. You've done good work so far."

I stared at the towel clenched in my hand. Sure, I felt confident in my idea to sneak into Lukas' place, but I was still no closer to being able to protect myself with magic in case things went south. I was playing with fire—figuratively and literally.

"Hey."

I was startled to find Jasper standing in front of me. His red eyes glittered as they searched my face. "You keep spacing out. What's eating you?"

He never used vampiric compulsion when he asked me anything. He didn't need to—not with those intense eyes that pierced me down to my very soul. I also knew he never would, at least not with me. When Jasper said he'd never hurt me, he'd meant it. That included forcing me to answer when I didn't want to.

Even still, those eyes...I wanted to tell him about Lukas. About what we were about to do. But I knew what the outcome would be. He'd put a stop to it. He'd play it safe. Or, at the very least, he'd want to keep doing what we were doing and training bit by bit until something that answered the prophecy fell out of the sky. We didn't have time for that.

"I'm just worried about the prophecy," I said.

Jasper held my gaze long enough that I could feel my face beginning to heat.

"About that." He stepped around me to grab a bottle of water. As he always did, he tossed one to me first. "I'm going to be gone for a little bit starting tonight."

I caught the bottle but didn't open it. "Where?"

Jasper looked like he was considering how much to tell me. "I'm meeting with the Deathless. Valencia and Farrar to be exact. You remember them from the Conclave?"

I shuddered. How could I forget? "Unfortunately."

Jasper nodded like he was thinking the same thing.

"Why on earth do you need to speak with them?" I said.

Jasper took his time answering, taking a long drink of water and then methodically replacing the cap. I saw it for what it was: stalling.

"Jasper, why are you meeting with them?"

There was a flicker of annoyance on his face. "Not a month in and you're already demanding to know where I go and what I do, huh?"

I realized then I'd taken a step toward him and checked myself. I was overreacting. I was sure Jasper had done stuff like this dozens of times before I'd ever arrived. It wouldn't be any different now that I was here.

So why did I feel so uneasy?

"The three of us have some business to discuss," Jasper said. "And I'm going to ask about the prophecy."

"You think they might know something?"

"That's why I'm asking. With the Northern Pack and the Deathless, you can be sure they always know more than they're letting on."

I barely held in a triumphant smirk. *My thoughts exactly.*

Jasper tossed his empty bottle into the recycling bin. "Don't you worry your frizzy head about it."

"Hey!"

"It'll be for the best."

I finished my own bottle and threw it into the recycle, barely missing Jasper in the process. "Whatever you say. Just…"

I was finding it hard to speak again. Why was it so difficult for me to talk like a normal person around him?

"Is Ari going with you?"

"No." I could have been mistaken, but I swore Jasper's expression darkened. "Just me. This is something I need to do alone." Then he flashed me a grin. "Like I said, you don't have to worry about me. I'll have news when I come back."

We both would. Good or bad, I didn't know. "If you say so."

Jasper waved as he left, leaving me suddenly alone.

I picked up my towel, worry festering in my gut. This was a new feeling, one that had grown stronger with each day I spent with the Outcasts. Not just my feelings toward Jasper—I didn't know *what* was happening with those—but for all the Outcasts. The closer we drew to finishing this prophecy, the more I felt the walls of danger closing in.

I gripped the towel tighter. We'd just have to meet it before it reached us. Starting with Lukas.

I had a wolf's den to visit.

CHAPTER FIFTEEN

We left a little after night had fallen, as soon as Sienna was able to cast enough of an illusionment charm to cover both of us. With the vamps watching the Loft now, we didn't have to worry so much about being smelled as we did about their excellent night vision. If either of us were spotted then word definitely would be getting back to the rest of the Deathless, and that'd be *no bueno* for a number of reasons.

"We good?" Sienna whispered.

We crouched in the mouth of an alley across from the Loft, having dashed there from the front door.

I scanned the Loft. As always, I was struck by how small it appeared from the outside. Only a few lights were on. Ari's room; maybe Collette. I thought I could pick out the dim flicker of Sawyer's screens.

But once my eyes adjusted I could see the vamps.

They stuck out from the shadows like smooth gargoyles, not even trying to blend in. One was leaning in the darkness of the building next door. Another in the small garden of the office beside us. I spied the creeper vamp that liked to peer in my window hovering just outside the reach of the Loft's improved defensive charms. I wondered if a good throw could knock him out of the sky. None of them seemed to be paying any attention to us.

"We're good," I whispered back.

We hurried from cover, still being sure to stay out of the light in case any overly perceptive vamps watching thought something looked out of place. The street the Loft was on had relatively low traffic, but the moment we turned onto the main road it became a challenge not to bump into anyone.

"Sorry!" Sienna hissed as she was shoved into me again. "Let's...just...Follow me this way!"

It took a few tries, but she finally grasped my arm and tugged me out of the flow of passersby. "Hold still."

I imagined her waving her hands. A moment later I felt a cold trickle down my neck as the illusionment charm dripped off me. Sienna did hers next until we both stood there, looking a little bumped and disheveled.

"Guess I should have done that sooner," Sienna said sheepishly. "Though I'm not sure how many more times I can pull it off tonight."

"It's okay," I said, starting to walk again, following the curve of the street. "We should stay more out of sight anyway. Who knows how many from Lukas' pack are hanging around right now?"

Sienna glanced around and sped up.

I didn't really think Lukas or the Deathless would have sent people to wander the city in the off chance they'd run into us, but then again, what did I know? They might be paranoid and power hungry enough to do just that. I'd have to stay on my toes.

We kept up the swift pace, diving down side streets, past pools of light emanating from the insides of shops and boisterous-sounding bars that had just opened for the night. Cars honked and in the sky were the strobing spotlights from the nearby convention center where a concert might have been going on. The night life of a city teeming with energy.

A strange sensation had started creeping up my back. One that told me we were being watched. I'd waited to see if it would go away once we passed more of the bars—after all, I'd been more alert than usual lately—but almost an hour later it'd only grown worse.

I stopped. "Sienna—"

"I feel it too."

She looked across a nearby beer garden's patio. Then to the quiet park where couples and families were taking late night strolls. "It's impossible to tell where it's coming from, though. You don't think one of the vamps saw us, do you?"

"I'm not sure. Quick, turn here."

We took a sharp left and the feeling suddenly stopped. I let out a small sigh of relief. Seems we'd temporarily lost our pursuer—

A burly figure stepped out, blocking the street we'd turned onto. "You ladies are out a little late, aren't you?"

The man leered down at us, a single sharp canine poking out from his upper lip. "I spotted you back there and thought, 'That's those Outcasts, isn't it? No way they'd be going out all alone, but here you are.'"

"Here we are," I said, taking a step back.

"We're just on a walk," Sienna said unconvincingly. "Let us by."

"No can do." The man's leer deepened. "You're in Pack territory and the boss has been wanting to speak to you." He jerked his head at me. "I think I'll do him a favor and take you to him."

I held out my hand and pulled from my magic until a decent-sized fireball sat in my palm. Already this night was *not* going how I'd hoped. "Let us through."

The man chuckled. Then he began to rapidly shift, until a wolf bared his teeth at us. *"Try your luck."*

I wound up, preparing to throw my fireball like an opening pitch when someone yelled, "Look away!"

143

I wasted a precious second trying to figure out who had spoken before Sienna clamped her hand over my eyes. There was a searing flash of white. Spots danced in my vision. I heard the high whine of a wolf then someone collapsing to the ground.

"Thanks," I gasped as Sienna let go of me and I wobbled in place, temporarily disorientated. I'd just managed to blink away the spots when someone grabbed my hand and yanked me after them.

"Hurry up and run!" a familiar voice hissed.

I caught a glimpse at the unconscious werewolf behind us before struggling to half run, half stumble after our savior. We dashed back one street then over a few more until I stopped counting, losing my bearings in a haze of neon lights and cool night air. After what felt like a mile we came to a stop outside a supermarket and slipped out of sight around the side.

"Okay," I said, breathing hard. "What just—*Collette?*"

The other girl had her hands on her knees, trying to catch her breath. I briefly marveled at how someone so slight had managed to pull both of us. "What are you doing here?"

Collette looked up and furiously brushed a sweaty strand of hair out of her face. "Following you. Idiot."

"Wait, was that you we felt following us?"

"No, that was the shifter who nearly attacked you. The one who probably already told all his friends that some of the Outcasts were stupid enough to go out on their own."

"Here." Sienna pulled a block of something strong-smelling from her pocket and wafted it beneath Collette's nose.

Collette knocked her hand away and straightened up, eyes blazing. "I can't believe you. When you talked about your stupid little plan, I didn't think you were serious."

"Of course I was," I said. "This *is* the best chance we have."

"This? *This?*" Collette motioned to where we stood, alone and exhausted in an unknown area. A few shoppers glanced our way as they left the store.

"Obviously not this exactly," I said.

"I'm so glad you had an ideal image of how this night was supposed to go. Now we're stuck in the city with two of the biggest paranormal groups looking for us." Collette took a moment to pin her hair back and straighten her clothes. "And you're lucky it was just one shifter. Any more and that pathetic matchstick you call magic wouldn't have cut it. What were you going to do? Roast them a marshmallow?"

"Hey, I didn't ask you to come!" I said. "And I don't hear you offering any better suggestions for what we should do."

"Guys..." Sienna tried to step between us. "Maybe we should discuss this somewhere else."

"Great idea," Collette said. "Now that we've all wasted our time out here, we can head back."

She turned and started in the direction of the Loft.

"No. We're not done," I said.

Collette froze. "Are you really that stupid?"

"If I am then it's by choice." I started walking in what I was pretty sure the direction to Lukas' den. "You can head back. I've got a prophecy to figure out."

"I'm with Riley," Sienna said, sounding torn. "Just...get back home safe. We'll be back before morning."

A moment later I heard a frustrated growl, followed by a "I can't *believe* this," and Collette started after us.

"I hope you know what you're getting into," she called. "The Deathless may be somewhat refined, but the Northern Pack is more brutal than any other. This Lukas guy? I heard he likes to kill his enemies slow, just for fun."

"If you're trying to scare me, you'll have to try harder than that," I called back.

"I talked to Jasper after that last Conclave meeting. He said even Valencia and Farrar are scared of him. You know how old those two are? You know how many paranormals *they've* killed to get to where they are now?"

Now Sienna was looking a bit frightened. I stopped to glare back at Collette. "Lukas won't be there. And if you're so worried, you should be happy to go along with us. You already saved us once. Maybe it'll happen again."

"That was luck. Everybody knows I'm not that good at magic."

I cocked an eyebrow. That sounded oddly modest of her. "How's that? Aren't you like part Fae or something? I would think they're good at magic."

Sienna sucked in a sharp breath. Collette's face began to color; first red, then purple. She shoved past us and stalked ahead. I stared after her, beyond confused.

"Did I...say something wrong?" I asked Sienna.

"I guess Jasper and Ari didn't tell you about it," Sienna said with a sigh. "Collette's technically a faerie. They're like half Fae. And to the Fae they're considered half-bloods."

"Is that bad?" I said. "Like Sawyer said, aren't a lot of the races half one thing?"

"Yeah, but the Fae are kind of jerks about it. Anyone who has Fae blood and isn't full Fae is considered lesser. Like second class citizens."

I watched Collette's ever-shrinking back. "That's horrible."

"Collette doesn't like to talk about it, but I know she didn't have the easiest childhood because of that," Sienna said. "I think her mom actually lived in the Fae realm. Collette lived with her until she was pulled here with us."

I tried to imagine what that must have been like, to have been cast out and looked down on just because of the way you were born. These past couple weeks I'd felt more out of place in some ways than I ever had before. I couldn't imagine feeling that way my entire life.

"I'll be right back," I said.

I hurried to catch up to Collette, who'd stopped at the top of the hill. Despite claiming this entire trip was stupid, she'd led us to exactly where we'd needed to go. Lukas' den was only a few blocks away, on the other side of one of the towering neighborhood gates bordering the sidewalk.

I felt Collette's glare burning into me as I reached her. She jerked her head over the nearest wall. "Here you are. Perhaps you have an access code to the front gate. Or maybe you'd like to pole vault over, add a bit of extra thrill to tonight."

"I'm sorry," I blurted out.

She sneered. "Whatever."

"I'm serious, I'm sorry," I said. "I didn't know about you and your family and I should have asked."

"Stop apologizing. That pisses me off." Collette kept her arms crossed, still turned away from me. "I bet Sienna told you all about me, didn't she?"

"Only a little. Only about the Fae and faeries. I figured I'd ask you about the rest."

"Screw that. I'm not dumping my story for you to sob over."

I didn't know what else to say. Sienna had stopped a little ways down the hill, giving us some space.

"The Fae aren't that great anyway," Collette said. "All they care about is appearances and partying. Why would I ever want to be like them?"

I thought of all the times I'd seen her in the gym. The countless hours Sienna told me Collette typically took to get ready each morning.

"You know, you're probably the most beautiful girl I've ever seen, magic or not," I said. "I haven't seen many—well, any—Fae. I bet they have nothing on you."

"Whatever," Collette said, but her tone had less bite. "I'm not even that great. My mom's the one I have to thank. She raised me all by herself in the Fae realm. My good-for-nothing Fae father was too busy sleeping around with every girl he could get his disgusting hands on to pay her any attention once he brought her there." Her jaw tightened. "Like I said, the Fae aren't that great, no matter what anyone else says."

She looked at me. "So are we doing this or what?"

I hadn't learned as much about her as maybe I should have, but it also didn't seem like she was eager to tell me anything more. Maybe I'd learn more in time, if she ever saw me as any more than someone to ridicule.

I looked up at the high fence. Obstacle number one of what I was sure was going to be many tonight. "We're doing this. Hopefully I won't have to roast too many marshmallows."

"Hopefully I won't have to save your butt again." Collette sighed as I gripped one of the thick metal bars and began to climb the fence. "But we both know that's not likely."

I couldn't help throwing a grin back at her. "And that's what makes it fun."

⋇

LUKAS' "Den" was swanky, a luxurious Italian-style villa complete with a wide, perfectly tended lawn, smooth marble edifices, and a small lake in the back with a gazebo on an island in the center.

"Is this one of his bases of operation or the world's most lavish bachelor pad?" I said.

"The vamps' places are almost worse," Sienna said. "Talk about luxury. Leon and I had to visit one once. You'd think, for beings trying to stay out of sight, they'd go for something a little more subtle."

Collette craned her head over the bush we'd taken cover behind. "They have any of that electronic security stuff? You know, magically shielded like Sawyer's computers?"

"I doubt it," Sienna said. "It took Sawyer a long time to make something that could do that, and he's probably the smartest person I know. I don't think they'd have it."

I didn't voice that, just because Sawyer's genius had trouble creating it, that didn't mean Lukas wouldn't have it. Though from what I'd seen so far of his pack, "genius" wasn't a word I'd use to describe them.

I scanned the rest of the outside. No shifters on guard, at least none that I could see. If Sienna was right and they didn't have any security, then this might be the easiest first break-in ever.

"One second." Sienna caught my arm right as I was about to step across the lawn. "They might have alarm charms."

She closed her eyes, then frowned slightly when she opened them a couple seconds later.

"Odd. No charms or hexes. Not even a simple jinx."

"Cocky," I said.

"Or dumb," Collette said.

I couldn't argue there.

With everything seemingly clear, we slunk across the yard, using the bushes as cover, until we reached one of the numerous back doors.

"Move." Collette pushed Sienna and me aside and put her hand on the lock. A moment later there was a click and we were inside.

"You'll have to teach me that," I whispered.

"Just melt the lock," she said. "If you can without blowing yourself up. Where now?"

I paused to listen. The house was silent. Sawyer must have been right and Lukas was away. "Let's find wherever he'd keep important information. An office or file room or bunker hidden behind a secret wall."

Collette glared at me, but I was already focusing on summoning a small ball of fire. The flame cast a little light as we set to work checking all the doors. None of them were locked, and Sienna triple-checked that there were no spells inside either. I suppose that was one unforeseen perk to not knowing spells and not trusting anyone who did: it sure made it a lot easier for novice thieves.

I checked each of the doors down the next hallway while

Sienna made her way toward the front door. I caught Collette checking out one of the weird statues Lukas had apparently thought perfect for creeping out whatever guests he had over. I almost told her that we didn't have time to play art connoisseur but didn't feel like getting snapped at. I felt like we'd overcome a low barrier of sorts between us—a temporary truce, if you will— but I wasn't under the illusion that we were best of pals.

I tried the next door and peeked inside. Books. An obnoxiously large chair behind an equally obnoxiously large desk. Filing cabinets. A study. Bingo.

I slipped inside and went immediately to the first file cabinet. I was legitimately shocked to find them unlocked, but when I fanned through them I could see why: they contained mostly notes on pack locations and recorded minutes from their get togethers. Nothing useful. Even his desk was pretty much bare of anything. No papers. Not even any handwritten notes or a picture. It was like the guy existed in a sterile environment. Though to be fair, it was hard imagining Lukas leaving heart-shaped notes across an adorable puppies calendar.

The final desk drawer at the bottom was locked. I pulled it again, just to be sure it hadn't gotten stuck but the thing was jammed tight.

"When one thing's not like the other..." I mused.

I looked for something to force it open. Maybe a letter opener or a stray crowbar—thugs like this had those lying around, right? —but found nothing. The guy probably didn't deal with his own mail. Or if he did, he used his claws.

I stared at the drawer, thinking about what Collette had said. I *could* melt the lock. That'd be blatantly obvious evidence that somebody had broken in, but it wasn't like he'd suspect me. After all, to him I was merely the easily manipulated new girl.

I turned my ball of flame toward the lock and pushed more power into it. At first the flame sputtered and sparked, then caught, growing bigger and turning blue as I coaxed it to slip between the crease of the drawer. I waited tensely as my fire slowly ate away at the metal.

At last the drawer popped open. I yanked it all the way out, being careful not to touch the slagged bits of metal that had dripped down the inside.

There was nothing but a couple manila folders near the back. They didn't even look all that full.

Confused now, I tossed the folders onto the desk and leafed through them. Maps. Tons of them. Torn from books and atlases, most with illegible scrawl in the margins. Some had lines sketched across them that had then been scratched out and redrawn in other locations.

I flipped through the rest of the papers, trying to make sense of it all. A few maps were of the world. Cities had been circled, then crossed out: Edinburgh, Copenhagen, Paris. Beneath those were city-level maps of Cliffside, the kind you might pick up from the city's visitor's center. This too had points circled on them, this time with huge lines drawn in marker across the city, all in different directions, all of them evenly spaced apart. No matter how many times I turned the map back and forth they didn't make any sense to me. The maps of the world were even more unclear.

I let out a grunt of frustration as I haphazardly began tossing the papers back into their folders. My fingers brushed across the last page. The layout of this one looked different than any of the others and my hopes briefly soared before I realized it was only a schematic of what looked like sewer tunnels and maintenance stations beneath Cliffside. A dried bit of crimson had stained the outside edge in a horrible splotch. I quickly dropped it back with the others before throwing it in its drawer again.

I stood, stomach a little sick from seeing the dried blood. It seemed Lukas was a budding archeologist. But that didn't mean he needed to keep his search a secret. What was he searching for? And worse, had he already found it?

I jumped as the door creaked open. Collette peeked in, eyes narrowing as she took in the office. "This room's as ugly as everything else." She looked at me. "We haven't found anything. I saw a sort of domed-looking room on the other side of the house as we came in. Sienna wants to check it out. I said we should leave while our luck holds, but…" She let out an angry huff. "Stupidity seems to be powering this little adventure."

"Let's check it out." I followed Collette through the kitchen to an entire other wing of the house I hadn't realized was there. My spirits sank. We hadn't even searched this and I feared Collette was right: we needed to finish up here soon while good fortune was on our side.

Sienna was already at a pair of double doors at the end of the hall. She tried the handle and the door easily opened.

"Kind of the theme for tonight," Sienna whispered.

I summoned another ball of flame and together we moved inside the dark room. It was slightly larger than Lukas' study, with a table in the center and the domed conservatory ceiling arching high above us. I felt my pulse quicken, though I wasn't sure why. This room appeared empty.

"Let's look quick," I said. "If we don't find anything here then we—"

The words died in my throat as my light reflected off a pair of yellow eyes set above a mouth of sharp, glittering teeth.

"I hope you found what you were looking for," Lukas said. "It'll be the last chance you get."

CHAPTER SIXTEEN

I immediately backed up, shoving the others toward the door before I heard it slam shut. I whirled to find two more shifters—what looked like a wolf and the same bear shifter from the tunnels, bandage covering his human nose and everything—blocking our way. My eyes stung as someone flicked on the lights.

"I wouldn't," Lukas drawled as we all raised our hands, ready to attack. "Let's talk like civilized paranormals, Riley. Otherwise I'll have no problem telling my pack to rip your friends apart."

I bit the inside of my lip hard enough to bleed, wondering if I could summon a big enough ball of flame to add a new scar to his face. "What do you want?"

"That's what I should be asking you," Lukas said. A growl of warning crept into his voice. "You've trespassed into *my* turf. By Conclave laws, I can administer whatever punishment I see fit. Not even those annoying Outcast rules can save you."

When none of us lowered our arms, Lukas' face twisted into a sneer. "Or I could kill you all right now." The other shifters boxed us in, snarling. "Your choice."

I met Sienna and Collette's eyes, trying to convey how sorry I was for dragging them into this. As one we slowly put our hands down.

"Wasn't that easier?" Lukas said. "You'll find a lot of things are easier when you do as I say."

"And you'll find I'm not the best at following instructions," I said.

"I know. You probably came here after someone explicitly told you not to. You probably came here without telling anyone else where you were going."

I felt the blood drain from my face. Lukas' grin grew. "I'm close, aren't I? How fortuitous for me that I was alerted to your presence, then."

"How did you know we were here?" Collette demanded. "The security sucks so much in this place I can't believe you found out that way."

"You can thank me for that."

Sienna let out a small gasp as Hayes stepped out from the shadows of the corner, as though he'd simply popped into existence.

"Yes, Hayes has proved his usefulness tonight," Lukas said. "He also did an excellent job getting a look inside your little Loft."

Hayes smirked. "It wasn't that hard. It's amazing what you can get when you flash a girl a charming smile."

Collette grabbed Sienna's arm as she took a step toward him. "I take it back," Sienna seethed. "You're not that cute."

Hayes pressed a hand to his chest in mock hurt. "*Oof*, that pierced my heart. I really thought we had something. At least you liked me well enough to completely miss that link charm I left on you."

"You—" Sienna's face splotched red. She turned to Collette. "Did he…"

Collette shut her eyes for a half second then nodded, glaring at Hayes. "You really left it on her, you creep."

Hayes shrugged, totally unrepentant. "I couldn't get it to stick to her." He jerked his head at me. "So her best friend would have to do."

Sienna let out a sound not unlike a cat wanting to claw someone's eyes as Collette's grip on her arm tightened.

"He could pick out some of your emotions through the charm," Lukas said. "When we learned you were coming here it was too perfect." His yellow, orb-like eyes pierced me again. "Did you have a nice tour? Find anything *interesting?*"

I finally understood. How incredibly easy it'd been to break in. The lack of other clues anywhere else in the house. They'd led us here like mice following a trail of cheese. Even finding the supposedly hidden folders hadn't been that hard. Because it wasn't supposed to be.

"Those maps should look a little familiar," Lukas said, clearly enjoying the fury I imagined was covering my face. "After all, you've been to the underground. You've seen something down there, haven't you?"

"What's he's talking about, Riley?" Sienna said.

I didn't answer, my mind clicking the pieces together. The underground. The drawn lines, perfectly spaced apart, seeming to crisscross at random along different points. They weren't marking coordinates or cordoning off places to search; the lines themselves were what he was following. Lines of power. Ley lines, hadn't that been what Sawyer had called them? And if Lukas was following those...

"You've been searching for the prophecy's tunnel, too," I said.

"And you're the dowsing rod that'll lead me right to it," Lukas said with a satisfied smirk.

I let out a humorless chuckle. "Sorry to be a party pooper, but the tunnel doesn't exactly come when called. I've tried looking and can't get it to appear again."

"It'll appear if given the right motivation," Lukas said. "After all, you're the only one who can find it."

"I won't use my magic to help you find it."

"No, not your magic. Your presence will be enough. What you *are* is what it's calling to. I'm terribly surprised you haven't figured that out yet."

The other shifters continued boxing us in, pressing Sienna and Collette up against my back. I couldn't take my eyes off Lukas, but not just because I was scared. Because there was something he knew. Something I needed to know. "And what am I?"

Lukas took a step closer, until I could see every sharp edge of his teeth. "An elemental. An ancient being of pure magic."

Collette let out a barking laugh. "I thought you were dumb before, but this—Agh!"

The wolf shifter had grabbed her arm and twisted it back, bringing his teeth near her throat.

"Get your hands off her!" Sienna yelled.

She cast a spell, but with a flick of his hand, Hayes sent it careening harmlessly off the ceiling. He slipped in between her and the bear shifter, holding a glowing hand at up at her face. "Let's not make things messy."

"You're not taking this seriously," Lukas said. I smelled raw meat as his breath brushed across me. "Maybe this will get your attention."

Collette let out another squeak of pain as the wolf torqued her arm harder. She glared up at Lukas, tears prickling the corners of her eyes.

"She's not taking it seriously because it's insane! The Fae are the oldest paranormals and they've never said anything about elementals!"

"Maybe it's because even the Fae don't know," Lukas said. "Or maybe because even they wanted to keep it secret. After all, what Riley is would be a threat to even their power."

Collette screamed as her arm was twisted harder.

"Stop it!" I said. "Stop hurting them! I'm—I'm listening."

Lukas stared at me for a long moment before jerking his head. Collette groaned as her arm was released. Hayes backed away from Sienna, hands still up.

My mind raced, torn between getting my friends to safety and wanting to know more. "Okay...Say I'm this elemental—"

"Part elemental," Lukas said. "True elementals are gone, lost to the eons of time back when the world was first formed."

Blood of mortals, blood of old.

"Part, then. What does that have to do with the tunnel? Why do *you* care?"

"Simple. I want power. You've only just joined our world and yet I know you've seen how divided and petty it's become. We squabble over useless matters. We stay confined to the shadows." He clenched a fist, making all the tiny white scars on the back of his hand pop. "We need a strong leader. Someone with a clear vision for all paranormals. Long ago, the elementals were the paranormals' true rulers, along with the true dragons of the air, and the leviathans of the sea. Beings of pure, chaotic magic. You are one of their last living descendants."

"But..." My head was spinning again. "How? How is that possible?"

"It doesn't matter how. What matters is that the tunnel and what resides at the end of it is calling to you. It wants you to take what it thinks is your rightful place."

"The throne," Sienna whispered. I glanced back to see her looking at me, eyes wide. "That second to last line. The ancients' throne."

I shook my head to cut her off before she could say more, but it was too late. A truly terrifying smile spread across Lukas' face. "Well, well, I was right after all. That tunnel leads to more than your supposed destiny. It leads to accession."

"Way to go, Sienna," Collette mumbled.

"I would have figured it out," Lukas said. "A throne... That sounds absolutely perfect."

He turned back to the table. This was covered in more maps like those in his study, even more detailed than the others.

I stared at them, temporarily too stunned to speak. I knew Lukas was conniving and a liar who would say anything to get what he wanted. Yet as crazy as he sounded, what he said resonated as truth in the deepest part of me. Not only was I supposedly this...this ancient creature that neither I nor any of the Outcasts had heard about, but there was a throne. Royalty. A *queen*. Supposedly the prophecy was calling me to become a queen. Me, a girl who up until a few weeks ago thought that getting her first part-time job was a huge step in responsibility.

"Listen to this guy," Sienna's voice broke through my thoughts, bringing me back to the present and the desperate situation we were still in. "You really want to work for this idiot?"

"Watch it..." the bear shifter growled.

"I'm just saying, people of your, er, talents have lots of opportunities that don't involve brutalizing helpless girls."

"You're hardly helpless," Hayes scoffed. "We all do what we have to. Maybe one day you'll see it from my perspective."

Sienna snorted. "Doubt it."

"Right or wrong it doesn't matter what any of you think," Lukas said, not turning from the table. "Riley and I will scour everywhere we need to find this throne."

"No," I said, forcing the word out. "I won't help you."

"You won't have a choice. You might be able to find this throne by yourself, but if you take your supposed place as elemental ruler, do you really think the other paranormals are going to give up power to a magical being most haven't heard of? The Fae, the vamps, the shifters, even the Horde. All of them will reject you. Hate you. You'll need allies. You'll need me."

"I'll figure it out when the time comes," I said, trying to catch Collette's eye. "The Outcasts and I all will."

Collette finally looked at me. I blinked rapidly, trying to emulate what it might look like if someone had just been stunned. At last she seemed to understand, right as Lukas let out a low chuckle.

"The other Outcasts won't be able to help, not when they're my captives. Think of it as an added incentive to cooperate. And if you don't, I'll make each of your friends suffer, starting with these two. I'll torture them until they plead for mercy."

"Who will you get to make them plead? These losers?" I said, trying to keep my voice from shaking. "You might not have noticed, but ugly mug over there already failed you once."

"Watch your mouth..." the bear shifter growled.

"And your other guys couldn't take us on before. Of course you'd need us as prisoners to beat us up. It's the only way they can beat girls."

"Don't take the bait," Hayes admonished as the wolf shifter let out a low growl. "She's just provoking you."

And it was working. I watched the two shifters' snouts elongate. Watched their eyes change from human to the far, far more light-sensitive eyes of an animal.

"Collette!" I yelled.

Collette was already thrusting her hand up as I turned Sienna away from the sudden blast of brightness.

I heard a pair of pained howls. Then Collette screamed. The light cut out sooner than I'd anticipated. I uncovered my face to see that Lukas had covered his eyes and crushed Collette's hand in one enormous fist.

"Don't touch her!" I roared, magic flaring to life.

Lukas had a second to spin out of my way as I swiped at him, fists spewing flames.

"Go!" I yelled to Sienna. "Both of you get out, I'm right behind you—"

"No you're not!"

I turned as Lukas lunged at me, shifting in midair as he came down. I rolled out of the way and came up facing a wolf bigger than any I'd ever seen before. If I'd thought Lukas was scary as a human, then his wolf form was terrifying: big as a bull with jaws that could easily break me in two. Cruelly intelligent eyes focused on me over a snout covered in scars.

I tried backing toward the door, but terror clenched my heart and my legs remained stubbornly in place. My entire body shook as Lukas stalked toward me, trembling the ground.

"You're an idiot if you think I'm going to lose my prize that easily," he growled. *"But I'm feeling generous: I'll let your friends go, for now. They can scamper back to that little Loft of theirs and warn the other Outcasts. It makes no difference to me. They'll all be mine in the end."*

I willed my body to attack, run, do something, but it refused to move as Lukas stalked closer. He let out a rumbling chuckle. He was almost close enough to bite.

"Is joining me really so bad, Riley? You have a destiny to complete. I'm just helping you get there a little faster. With me, you won't have to fear anyone ever again. With me, you could have anything you ever wanted. All I'm asking is for a little help in return."

"Riley!" Sienna sounded desperate. She sounded just like Iris had, the last friend I'd failed to protect. That same event was happening all over again. I couldn't see her or my family anymore because I hadn't been strong enough.

I clenched my fists, fire spewing between my fingers. "You have no idea what I want."

The scars on Lukas' snout twisted as he frowned. *"Don't you dare—"*

I threw a fireball but Lukas leapt at the last moment, the flames just singeing his fur and igniting the table behind him. I spun as Lukas snapped at me. I felt a burning sting on the outside of my left hand where his bite barely missed. He pivoted to attack again but my fire had caught unnaturally fast onto other parts of the room and cut him off from me. In seconds, the conservatory had become a near-inferno.

"Hurry up and get your butt out of there!" Collette screamed at me.

I waved away the nearest flames to create a small channel for me and I sprinted after them. The ground trembled as Lukas pursued.

"No you don't!"

"Stay back!" I threw a burst of flame as he leapt through a barrier of fire, barely missing me and bulldozing a cabinet I'd barely avoided. I threw myself out of the room after Sienna and Collette. An enraged howl followed me, but there was no time to celebrate. The rest of the house was filling with howls; more shifters that Lukas was calling in. Hayes had disappeared, but I didn't really care where he'd gone. Just as long as he wasn't in our way.

"Gotta get out right now. Right now!" Sienna said as the howling increased.

A panther shifter cut us off at the end of the hall and we went right, trying desperately to find any opening to escape.

"Any other brilliant ideas?" Collette yelled back at me.

"Just keep running!" I panted.

Easier said than done. The house had somehow become more of a maze than it was before, every new corner leading to some-where unrecognizable. The shifters closing in weren't helping my nerves any. Where were the freaking doors out of here? Or windows? Hadn't we seen a billion of them on our way in?

"Guys!" Sienna pointed down an empty hallway. At the end was a blessedly shifter-free door. Our salvation.

Sienna dashed ahead, Collette and I hot on her heels.

I didn't see the panther until it was too late. It blended perfectly with the shadows, the only thing giving it away was the golden glow of its eyes as it pounced on Sienna.

"Watch out!" I screamed.

The panther slammed into Sienna, knocking them both against the far wall. Sienna screamed and her leg twisted beneath her. Collette yelled something I couldn't make out—maybe a spell, maybe a curse. I lost all sense of my surroundings, my focus only on helping free my friend.

"Get off her!" I drove a fist into the panther's muscular side. I didn't expect it to do much, but the panther snarled and stumbled off her. Yet almost immediately it recovered and lunged for me. I braced for the hit.

There was a whimper, then the sound of a body hitting the wall. I opened my eyes to find the panther out cold on the other side of the hall, the last remnants of a spell drifting off its fur.

"Bullseye," Sienna said weakly, dropping her hand. She looked up at me, blood trickling from her forehead down the side of her face. "Help me up?"

I wasted no time looping my shoulder beneath one of her arms. Collette did the same on the other side. Her eyes flickered to the panther. "Nice hit. Didn't think you knew much offensive magic."

"I don't. I...might have overdone it with that one. I didn't want him to hurt you guys."

"Fine by me," I said.

"Same," Collette said.

Sienna's twisted leg must have been worse than I'd thought because she winced every other step. I wished we could have stopped to address it but we were already moving slowly enough as it was. I was sure another shifter would come across us any second.

We took the next corner. Right as two more shifters appeared in the hallways ahead of us.

"Hex it all!" Collette yanked us to the right, straight into a dead end.

I gently slipped from beneath Sienna's arm and tried both doors of the small annex. Locked. Of course. No windows either. If any shifters—or Lukas—found us here we were beyond screwed.

"Let me try to unlock one." Sienna's hand was shaking so much that Collette put hers over it and gently pushed it back down. She looked at me.

"Tell me you can do something useful."

"I'll try to melt one of the locks."

I went over to the first door again, gently coaxing my magic to work and not blow up in my face. I was so on edge right now I worried I'd have more trouble controlling it than getting it to answer at all.

I'd just put my hand to the doorknob when I heard a grinding sound. I spun around to find one of the walls beside the door sliding away, revealing a single narrow staircase down.

I glanced at Collette.

"Don't look at me," she said. "I didn't touch any secret switches."

"Then who...?"

There was a mournful howl close by, followed by two more, and a distinctively pissed-sounding bear growl. Seemed our partners in death tag had found their downed panther friend. They'd be here any second.

"We should take it," Sienna said, peering down the steps. She looked worriedly at the mouth of the hall. "Preferably now."

"It could be a trap," I said. "It's *probably* a trap."

"Better than staying here. Help me," Collette said.

I grabbed Sienna's other side and we started gingerly easing ourselves down the first steps. I jumped as the wall began grinding closed behind us. I looked back just in time to see a figure framed in the doorway, looking down at us. Their outline looked vaguely familiar. Was it...Hayes? No, this person was wearing a hood, and his face was—

"You!"

"Watch it!" Collette hissed as I nearly sent us all tumbling down the stairs. "What's your problem?"

The wall slammed shut. I stared at the dark wall of black

where the figure had stood. Where I *thought* someone had stood. I must have been wrong. It couldn't be possible that my killer was here. It must have been my hyped-up imagination. That was the only logical explanation.

"Riley?" Sienna was looking concernedly at me.

Even in the dim light, the blood and pain on her face stuck starkly out at me and I mentally kicked myself. I didn't have time to mess around with phantom figures. Not here. Not now.

"You good?" Sienna said.

"Peachy." I started helping her down the next steps. "Let's blow this popsicle stand."

LUKAS MUST HAVE BEEN USING these tunnels for his little scavenger hunt. We saw signs of recent activity; piles of spent batteries and dead flashlights. Empty bottles of water. There was no rhyme or reason to their placement. No sense of where he'd searched and what places he still had to investigate. Lukas might be vicious and calculating, but organized he was not.

"So far so good," I dared to whisper when I felt we'd walked a good ways from the entry of the tunnel. "I don't hear anything following us."

"Lukas uses these to travel between dens, but the shifters aren't the only ones who do," Collette said. "If the Deathless or any of the Horde were here, we wouldn't know."

"Positive thoughts, Collette, positive thoughts," Sienna said. She sounded exhausted. I'd helped Collette wash off most of the blood from her face with one of the half-spent water bottles we'd found. Thankfully Sienna hadn't lost as much blood as we'd thought. But she still needed help. And soon.

We rounded a corner. I felt the light brush of air on my face. I freed one hand and cast a ball of flame. A door jumped out at us, set at the top of a jagged set of stairs. "There!"

Each step seemed to be agony for Sienna as we took it. I forced us all to stop when we reached the top. "Wait." I used my shoulder to shove the door open and peeked out.

We'd come up between two pillars on the abandoned side of a subway station, one I recognized that wasn't too far from the Loft. There were only a few other people on the working side of the platform, on their phones and oblivious.

"Okay, it's safe."

We snuck through and managed to make it to the street without running into any trouble. Sienna's limp was growing worse by the second.

"Almost there," I coaxed her as the Loft came into view. I nearly sagged in relief. The lit-up windows and promise of safety had never been so inviting.

We waited until a pair of police cars and an ambulance, lights flashing, screamed past us before crossing the street. Collette looked suspiciously around as we made our way up the Loft's front steps.

"Where are the vamps? Don't those bloodsuckers usually watch us at night?"

"I'm sure they're there," I said. "We just don't see them."

Though it was strange they hadn't stopped us. I was apparently whom they were most interested in and here I was, injured and at a disadvantage. Easy pickings. Still, I wasn't going to throw back what luck had offered.

"Here we are," I said to Sienna as I went to unlock the door. It swung open before I touched it. I blinked at it, confused. The "something's wrong" bells were going off in my head as we eased our way inside.

"Ah, the guest of honor."

I froze. Collette gasped.

Valencia and Farrar stood in the center of the living room, both grinning at us like cats that'd found a bird with a broken wing. Jasper stood between them and Ari, looking truly murderous. Sawyer lay at Ari's feet, a small pool of blood beneath his head.

"Welcome home," Valencia said, showing every row of her sharp teeth. "Now we can truly get started."

CHAPTER SEVENTEEN

"What the hell is going on?" I demanded. My eyes flew to Sawyer as Ari tended to him. His breathing was strained and skin pale. My chest tightened. "What did you do to him? What are you doing here?"

"It doesn't matter what *we're* doing here. It's you three who have had quite the night, haven't you?" Farrar purred. "The news we've heard…Breaking into Lukas' private den. Assaulting him." He clucked. "That's against some of our most sacred rules."

"He attacked us first." My mouth was dry. I couldn't seem to make sense of everything that was happening. "Part of his pack attacked Jasper and me after the Conclave meeting."

"Unfortunately there's no proof of that," Valencia said.

"Riley."

It hurt to look at Jasper's terrified, almost pleading face. "You guys didn't go to Lukas' den, did you? Tell me that isn't true."

Sienna shifted herself away from my side and slumped heavily into a chair. Jasper's eyes followed her, her movements answering what I couldn't.

"Lukas had information that rightfully belonged to all the Outcasts," I said, unable to look at him. "He's been planning—"

"We know what he's been planning," Farrar said. "We have eyes and ears everywhere."

Before I could fully grasp that Valencia and Farrar knew as much about Lukas' plan as I did, Jasper rounded on them again. "Whatever she's done isn't the problem. You broke the charms and entered the Loft without an Outcast's explicit permission. Our Outcast laws state—"

"You have no laws except for the ones the Conclave upholds," Valencia said. "I'd say what that girl's done this night is far worse than any crime we've committed."

I tried not to let that sting: what *I'd* done. This was my fault. If I'd been here instead of making more of an enemy out of Lukas, maybe I could have prevented it.

"You should see to your friend," Valencia said, nodding to Sawyer. "The little fool shouldn't have attacked us."

A growl ripped from Ari's throat. I saw Jasper shoot her a halting glare before she did what we all wanted to and ripped these two bloodsuckers a new one.

Collette went over to Sawyer and brushed Ari aside. She placed her hands on his chest, fingers glowing. The pain on Sawyer's face eased just a bit.

"I've got him," Collette said to Ari.

"We figured you'd want to hear our offer," Valencia went on. "Lukas is powerful, and you've enraged him like no other paranormal in this city. He'll be after you even more than usual now, if not for his own personal gain then at the very least for revenge. You'll need protection."

"We have protection," Jasper said. "The Loft's charms—"

Valencia gestured to herself, her very presence picking apart his argument. "You need *more* protection. Protection the Deathless are willing to provide."

I didn't like where this was going. I hadn't had many dealings with vampires, but I knew there was a lot of fine print hidden behind their honeyed words.

"And what do you want in exchange for it?" I said. "My blood?"

Farrar's face twisted in disgust. "You think too highly of yourself, my dear. What would we do with the blood of an unknown paranormal?"

I didn't miss the sharp look Sienna shot me. Apparently they hadn't learned of *everything* we had tonight. That was a small victory at least.

"You came to speak earlier about us giving you assistance, Jasper," Valencia said, voice turning silky. "We're going to take you up on that offer."

"How so?" Jasper said warily.

"The night children are all of our family, and we must stick together. You will join the ranks of the Deathless, and in return we will protect the Outcasts from Lukas and any other threats that present themselves."

I waited for Jasper to immediately turn down their offer, but he just stood there, thinking.

"Jas…" Ari said warningly.

"You can't be seriously…" Sienna said.

"Why would you want me?" Jasper said.

"Jasper!" Ari gasped. "Don't even think about it!"

"And why not?" Jasper snarled, turning on her. "Even without tonight, Lukas isn't the only paranormal who's after us, and it's only going to get worse the closer we come to the prophecy. By ourselves, sooner or later, one of us is going to get seriously hurt."

"Now you're seeing it from our perspective," Farrar said. "And a wise perspective it is. As for why we'd want you? Jasper…Jasper…If this girl gives herself too much, you give yourself too little. An Outcast, a Forsworn vampire who feeds on magic, not to mention an excellent fighter. These are enviable qualities."

"We'll even sweeten the deal," Valencia said. "You would join the Deathless as one of our most prized valets. No groveling for rank for you. You would immediately be exalted among others."

"Please consider carefully..." Farrar's eyes flashed. "You wouldn't want to make a hasty decision you'd regret."

I bit my lip. Farrar's threat was beyond obvious, but we weren't in any state to fight two of the head vamps of the Deathless. Not as we were right now. Not without another one of us getting hurt. Even still...

"Jasper?" I said softly.

He continued looking at the ground, conflict raging across his face. At last he lifted his eyes to meet mine.

"I screwed up, I know," I said. "But there has to be a better way. I can ask them if they'll—"

"We don't want you," Farrar butted in.

"Yeah, you made that clear," I snapped. "But maybe I have information you want. I'm the thirteenth Outcast with an entire prophecy behind me. Maybe I'd be worth more than Jasper."

I swore Valencia hesitated before her expression became unreadable once more. "I doubt that. The Deathless would never accept a non-vampire, no matter how much she thinks herself important. That is our offer, Jasper. And our patience is running out."

"I accept," Jasper said. "Yes, I accept," he said when Ari and Sienna started to protest. "The Deathless will protect us. We can't do this alone. You both have known that for a while."

"Yes, but we always said we'd figure it out," Ari pleaded. "How are we supposed to do that when you're gone?"

Jasper turned to the head vampires. "I accept, but on the condition that I only join after the Outcasts fulfill the prophecy."

"Absolutely not," Farrar said. "That could take years."

"Very well," Valencia said, and Farrar gaped at her. "Although we trust you won't use our generous time to stall."

"I won't," Jasper said firmly. "Too many of us are relying on this."

"Then we accept your terms," Valencia said. Farrar looked like he was going to argue more but jerked an affirmation.

"The Outcasts come first," Jasper said to us. He forced a grin, and I felt an uncomfortable pain in my chest. "Besides, we've sucked at solving the prophecy so far. At this rate, I won't be gone for a while yet."

"Kneel," Valencia said.

Jasper knelt before the two of them and I wanted to scream at him to stop. He'd barely put up a fight. Why had he not argued more? Had he gone to them tonight knowing something like this might happen?

Valencia bit the inside of her wrist until a bright red stream of crimson ran down her arm. She held her dripping palm above Jasper and I felt sick as he let a couple drops fall onto his tongue.

"Blood magic, strong and binding," Farrar said. "This will ensure you keep your allegiance where it belongs. If you do not keep your word to join us, you will die."

Jasper wiped his lips and stood. "Good, that's done. Now get out."

Valencia and Farrar gave short bows, both looking sickeningly pleased. My magic stirred, wanting to rise up and consume them both but I stuck my fingernails into my palms until the feeling subsided.

"You all have a wonderful rest of your night," Valencia said before they drifted out into the darkness. The front door slammed shut behind them.

※

"THAT WAS STUPID, JASPER." The words were out of my mouth the moment the vampires had left.

Jasper swelled with anger, straightening up to his full height. I kept forgetting how tall he was. "And what would you call what you did? You dragged two Outcasts into the worst, most dangerous—"

"Technically I went willingly," Sienna said weakly.

"And for what?" Jasper exploded. "Now Lukas wants you more than ever!"

"Like you did any better!" I shot back. "You went right to them to…to…I don't know, ask for help? You knew they'd never do it without wanting something in return, and you didn't bother telling any of us."

"I knew," Ari said.

I threw up my hands. "Great. Wonderful."

"And I told you," Jasper said to me. "But I don't remember asking for your input."

"And I don't remember needing yours. If it were up to you, I'd stay in the Loft like a good little girl while everyone else puts themselves in danger. I know you think you can keep all of us safe, but I've only been here a short time and can already tell that you can't."

"Okay, stop," Ari grabbed Jasper's arm.

"You agree with her?" he snarled. "You think I'm just giving up on you all, is that it?"

She didn't back down from his fierce look. "I'm on your side, Jas. We all are. I know why you had to make a deal with the Deathless, really I do. But without you we're at a severe disadvantage."

Jasper looked at all of us, betrayal covering his face. "So that's what you all think? That I wanted to give myself up like that?"

"Don't put words in our mouths," Collette said. "No one here's blaming you."

"Really? 'Cause it sure feels like it." He jerked his arm out of Ari's grasp and stormed upstairs.

"No," Ari said when I made to go after him. "Both of you need some time to cool off."

I stared up at where Jasper had gone, aching to follow and

continue defending myself to him. I knew Ari was right, though. I was fired up. As I was, I might end up saying something I'd regret later.

"That son of a..."

Sienna opened her eyes, looking even more exhausted if possible. "That ponytailed prick really did put a link charm on me. Tough one to break, too."

"Not so cute anymore, is he?" Collette murmured, hands still roving over Sawyer.

Sienna frowned. "I didn't say that..."

"Okay, out with it," Ari said. She folded her arms and gave me a withering glare. "What the hell did you three do tonight?"

I recounted everything that'd happened, Sienna filling in any details I missed. As we laid it out, Ari's face grew more and more pale, turning nearly milk white as I recalled our time in Lukas' den.

"If he'd caught you...kept you..." She let out a shuddering breath. "I really, *really* hope doing that was worth it."

"We know what he's up to now," I said. "And...he knew what kind of paranormal I was."

Ari looked up sharply. "What?"

"Yeah, he said I was part elemental. That I was destined to take some sort of throne like the elementals from a billion years ago."

Ari's disbelieving face looked like she'd taken a particularly vicious roundhouse to the gut. "What are you talking about? Elementals don't exist."

"That's what he said," I said, suddenly feeling exhausted and not wanting to argue about what may or may not exist in the paranormal world. "I don't know what else to tell you."

"No," Ari was still shaking her head. "He probably meant something else. Elemental magic maybe. Or..."

"It's possible," Sawyer croaked.

I looked over to see he was trying to sit up. The dried blood on the neck and collar of his hoodie looked so gruesome I almost couldn't stand looking at it. Another knife of guilt twisted into me.

"There're a lot of things from a long time ago that we don't know about. Give me a little time and I'll look into it."

"No, you have to *rest*," Collette said firmly, trying to make him lie back down. "Don't be stupid like Jasper and Ari and think you can just hop back up from an attack no problem."

Sawyer reluctantly put his head down, still grimacing. "Lukas isn't an idiot. It sounds crazy, but I'm sure he's done his research. He's probably right."

"Sawyer..." Ari contemplated this, and it struck me at just how right Sawyer must have been on many things if she was so willing to take his word for it. "If it's true, then the vamps *cannot* know. It's bad enough having one of the races after you and whatever your prophecy is, Riley. I really don't think we can deal with two."

She looked up at where Jasper had gone. I could tell she, like me, was thinking we'd barely handled one properly. Not without essentially losing one of our own.

"What about the Horde?" Sienna said. "We could talk to Kaia about it. They spoke to Riley right after the Conclave meeting. I really think they're on her side, part elemental or not."

"Is that true?" Ari asked me. "You think they'll side with us?"

"I'm...not sure," I said honestly. "I trust Kaia. Uko and the rest of the Horde could be in it for themselves just like everyone else. I think..." The possibility didn't feel good, but a deep part of me knew it was a risk we may have to take. "We might have to tell them. About everything. I have a feeling we'll need their help."

Ari let out a long sigh. "I hate to say it, but I agree. Anything else you learned tonight that's going to suddenly make our lives a lot more complicated?"

I recalled the shadowy figure I thought I'd seen as we'd left Lukas' den. In my memory, it changed from Hayes to my killer and back again, switching so many times I wasn't sure who was who. Or which one was worse. We knew Hayes was Lukas' lap dog. But what if my mysterious killer was, too? That'd be flippin' perfect.

"Nothing else," I said.

"Then the goal remains the same," Ari said. "Find this throne or whatever before Lukas does and fulfill the prophecy." She paused for a moment. "I hope that'll solve some of our problems, but I really don't know. Go see Lucinda, Sienna. She can help with your leg—"

Collette let out a barking laugh. "You think figuring out some dumb lines of a poem will solve our problems? The only thing we've gotten since Riley arrived are problems."

She picked up Sawyer, cradling him gently in her arms as she glared at me. "You might find this throne, but if you think we're following some fake queen or elemental or whatever you are then you've got another think coming. Nobody is going to listen to some reckless nobody they've never heard of, prophecy or not."

She stomped up the stairs before I could think of a retort. Not that I had any. She was right. I just wished she wasn't.

CHAPTER EIGHTEEN

I didn't sleep. How could I? There were only about a hundred and three things running around in my head, starting with Sawyer and Sienna's injuries, taking a quick pit stop when Jasper pledged himself to the Deathless, and ending with me supposedly being an elemental. At the rate I was taking to process all of it, I'd be lucky to catch any Z's by the end of the year.

I lingered in the living room, watching the faint pulse of the prophecy's fiery letters. Rodge had come down a couple hours after everyone else had left. He'd jumped at finding me sitting there in the dark.

"Uh, you okay?" he'd asked.

Not even close, but I'd nodded. He'd fished a soda out of the fridge, then held one up as though offering it to me.

"No thanks," I said.

"Okay, then...Okay."

I'd been grateful when he'd left me alone again. I wasn't in the mood to talk to anyone.

I didn't move until the ticking clock had softly chimed five o clock. I couldn't stay here moping forever. I needed to clear my head.

I made my way up the stairs, heading for where Sienna had once told me the Loft's rooftop terrace was. It was where the Outcasts had used to have themed party nights during the summer, before everything got so crazy.

Basically, before I'd arrived.

I stopped, about to head up the final stairwell to the roof. The door to the Gargoyle's Roost was cracked open and Jasper and Ari's voices spilled from within.

"Don't expect me to be happy about what you did," Ari said. I leaned against the wall outside, feeling a little guilty about listening in.

"I don't expect anyone to be happy about it." Jasper's voice was low and distracted, like he was messing with something while he talked. "I expect you to continue watching over the others when I have to leave."

"Do you understand what that means? When you *leave*. For *good*. This isn't some side trip you're taking, this is the Deathless. Lifetime servitude, which for you could mean forever."

"We'll have fulfilled the prophecy by the time I'm gone. The Outcasts won't need to exist anymore."

"Oh, I get it," Ari said in a tone that implied she definitely did *not* get it. "When we're done then we'll all go our separate ways. Drift back to the families we may or may not have left."

"You know that's not what I meant."

"You put yourself in danger and you think it's noble. You *always* do this even when I tell you not to. Even when it's not worth it."

There was a loud *clunk* as someone—Jasper probably—dropped something on the table. His voice took on a biting edge, "Don't patronize me. I had to do that. For all of us."

"That's what you keep saying, but sacrificing yourself isn't helping any of them. It's certainly not going to help Riley."

I leaned in, throat tightening.

"Riley will..." Jasper's voice was soft. "It's better I'm gone. She won't need me anymore once this entire thing is over."

Is that what he thought? That I'd have been better off this entire time without him or Ari or Sienna or every one of the Outcasts?

"Jasper..." Ari said consolingly. "I know why you really do these things, but making yourself suffer isn't going to make up for—"

"Don't," Jasper said sharply.

"Then start freaking listening to me. You can't play it safe and coddle us, then go throw yourself in harm's way. That won't change what's happened. That won't bring—"

Thunk. It sounded like someone had hammered their fist against the wall, so suddenly that I jumped.

"Maybe you're right and I do think that," Jasper said after a moment. "But what's done is done. We have to move forward."

I'd heard enough. I began backing away, heading toward the stairwell again.

The early morning air kissed my skin. The faint blush of dawn colored the horizon, starting to leak into Cliffside's streets.

Ari must have been talking about Jasper's family; the one she said he'd barely told anyone about. I could get why he thought protecting us was somehow protecting them, but Ari was right. The Outcasts would be disbanded once the prophecy was finished, but that didn't mean we'd be safe. And with Jasper gone we'd be at a serious disadvantage. Even more than we already were.

And I...Without him, how would I...?

I shook my head. It didn't matter right now. Like Jasper had said, what was done was done. We needed to be stronger. *I* needed to be stronger.

I pushed all the lawn chairs behind the mini bar to clear out a training space, then set to work. My fatigue from lack of sleep was catching up to me, but somehow it helped me focus. I went through the sparring moves Ari had taught me, then the sequences I'd been working on with Jasper.

With each move the magic in my core grew stronger, but I held it back. I needed control. Right now my magic had two settings: too much and not enough. I needed to be better than that.

I trained until I was a sweaty mess, the dawn truly arrived and blistering, before stopping to catch my breath.

"You're getting better."

I straightened up and calmly turned to face Jasper. He grinned. "Seems I can't scare you quite like I used to."

I wondered if he could hear my heart going. Probably. "What a shame. Guess you'll have to be more creative."

"I'll remember that."

He pushed off from the stairwell door he'd been leaning against and stepped over to me. "You always get this part of the sequence wrong. Here."

"I'm really sweaty!" I blurted out, shrinking from his outstretched hands.

Jasper's hands paused inches from mine. Then his grin widened. "I see that. Shockingly, getting a little dirty doesn't bother me that much. But if you're sure..."

I could have smacked myself. "No. Never mind. It's fine."

Jasper held my gaze a moment longer before reaching around and moving my left arm a tad farther down. His other arm slid around my waist and adjusted my footing. Even with those minute changes my position did feel stronger. But I wondered if he'd really needed to adjust, or just needed an excuse. I wasn't complaining either way.

"There." Jasper's hands lingered on my skin for a beat longer than was probably necessary. His voice sent rumbles into my back and chest. My senses were going wild. I tried to bring myself back down to reality. "Thanks."

"You heard Ari and me talking, didn't you?"

My first instinct was to immediately deny it, but I nodded. "It was kind of hard not to."

"Ari can get very…passionate when she's upset."

"I think she has a reason to be."

Jasper frowned. "Don't you start on me, too."

"Did you go to the Deathless last night planning to offer yourself to them?"

"I went willing to do whatever I had to. I hoped it wouldn't come to that."

"You should have told us what you were planning."

"That's what I should be saying to you." I waited for him to continue chewing me out, but he stepped across from me and put his hands up in a fighting stance.

I attacked without waiting for another invitation. He easily ducked my first kick, but I was able to evade his counterattack as he swung his fist around. I could tell he was tempering his speed for me, but I also wasn't using my magic. This was about as fair a fight as we were going to get.

Jasper feinted but I'd seen him pull that move before and punched where I knew he'd be. He caught my fist in his palm, eyes alight with devilish delight. "Seems the kitten has grown some claws."

"Piss me off and you'll see the tiger," I promised.

"No thanks." He dropped my hand and straightened up. "Ari also told me what Lukas thinks you are. About the throne the prophecy believes you have to take."

"I can't be a queen," I said immediately. "Do you know how crazy that sounds? I don't even want to lead the Outcasts and now there's supposedly some stupid, insane royal destiny I apparently have to fulfill and it's all so…so…"

Jasper let me rant, the corner of his lip quirking up just a bit.

"Well?" I demanded. "What do you think I should do?"

"What do you want to do?" he said.

I thought that over. I could never go back to whatever normal life I'd had. But moving ahead with this was so far beyond my comfort zone it wasn't even funny. If that's what it took to free the Outcasts and see my friends and family again, could I do it?

More importantly, did I really have a choice?

"I still don't know about being queen, but I can't let the other Outcasts down," I said, resigned. "This prophecy, this curse, needs to be broken so they can all go see their families." Jasper's expression had darkened. "So you can go back to your family, too," I added.

"I don't have much family to go back to."

"Can I ask...?"

"I hurt them. Badly," he said, anticipating my question. He turned away, staring off the edge of the roof. "I'm sure they still hate me for it and I don't blame them. They'd never accept me if I ever saw them again."

"Jasper, you don't know that."

I hesitantly lay a hand on his arm. He didn't pull away. "Families can suck sometimes, and yeah you can really hurt them, but they're family. Like the Outcasts. They stick together no matter what."

That managed to get a smile out of him. "Sounds like you've had some personal experience of your own."

"Let's just say I may or may not have caused my parents unnecessary grief as a child. But they took me back no matter what because they loved me."

"And what makes you think mine will still love me?"

"Because I know you. You're brash and hot-headed and passionate and listen to me way less than is good for you. But you care, truly care, about those closest to you. They wouldn't be your family if they didn't understand that."

Jasper chuckled. "I could say the same thing about you. You..."

He turned to face me and I realized how close we stood together. The sunrise haloed his frame and ignited his eyes in a way that was positively unreal.

"You're too hot-headed for your own good." His voice dipped deeper. His face had moved closer to mine, but I couldn't tell if he was the one doing it or I was. "But I'll admit, I find that to be almost...intoxicating."

And then the edges of his lips brushed mine, sending a shockwave all the way down to my toes. I'd been kissed once. Freshman year by a guy I didn't even like that much. This was different. That kiss had been nothing more than a speck of space dust and this, just barest touch of Jasper's skin, just this tiny brush of his lips against mine, was an entire galaxy.

I closed my eyes as our lips brushed again. I tried to take a breath, but it lodged in my throat. My hand tightened on his arm. I was feeling weak. What was going on? We hadn't even actually kissed and he was already making me lightheaded?

I cracked open one eye and nearly gasped.

Fiery tendrils of magic were lifting off my skin and being drawn into Jasper's mouth. With each passing second I could feel a growing edge of fatigue pulling me down. Like my strength was being taken straight from the hot core of power deep inside me, and I couldn't shut it off.

I let out a faint gasp. Jasper's eyes flew open. In a second he'd left my side and was backing away, horrified. The feeling of being drained immediately subsided. I put my hands on my knees, trying to catch my breath.

"Riley." Jasper's voice was a raw gasp. In another instant he was beside me again, hands pressed against my back as though to keep me from toppling over. "That wasn't—I didn't mean for that to happen."

I coughed again. "It's okay. I feel okay."

Jasper's eyes narrowed like he didn't believe a word of it, but I wasn't lying. At least not completely. I already felt back to normal. I checked my magic and couldn't see anything different about it. Seemed the only problem was that I apparently couldn't kiss the guy I probably—no, definitely—wanted to without, well, this happening.

That was just grand.

"Guess I'm just too irresistible, huh?" I said, at last straightening up and giving him an awkward wink.

Jasper grew even more pale. "Don't even joke about this. I shouldn't have lost control like that. I've never...that's never happened with anyone else."

Probably because you weren't trying to kiss them, I wanted to blurt out. But Jasper looked so upset that joking about it felt callous. Still, I didn't completely get what the big deal was. So he'd started to take some of my magic. I could get that back, right? No harm, no foul.

As soon as he was sure I wasn't going to keel over, Jasper took his hands off me. "That was a bad idea."

"Seemed good at the time," I said, growing a little annoyed now.

Jasper continued shaking his head. He looked like he wanted to say more—maybe explain why whatever had almost happened was a "bad idea"—but instead turned and stalked to the door.

"I think we should meet the Horde," he said.

I blinked, confused at the screeching one-eighty the conversation had taken. No transition. No explanation. "Okay..."

"We need allies," Jasper went on. "The Horde are usually neutral in all affairs of the Conclave, but they seem to like you. I'll talk to Ari. We'll find a time to meet."

Before I could respond and, oh, I don't know, get him to slow down and explain a few things, Jasper left.

I stood there, baffled. The wind was suddenly chilly on my skin.

I angrily pushed an empty flowerpot over with my foot.

CHAPTER NINETEEN

My worry about Sienna and Sawyer had gnawed at me for most of the day. The pool of blood beneath Sawyer, so starkly red, had imprinted itself in my head. Though Ari had assured me he'd be fine, I still feared the worst.

But all my fears were laid to rest when I practically barged into his room, demanding to see him.

Sawyer wasn't in bed where Ari and Collette had commanded he stay, but instead perched in front of his computer, one hand fumbling for an open bag of Bugles beside him, never pulling his eyes off the screen. Collette's healing magic must have worked better than I thought. Now he could go back to doing more damage to his body than any vampire ever could.

"Why aren't you resting?" I said.

"I'm all better." He lifted first one arm, then the other, as though movement of two of his four limbs proved it. He hadn't put his hoodie back on yet, and I saw the faint white line at the base of his scalp where the vampire's cut had healed up. Hopefully it'd disappear given enough time. "And I was bored."

I peered at the lit-up screens, watching images of immense, raging creatures flick by. Some were as large as cities, with clusters of tornadoes around them; others weren't much bigger than I was but had mountains as big as Everest crumbling behind them. Each one was mesmerizing and terrible and...

"Are those supposed to be elementals like me?" I said.

Sawyer didn't answer. Another image came on screen, this one of a being made of pure lava, leaving a swatch of scorched earth and bubbling ground in its wake.

"Sawyer?"

"Artist renditions of true elementals. At least what the fantasy community thinks of beings like this," Sawyer finally answered. "There's no way to tell if they're accurate since, as you know, nobody was alive to see them. Or not alive anymore."

Maybe because they were so old. Or...I thought as I looked at the picture. "No one survived an encounter to write about them."

I peered into the soulless eyes of the elemental as it continued to forge its path of destruction. I'd felt that kind of fire deep inside. Felt that extreme lack of control as the tiger had risen up to defend me. Was this what I was, truly? Or was this what I was destined to become?

"Don't stare at the screens too long," I said, swallowing my fear before it could manifest into full-blown panic. "And try to get some more rest."

"Uh-huh."

I grabbed the bag of Bugles and swapped it out with a bowl of carrots and celery sticks one of the others must have left. Sawyer's fingers brushed against them before recoiling.

"Hey...where'd...."

I dumped the Bugles in the trash as I left.

My next stop was to check on Sienna. Ari had told me (after my more-than-a-little confusing rooftop sparring session with Jasper) that I should go see her and Lucinda, the one who was apparently helping her heal.

I immediately headed up to the second to last floor, wondering why I hadn't seen Lucinda before. Granted, I hadn't seen some of the other Outcasts either, but even Rodge had made an appearance, and Ari had said that he could die in his room and nobody would be able to tell the difference for a month. Lucinda liked to hang out by the pool I had forgotten the Loft supposedly had. Maybe she used it as much as Collette used the gym.

On the second floor I found a side hallway I surely would have missed if I hadn't been looking and finally reached a clear glass door completely steamed over.

The moment I walked inside my skin beaded with moisture, my hair undoubtedly preparing to become even more of a frizzy monstrosity. But I wasn't paying attention to that—I'd entered paradise.

A beach of picture-perfect white sand ringed a pool of sapphire-blue water. An island on the other side of the glass-still blue held more sand and real palm trees. The sound of tropical birds squawked over my head, though I couldn't see them.

I spied Sienna and Collette sitting at the edge of the deeper end of the pool. Sienna dangled her injured leg in the water. I could make out a strangely distorted shape in the water beneath.

Sienna's eyes grew wide when she spotted me coming over. She began to awkwardly get up, trying to free her leg from whoever—or whatever—had hold of it below.

"Riley! I didn't expect—How'd you get here?"

"Ari told me," I said. "Don't get up. I don't want to stop your healing."

"No, my leg's fine now," Sienna said, still trying to free it from the thing below, which seemed to have a firm grip on it.

"Stop spazzing," Collette grouched, brushing off beads of water Sienna splashed on her arm. "Not like she was never going to meet her."

I suddenly realized who the shape below must have been. "Is that Lucinda?"

There was a splash. My upper body was suddenly drenched in saltwater as the person below broke the surface.

"Sienna! I'm not done yet! Give me your leg—"

Lucinda spotted me, and I got a good look at her. She had lustrous, coral-green hair, sheeny like a pearl. Short, pointed teeth filled her mouth, open in surprise. But the most shocking thing was the enormous fish tail comprising the lower half of her body, scales glittering as she pumped it to stay above the surface.

"Hey," I said, giving an awkward, soaked wave.

"*Eep!*" Lucinda answered and dropped beneath the surface once more. I watched her fractured form dart across the deep end and vanish around the other side of the island.

"That's what I was afraid of," Sienna said, letting out a long sigh. "It's not your fault, Riley. Lucinda's just really, really, shy. I wanted to give her a chance to hear more about you before meeting you in person."

"She'll get over it," Collette said. "Just give her a minute."

"Okay. Uh..." I took a damp seat beside Sienna. She watched the island for a moment before beaming at me. "Welcome to paradise!"

"Probably the only bit of it we're going to get any time soon," Collette said. I didn't miss the disgruntled look she shot me. Sienna frowned at her.

"We already talked about that. What the shifters and vamps are doing isn't Riley's fault."

"Whatever," Collette said. She skimmed the surface of the water with the tips of her fingers. "Not like she helped much."

"That's not fair."

"No, she's right," I said.

Collette cocked an eyebrow at me.

"I'm sorry for putting you guys in danger. It was selfish of me. I needed answers, but I should have come up with a better way to get them."

"Don't *worry.*" Sienna gave me a soggy side hug. "I'm totally fine, Sawyer's back to his usual reclusive self. Collette's still..."

Sienna practically withered beneath Collette's venomous

glare. "Well, you know," Sienna said. "It's not like this is the first time we've ever been in danger before."

"Still, what I am is my responsibility to understand. You shouldn't have to—"

"Would you shut up already?"

I gasped as Collette splashed water at my face.

"I'm so freaking tired of you acting like you're the only person who has to solve this thing," Collette said. "Like, seriously, how conceited can you get? I'm not saying you're this queen or anything, but you're still an Outcast. We all have to deal with the prophecy."

She glared out across the water. "So stop taking all the blame. It's unattractive. And it's pissing me off."

"Yeah." Sienna said brightly. "We're all big girls and boys. We can make questionable decisions on our own."

I felt tears prickling the corners of my eyes and quickly wiped a wet hand over my face. When I was done, I noticed a coral-green head peering around shyly from behind the island. "Thanks, guys. I'll remember that."

"Good!" Sienna said.

"You better," Collette said.

"Lucinda!" Sienna waved at Lucinda's head, which immediately popped out of sight. "Give her just a bit longer," Sienna said apologetically.

I took off my shoes and let my feet dangle in the warm water. It smelled like the ocean, and the warm air was giving me flashbacks to what felt like another life, where I'd been able to go to the actual ocean and sit in the actual surf. Iris and I had gone a few times last summer. It'd been a while since I'd thought of those trips. Heck, it'd been a while since I'd had time to slow down at all.

Little by little, Lucinda floated out from her hiding spot: first her hair, then her glimmering tail, cutting through the water as she drifted back over to us.

"I'm Riley," I said when she floated in front of me, half her face submerged, pearl-like eyes peering at me. "I'm the thirteenth Outcast."

Lucinda gave a short nod like she knew that already. "I'm...Lucinda."

Bubbles came up when she spoke, but I could make out her words perfectly clear, even underwater. "Sienna told me you're going to solve the prophecy."

Collette snorted. I ignored her. "I'm trying. *We're* trying. I'm not doing a very good job, though."

"That's okay." Lucinda's voice was like the sea breeze, lighter and more breathless than even Sienna's. "I wish I could help more, but I..."

Her tail flashed beneath the artificial sunlight.

"You're a mermaid?" I guessed.

Lucinda nodded.

"And I'm guessing you can't leave the water."

"Well..."

"She technically can," Sienna said. "Mermaids with enough magic can change their flippers to legs, but she dries out really fast if she's not in water."

"That's why I like when it rains," Lucinda said. "Otherwise we have to bring spray bottles and lots of bottled water for my skin. It's a hassle for everyone and I don't want to be a bother."

"We already said it wasn't a bother, so don't harp on it," Collette snapped. Lucinda shrank back just a bit, but she kept those luminous eyes fixated on me, like she'd never seen anyone like me before. Or had rarely seen anyone new.

"Did you fill Jasper in on everything you told Ari?" Sienna asked me. I could tell she was trying to change the subject in order to make Lucinda feel more comfortable.

"She told him most of it," I said. "He and I just talked, actually."

"And?"

I thought back to our sparring, to our argument, to our...

Whatever that last part had been about. "We're good. We're gonna figure this thing out with the vampires, and in the meantime try to keep Lukas off our back."

"You talk about anything else?" Sienna pressed. She was giving me a knowing look and I felt my cheeks heat.

"I mean...We might have...I didn't think it was that obvious..."

Sienna's impish grin grew. "Maybe not to some, but I'm more perceptive. Your aura's positively radiant. Plus, I've noticed those smoldering glances you two throw each other's way."

My face felt like it was going to ignite.

"*Gro-oss!*" Collette said.

"That's so romantic!" Lucinda sighed, performing an underwater backflip.

"Okay, first off, no one is throwing smoldering anything except for punches when we're training," I said.

Sienna's grin didn't drop. "Whatever you say..."

"Secondly, he...even if I wanted him...Even if he..."

Collette rolled her eyes so hard I was worried they'd disappear into her skull. "This is pathetic."

"We tried to kiss," I blurted out. "But it didn't work."

The three of them stared at me.

Collette furrowed her brow. "I can't believe I'm saying this, but even you should be able to figure out how kissing works. You each take your lips and..." She pressed her palms together and twisted them back and forth.

"*That* wasn't the problem," I said. Yep, my face was definitely on fire. My eyebrows were going to combust at any moment.

"It's because he's a Forsworn," Lucinda said quietly.

Sienna nodded. She wasn't smiling anymore. "I was worried that'd be the problem. I've never seen Jasper get close to anyone. Not that any of us Outcasts really have. Dating outside our group is tough. And dating inside..." She shrugged. "Not for me. I didn't think that the reason Jasper might not be with anyone was because of what he was."

"He started draining my magic as soon as we got close," I said. "I don't think he even meant to do it. It just...happened."

The others were silent. I was pretty sure none of them had run across a problem like this. You like boy. You hope said boy likes you. Said boy also sucks away your magic every time you get too close. Not exactly a typical romantic hurdle.

"Riley, I don't want to dampen your spirits, but Forsworn like Jasper are very rare and very strong for a reason," Sienna said. "If he takes too much of your magic it could permanently hurt you. I feared this might be a problem with your magic being as strong as it is. With a normal paranormal it may be easier for him to resist."

"There are probably ways he could learn to control it," Lucinda said hopefully. "And you could learn to shield your magic."

"You think that's possible?" I said.

"I'm sure it is. Maybe..."

I pulled my legs up to my chest. "Him draining my magic wasn't even the worst part, it was what he did after. He looked so...I don't know, not disgusted. But it was like I'd slapped him."

Sienna put her hand over mine. "I'm sure he wasn't mad at you. He was probably scared. He doesn't want to hurt you."

"I don't even know why you're bothering at all," Collette said.

"Seriously, Collette?" Sienna said, annoyed. "Hasn't there ever been anyone you've liked?"

Collette blushed. "T-That's not the point, dummy."

"Please don't be mean," Lucinda said meekly.

"I'm not being mean, I'm being realistic," Collette snapped. "Seriously, this isn't the problem we should be focusing on right now. Hello, we kind of still have a prophecy to figure out." She leveled her gaze at me. "And someone supposedly needs to become royalty or something equally stupid."

Biting final comment aside, Collette was right. Compared to the other things I—all of us—were dealing with, my disappointment with Jasper seemed selfish and trivial.

Still, it sucked. No pun intended.

"Maybe things will change," Lucinda said cheerfully. "If you're meant to be together, it will work out. The best romances always do."

I gave her a smile, trying to feel optimistic about that. I didn't know about true love, but I'd hold out hope that I could at least kiss a guy I was growing to like more.

"Riley?"

I was surprised to see Ari at the door. She motioned for me.

"You have to go already?" Sienna said.

"Yeah, sorry, we're—" I almost told them that we were going to pay a visit to the Horde, but I figured that'd only worry them. "See you soon."

"Thanks for not saying too much," Ari said when I joined her outside in the hall.

"Though we should tell them soon," I said. "Wasn't a lack of communication what got us into this mess in the first place?"

Ari grimaced. "True. But this is different."

"Maybe tell Jasper that."

"Are you kidding? That boy has a skull as thick as granite. Maybe *you* could. You seem to have just the right hammer to crack it."

I wasn't positive, but I could have sworn she shot me a significant look. Seriously, was it *that* obvious I liked him?

"Besides," Ari went on. "We're just meeting the Horde. It won't be dangerous. At least, it's usually not."

"Sounds comforting."

"We'll be fine," Ari said, this time with more confidence. "Now come on. We have one stop to make before that. I'll let Jasper explain on the way."

192

Jasper was confident Lukas wouldn't attack us. Apparently he'd pulled away his shifters from outside the Loft. He was definitely planning something, but at least for now he was off our backs. The sun was still high enough in the sky, meaning the Deathless would be none the wiser that we were going to meet the Horde. Plus...

Jasper, Ari, and Leon strode confidently beside me. A Forsworn vamp, a lion shifter who looked like a WWE wrestler, and a cheetah shifter who could use weapons as well as some people used forks. With these sorts of companions, I was sure even Lukas would think twice about causing trouble.

Jasper didn't actually explain much about what we were doing as we took the ten-minute walk from the Loft toward the heart of downtown. We bypassed the Art Institute and were swallowed beneath the looming shadows of the skyscrapers before we took Rines street straight into the historic district. Here the buildings changed from the modern gray slabbed stone and glass to more russet brick and spiraling, asymmetric towers crowning shingled rooftops.

"Are we going to have trouble?" Leon murmured as we began to slow.

I looked ahead to where he'd nodded and realized we'd wound up in front of the Cliffside History and Natural Sciences Museum. I'd only been here once as a kid when my parents took me for an exhibit of Paleolithic archeology. Riveting stuff for a six-year-old. I remembered the plush dolls in the gift shop the best.

It sat connected and opposite a colossal cathedral on its northern end, the two squashed together buildings creating an almost palace-like facade. A couple police cruisers and another unmarked car sat at the foot of the museum's steps.

"Not our problem," Jasper said. "Just as long as Biblion's available."

Despite not quite being closing time, the steps were empty as we made our way up. I found out why when we reached the top and found yellow police tape barricading the front doors. Jasper brushed under it without a second thought, and after a moment's hesitation I followed the others inside.

The moment I entered I felt the prickle of magic on my skin, something I couldn't remember feeling here before. The interior of the museum stretched broadly on either side as if to envelop us in a welcoming hug. The interior was more of that russet stone and multicolored columns halfway embedded in the walls. An arched ceiling made almost entirely of skylights highlighted the blindingly white skeleton of a blue whale hanging suspended over our heads. A grand staircase at the far end beckoned us to the second floor, while vaulted entryways on either side of the first floor indicated the entrances to the museum's various exhibits. Three of them were blocked off with more police tape. The museum's foyer was eerily empty.

"Find Biblion," Jasper said.

Ari and Leon split off to check two of the cordoned off wings while Jasper and I went to the third on the other side.

"What exactly are we supposed to be asking this Biblion guy for?" I said, keeping my eyes peeled in case any police decided to question why we were clearly violating some sort of crime scene.

"He's the curator here and he's going to help you with your magic. Well, not him specifically, but he'll take you to a place that can help. Hopefully."

"There was a lot of hesitation in that sentence. I didn't think I was having that much trouble with my magic. It's not as strong as I'd like, but…"

"It's not enough," Jasper said. He said it casually, distracted as he probably was, but I still felt a little stung.

"I am trying, you know."

"I know. It's nothing to do with you. Some paranormals just need a little extra…push."

"And that's what we're here for. A little extra push?"

"Something like that."

The wing we entered was empty. The usual tall display cases lined either side, except that more than a few of them had been smashed open. Shattered glass was spread across the floor, creating sparkling halos.

"A break-in?" I said, shocked. I'd never heard of that happening in the museum. In action movies and stuff, but not real life.

"Seems like it," Jasper said. "I wonder—"

"Jasper!"

We crossed back over to where Ari was waving us down outside the second wing. A couple police officers stood guard in front of the few still-standing display cases, overseeing a similar scene of destruction. Whoever had broken in here had done a thorough job.

"Mr. Biblion," Jasper said.

We approached a slightly heavyset, grumpy-looking man standing outside of the crime scene. His entire face seemed to be stuck in an eternal frown, gray suit wrinkled. A middle-aged woman with curly blonde hair and a smile so wide it looked painful appeared delighted when we joined them.

"Jasper! Ari! Leon! Oh, and..." She smiled wider at me. "You must be the new girl!"

"Mrs. Roberts, please," Mr. Biblion groused. "I'm afraid this isn't a good time, Jasper. As you can see." He waved a pudgy hand across the scene of destruction and on the two people in tan khakis and crisp blazers with badges pinned to their chests moving through it. "We had a very brazen robbery last night and have only now gotten around to looking for any clue as to who might have done it."

One of the khaki-dressed people—I was guessing a detective of some sort—looked over at us. He frowned. Uh-oh.

"What about the magical wards you had in place?" Leon said.

Mr. Biblion pulled at the collar of his suit. "They were, unfortunately, quite deteriorated and whoever the thief was managed to circumnavigate them without a problem."

"That means it wasn't just a normal mundane robbery," Ari said.

"Hold on," I said. "You know about us, Mr. Biblion?"

"Mr. Biblion and Mrs. Roberts are two of a few mundanes who do," Jasper said. "They provide a variety of invaluable services." Jasper nodded his head apologetically. "As much as we'd love to help, Mr. Biblion, we're here on Outcast business."

Now the detective was making a beeline for us. "Trouble incoming," I said.

"This is an active crime scene, Mr. Biblion," the detective said, scanning over each of us as though we were potential suspects. "I don't recall allowing anyone else in."

"It won't take long," Jasper said to Mr. Biblion. "Please."

"Excuse me." The detective tugged on his badge as though it wasn't already glaring at us in the face. He was tall, with slicked back hair and the faintest wisp of a five o' clock shadow. "Detective Ramirez. You're encroaching on Cliffside PD business. I'll have to ask you one more time—"

"They're guests of mine, detective," Mr. Biblion said with a labored sigh. "They have a standing appointment with me that will only take a minute, and then they'll be on their way." He gave us a look as if to say, "You'd better.".

"Don't worry, I'll keep you all company," Mrs. Roberts said, beaming at Detective Ramirez. "I don't mind watching."

Detective Ramirez grumbled something as he dropped his badge back against his chest. "Just make sure they don't interfere. We're having enough trouble uncovering any leads as it is."

Ari jerked her chin toward one of the broken cases. "Looks like they took one of the necklaces of a Macedonian shaman."

Detective Ramirez looked back at the case, then suspiciously at her. "So it would seem. How did you know that?"

"I'm a history buff," Ari said. Then added in a lower voice as we followed Mr. Biblion out of the wing, "And it supposedly curses anyone who steals it. Whoever did this has guts."

"I wish you wouldn't provoke him like that," Mr. Biblion said. "This is already stressful enough. And really, coming here is just a waste of time."

"Why's that?" I asked as he led us back into the main hall and through one of the doors on the side of the grand staircase. We ended up in a smaller hall, though no less lavish.

"I'm assuming you're here for the spring and not just an amusing side trip?" Mr. Biblion said.

"Yes," Jasper said.

Mr. Biblion nodded. "Outcast or not, the spring won't work for just anyone. Have you explained to her how dangerous it could potentially be? And how *it* may not let you drink at all?"

No, they hadn't. And now I was growing nervous. This entire trip was becoming more and more of a surprise, and I was beginning to understand why no one had said anything prior to us coming here.

"I'm sure whatever it is I can handle it," I said, trying to sound confident.

"We shall see," Mr. Biblion said. We'd reached another door at the far end of the smaller hall. He took out a ring of a dozen keys, unlocked the door, and pushed it open.

We entered a storage room, clearly where they kept all of the artifacts and exhibits that were preparing to be shipped out or put on display. Enormous suits of armor from various eras stood straight as a line of soldiers, their headless helmets seeming to silently judge us from across time. There were tables covered with more artifacts carefully sorted into boxes or with thin clear film covering them. I felt an even stronger prickle of magic here. Either this room was full of more magical objects, or wherever we were headed to was strong. Very strong.

We passed through the storage room and down a short flight of stairs, entering what I could only describe as a little slice of catacombs, with rough stone walls and strip lights along the low ceiling. A woman stood at the other end of the hall. She had short, spiked hair and a face that was so tanned it looked golden. A slender silver chain hung around her neck, a cross dangling from the end.

"Pastor Kegan—Cassandra—thank goodness you're available," Mr. Biblion said. "I'm sure you sensed it earlier, but they're here for the spring, and as much as I'd *love* to take part in another of the Outcast's riveting tasks, I simply must get back to my museum."

Pastor Kegan gave him a sympathetic smile. "I'm sure those detectives will appreciate your presence. I hope they recover the stolen objects."

"As do I, pastor, as do I. You are all fine, then," Mr. Biblion said, backing away down the hall. "I'll just leave you to it."

And then he'd waddled away before I could thank him for... well, whatever it was we were doing.

"Good to see you all again." Pastor Kegan gave the others brief hugs, then clasped my hand in hers with a warm smile. "And of course I've heard of you. We get lots of paranormals seeking sanctuary within our walls. There isn't one recently who hasn't talked about the massive changes happening in the paranormal community. Congrats, you've made quite the stir."

I wasn't sure how to respond to that. I knew me showing up had changed some things, but Pastor Kegan made it sound like I was some sort of celebrity.

"Uh, thanks, I guess. Jasper said I'm here to use some kind of spring?"

The smile on Pastor Kegan's face became a little forced. "I'm sure they explained to you that, just because you want to use the spring, doesn't mean you'll be able to."

"I don't think they were completely clear on the specifics..."

"Can you take her?" Jasper said. "Not to rush, but we're kind of on a tight schedule."

Pastor Kegan nodded and motioned for me to follow her through an archway. After a brief hesitation, I did. The words "Hope Springs Eternal Church" were etched into the stone above my head.

I noticed the others weren't following. "You guys coming?"

Ari glanced at Jasper, who was looking up at the words as though they were a rabid dog he was wary of biting him.

Right. Wasn't there something about vampires and churches?

"You're free to enter, Jasper," Pastor Kegan said. "You've always been welcome."

Jasper shook his head. "Thanks, but no thanks. I think whatever your church is offering is already too far gone for me."

Ari tried to touch his shoulder but he slipped away from her and started walking back the way we'd come, giving a short wave over his shoulder. "I'll go check out the museum. Maybe see if there's anything those stellar detectives have missed."

"Go ahead, Riley," Leon rumbled. "We can't help you with this part anyway."

I stared after Jasper as he disappeared up the stairs. "Can he not..."

"Oh, he can," Pastor Kegan said sadly. "It's not something physical or magical that's stopping him."

I decided not to press right now. There was clearly a lot more history behind this than I was aware of.

I gave Ari and Leon a brief wave before following Pastor Kegan through more smooth tunnels. I tried to push Jasper out of my mind and focus only on what was coming up. *Whatever* was coming up. I watched Pastor Kegan's confident stride. She hummed something that sounded like a hymn under her breath.

"No offense, but I didn't think pastors believed in this sort of thing," I said.

Pastor Kegan's smile was teasing. "What sort of thing?"

"You know...magic." I summoned a ball of flame and held it out. She didn't even bat an eye, and I wondered just how many things she'd seen to get to the point where two shifters, an elemental, and a vampire could walk in and she'd greet them as though they were anybody else off the street.

"I choose to see magic as just another spiritual gift. One of many," Pastor Kegan said. "Look at the Bible. It's full of miracles. I'd argue that's just magic of a different kind."

I paused for a moment as the strong, reverberating notes of an organ drifted down to us through the ceiling. A choir of voices rose up to join it until the entire tunnel was enveloped in rapturous music.

"So we're in the church," I said.

Pastor Kegan nodded. "Under it, technically. Hope Springs was originally founded on, what else? Underground springs. This spring, in particular, is one of immense spiritual and magical power, but over the years as more people tried to forcefully take what the spring offered, the church continued building atop it. Today, hardly anyone knows the church's namesake is real and right below their feet. Even fewer know what it can actually do."

"And what is that?"

Pastor Kegan glanced over at me. "Hopefully free any inhibitions you might have on that magic of yours."

I held in an annoyed grumble. "Wish we'd done this earlier. Would have made things a lot easier for me."

"Not necessarily. Not everyone reacts well to it. If Jasper and the others brought you here that means it's—to take the words of my Catholic brothers and sisters—a Hail Mary of sorts."

We reached a small stone door, completely smooth, without even a seam to show where it split. Pastor Kegan ran her fingers down a small, worn groove on the right side of the wall. The door shuddered, then began opening outward.

The room beyond was low-ceilinged and didn't seem to have any other exits. Fat columns, three on each side, funneled the narrow walkway toward a back wall. In the glow of more strip lights I could see the wall was slick with water.

"This is where you'll have to go it alone," Pastor Kegan said. "The waters of the spring cannot be taken by force and are freely given to all. But not all react well to it. Just walk through, let them see you, and you'll be fine."

She gave me a less-than-reassuring pat on the shoulder. "I'll see you in a little bit."

Then she started walking back, as though I had a clue what any of that was supposed to mean.

I stepped inside and started slowly walking up the center aisle toward the far wall. What was the *them* she was referring to? Something dangerous? It couldn't be. Jasper and the others wouldn't throw me into something like that without telling me. Then again, information wasn't always forthcoming from them...

I froze as I heard the sound of grinding stone. Trying my best to move slowly, I turned to look to my right, then my left. I couldn't see anyone. It'd sounded like another door opening, but the walls remained smooth.

Then I saw the columns begin to move. They were sectioned

like the layers of a cake, each section a slightly different shade of stone. The top layer of the nearest column rotated until I could make out a pair of eyes gouged into the stone. The layer beneath that was a large stone mouth filled with teeth not unlike jagged pieces of broken pottery. Another set of eyes were on the section below it, then another mouth, interchanging back and forth all the way to the floor.

The teeth ground together. I winced as the horrible sound grated my ears. I took another step and the columns rotated to follow me. They looked immovable, but I didn't want to imagine what they could do if someone broke their way in here.

Freely given, but never taken by force.

I let out a long breath. I was fine. I hadn't done anything wrong. I would take what I'd come here for. Then would kill the others later for not telling me about this.

The columns continued to follow me as I walked to the far wall. The "spring" was really nothing more than a trickle of water leaking from a hole in the ancient-looking wall and collecting in a small basin at my feet.

There was only one thing left to do. I knelt, cupped a small amount in my hands, took a deep breath, and drank. It tasted metallic, with a hint of grit that rubbed down my throat the wrong way.

I took another drink for good measure, then stood, waiting for something to happen. I peered down into the pool and let out a small scream.

Lucinda the mermaid was staring back at me.

"Did it work?" she asked.

Either the water was doing *something,* or she was using some sort of water magic. I quickly knelt again. "What are you doing here?"

"I can travel between different bodies of water." She wriggled as though stuck. "Mostly. This one is kind of a tight fit."

I looked over my shoulder as the columns' grinding grew louder. "I don't think it's a good idea for you to be here."

Lucinda slipped shyly back down the basin. "I don't think they mind. I came here when Daniel drank and they didn't run me off that time. Do you...feel any different?"

I looked down at my arms; closed my eyes to take stock of my senses. Nothing felt all that different. "I don't think so. Is that a bad thing?"

"I'm not sure. Maybe it doesn't work right away. Or maybe it doesn't work at all."

That was an encouraging thought. Even the great and powerful spring o' magic couldn't do anything for me. I let out a sigh. "I guess we'll just have to wait and see."

"Don't give up," Lucinda said. She wriggled a bit more, clearly trying to unstick herself. "I'm sure it'll work out—"

One of the columns made the loudest grinding sound yet. Lucinda shrank farther back into the pool. "Maybe they do mind. I think I should go. See you later!"

Then she shoved herself backwards and the surface of the water was clear once more. I stood, trying not to feel too disappointed that the spring hadn't worked as advertised. Hopefully Lucinda was right and it was just a delayed—

I toppled like I'd been sucker punched, feeling the ground come up to meet me as I collapsed. I couldn't move, couldn't speak as images flashed across my vision. A dark night full of stars and figures cast in the shadows made from an enormous bonfire. The figures danced and chanted as they circled it. Somehow I knew there were twelve of them. As they circled, a thirteenth figure rose in the center of the fire, licked by the flames but not burned by them...

The vision shifted and now I was looking at the surface of the earth. Only it wasn't the earth I knew but primordial and barren, covered with pools of magma and erupting volcanoes. The atmosphere was thick with smoke and ash. The light illuminating it grew so bright it was nearly unbearable, then shifted to total darkness as the earth hurled through the cosmos, whipping around the sun alarmingly fast as eons passed.

The surface shifted and now I saw dragons—they had to be dragons—perched atop the volcanoes, roaring to the heavens. Their leathery wings spread wide, ground cracking beneath their talons. And then from the oceans came a deep, answering call from something so old it almost hurt. Something ancient and wondrous and terrifying that rattled the oldest parts of my soul.

I gasped as I snapped awake again. My palms stung from where I'd tried to catch my fall, my face slick with water and grit. I didn't dare move for a moment, afraid that whatever had just hit me would come back for round two, but after a moment it seemed I was safe.

I pushed myself to standing, wobbling a bit on my feet. It had felt so real, so tangible, like I could have reached out and run my fingers across the dragons' scales and burned myself from the heat of the bonfire. Was it some sort of premonition? Or a glimpse of the past?

The stone columns ground out their annoyance that I was still lingering here. With a slight headache, I walked out and made my way back to the museum.

Jasper stood at the plaque of the blue whale, Pastor Kegan beside him. I could see they were talking about something so I slowed, giving them a little more time. After a moment Pastor Kegan noticed I was there. She smiled brightly.

"How'd it go?"

Jasper's piercing gaze snapped right to my slightly bloody, scraped hands, as though he had injury-seeking vision.

"It went...all right," I said honestly, sure that Jasper would pick up on anything outside the realm of truth. "It wasn't quite what I expected."

"I hope it helped you," Pastor Kegan said. "From what Jasper tells me, you've got a big destiny ahead of you. One I'm sure you'll rise to meet gloriously."

She patted him on the shoulder. "You are welcome at Hope Springs anytime. Both of you. Now I'm afraid I have to leave you and the flustered Mr. Biblion. Let him know I'll bring a broom and dustpan over once they're done with their investigation."

"All right?" Jasper said once Pastor Kegan had left. "I feel like something more than just 'all right' happened."

"You *feel*, or are you listening to my heartbeat again?" I said.

Jasper grinned, totally busted. I rolled my eyes and told him about the vision I'd seen.

"It was so real," I said. "I wasn't just watching it, I was *there*."

"I'm sure it felt that way," Jasper said. "The spring taps into the core being of who you are. Chances are it was showing you some of your history in an attempt to unlock parts of your latent magic."

I shuddered. If that was true, then my history was terrifying. "I don't feel any different. How do we know if it worked?"

"We'll have to wait. You could see changes in an hour, or never."

I noticed Detective Ramirez staring at us from the archway of the wing they'd been combing through. He turned away when he caught me watching, but he didn't leave. Jasper smirked.

"I did a quick look around the museum. Mr. Biblion was right, everything stolen was magical in nature. Lots of stuff from a collector named Mr. Morian. But what they took doesn't have any rhyme or reason to it. It's like they just grabbed whatever they could get their hands on."

"What were some of the items?" I said.

"Ari told me one was called the Goblet of Smarkand. It detoxifies whatever's in it so you never get poisoned. Then there's something called a transference stone. Transfers magic from one object to another. And a crystal egg. Smash it over a charmed object to break the charm."

He glanced over at me as though he hadn't just listed off a bunch of items from a mad wizard's treasure chest. "See what I mean? No rhyme or reason. A few weapons were stolen too. Either someone's planning for an attack, another heist, or a massive magical experiment."

"Sounds like a diversion," I said.

"How's that?"

"Well..." I tapped my chin in thought. "The thief grabbed a bunch of different things to throw the detectives off the trail of the one thing they actually wanted."

Jasper nodded, considering that. "Makes sense. Normally it'd be in the Outcasts' interest to help find the objects, but we're on a time crunch. Come on. Ari! Leon!"

Ari and Leon both stopped sparring with the toy swords they'd grabbed from the gift shop. As we headed to the exit, Detective Ramirez began making a line straight toward us.

"For real?" I muttered. "Can't this guy take a hint?"

"One second!"

All of us turned to glare at him. It would have been more intimidating if two of us hadn't just been trying to impale each other with foam swords.

"I'd like to ask you all a few questions," Detective Ramirez said, pulling out a phone. "It seems a little odd that you'd come in here now of all times and have such a close relationship with the curator. Where—"

"Are we suspects in your investigation?" Leon said.

Ramirez paused. "What?"

"Do you have probable cause to detain us as suspects in your investigation?" Leon said. He crossed his arms, glowering at the detective.

"I'm *making* you suspe—"

"Ramirez!"

His partner, a sharply dressed woman with mocha colored

skin and a piercing glare stood beside Mr. Biblion. She waved to us. "Don't mind him. You all have a nice day."

"We'll send Sienna and Sawyer over later to help you out," Jasper said to Mr. Biblion over Detective Ramirez's steadily growing protests.

We left Detective Ramirez sputtering in our wake as we stepped back outside.

"Nice going with the cop terminology," Ari said, elbowing Leon. She held her arms out wide to her sides, puffing her cheeks in an impersonation of Leon. "'Do you have probable cause to keep us? Do we have the right to remain silent?' Real Law and Order type stuff. That's thinking on your toes."

"I've watched my share of cop shows," Leon said.

"Focus," Jasper said, snapping us all back to the present. To what we still had to do, and who we still had to meet. "Let's not keep the Horde waiting."

CHAPTER TWENTY-ONE

T he designated meeting spot was beneath an old bridge on Cliffside's south side, not too far of a walk from the museum.

"Doesn't seem too bad a place to meet a bunch of the undead," I said.

"They're doing it for our benefit," Jasper said. "They don't want to scare you off the first time."

Ah. Okay then.

We hopped over the sidewalk's wooden railing at the waterfront and picked our way down the rocks until we hit the gravelly beach below. A rusted steel bridge branched across one of the river's many channels.

"What am I supposed to say when we get there?" I asked Jasper.

"We're asking for their help. Try to do that without giving anything away. See if they know anything more about the prophecy like Lukas did."

"And if they don't? And they don't want to help?"

"Then this was a waste of time."

"But the Deathless will still uphold their end of their deal and protect us for now."

Jasper's expression tightened. "Yes, but we don't want to rely only on that."

I watched his face in profile for a moment, wanting to bring up what we'd begun to talk about on the rooftop, but knowing it wouldn't do any good now. Jasper seemed totally chill about it, not letting a hint that it'd affected him slip through. I'd managed to take all my confused emotions and stuff them neatly in place until I could piece them together later. Collette had been right: we had bigger things to think about.

We stopped under the bridge. It rumbled every so often as the traffic passed by overhead. The support beams were slick with algae and grime and the entire thing smelled a bit like fish gone bad.

"Atmospheric," Leon said, gazing around. "The Horde sure knows how to pick 'em."

"Keep your eyes open," Ari said. "They'll be here any minute."

Jasper tugged me aside, until we could speak mostly privately to one another. "Don't tell them I pledged myself to the Deathless."

The urgency in his tone immediately put me on edge. "Why not? They've probably already heard."

"They might have. But we don't want them knowing if they haven't. If they find out one Outcast can be blackmailed away..."

"Then they'll try to do it to others," I finished grimly.

"Mainly you," Jasper said. "And I don't—we don't—want that to happen."

There it was, just a brief flicker of the look I'd seen on the roof. Proof that he hadn't disregarded what had almost happened as much as I'd thought. "Believe it or not, I don't want that either," I said.

He nodded, the look vanishing and being replaced with his normal steely expression. "Then they can't know."

"Know what, vampire?"

I spun. Ari and Leon crouched on instinct, prepared to shift. Uko and Kaia were suddenly *there*, having seemingly emerged from the darkness of the deepest part of the bridge.

Uko's ice-chip blue eyes roved over us, glittering with curiosity. "It seems there's something you want to tell us."

There was an awkward pause. I quickly wrangled my thoughts together and stepped forward. "Thank you for meeting with us."

"The Horde is always willing—" Kaia started.

"The Horde has great interest, and trust, in the Children of the Prophecy. And they hope the Children of the Prophecy have great trust in them," Uko said.

I wasn't sure whether ghouls had the power of compulsion like vampires, but Uko's gaze felt as though it was slowly drawing from my lips the one thing Jasper hadn't wanted me to tell.

"You said you were on my side before," I managed. "You said you'd ask around for anything that might help us figure out the prophecy."

"That we did," Uko said. "And we have."

I waited for him to go on. "And…?"

"While I am always on the side of those the prophecy has chosen, I am curious what the Horde will receive for their efforts."

"Of course," Leon grunted.

Kaia threw Uko a sour look. She was clearly as surprised to hear this as we were. "Surely you can make an exception for the Outcasts, Uko."

"You do not speak for the Horde, because you are not fully one of us." Uko's long tongue lolled in his mouth, making the peeling skin of his face flap. "Your allegiance will always be, at least in part, to them so you will always have something to gain."

Kaia looked furious, her usually somewhat-solid form flickering in and out of sight. "I've only ever done what I think is best for the Horde!"

"Then you understand that we must first and foremost look after ourselves," Uko said, still not breaking eye contact with me. "This is a world of give and take."

"Then it appears we've wasted each other's time," Jasper said. "We don't know what we could offer you—"

"You want to know what the other races are doing," I said. It was obvious, really. What I was quickly learning was that very little happened in the paranormal community without one of the other factions wanting to know about it. They might not have been in all-out war, but being in the loop about what your "ally" was doing was something that could potentially come in handy when you needed it most.

"We may have a few things you'd like to know," I said.

I caught Jasper's eye. He was looking at me like he wasn't sure what I was about to say. Almost...pleading.

"Just to be clear," I said to Uko, "we're on the same side."

Uko's grin was too wide for his face. "We're always on the side of the Children of the Prophecy."

Of course.

I told them what we'd learned from Lukas. Not *how* we'd learned it (I still wasn't sure how many Conclave laws I'd potentially broken) but enough that I was satisfied Uko believed us. I told him about the other lines of the prophecy. Ari seemed ready to cut me off when I'd done that, but really, what did it matter? Everyone else probably knew—including Kaia. Better to use it now in a gesture of goodwill than have them find out another way and lose any potential leverage.

"This is all very good, thank you." Uko gave a short bow. "We were not aware that Lukas was being so aggressive in his search for the prophecy's end. He must be very eager to have it for himself."

"He's power hungry is what he is," Kaia said darkly. "I've told you before, Uko, if left unchecked, those like Lukas will only grow to cause more and more trouble."

"And as I've said, there's little we, the Horde, can do about it. We have been stripped of what little authority we had by the Conclave, and those same ones on the Conclave appear to have no intention of checking themselves. If only…" He was looking at me again, and I felt not unlike an insect pinned to a cork board. "We had a leader to step up. One to help quell the strife within the paranormals."

"I'm not a queen," I said, positive that was what he was referring to. "I'll do what I have to in order to complete the prophecy but I won't—can't—be a ruler. Besides, monarchy's a little old-school, don't you think?"

"Not among paranormals," Kaia said. "Many come from ancient lines of power that only recognize authority when it's ultimate authority. If you were queen—"

"Which I'm not going to be," I said. I hated to cut her off, but there was no way I was even considering this right now. All I wanted to do was finish the prophecy. Whatever happened after that queen-wise wasn't my deal. "Lukas seems to really want to complete the prophecy for himself, but I don't understand how. How can he complete it without the Outcasts?"

"Even strong, ancient magic can be altered," Uko said. "Lukas is crafty enough I'm sure that even if he did not find a legitimate way to fulfill it, he would break the rules to make it his own."

That sounded *exactly* like what Lukas would do. "And if that happens? If he manages to fulfill the prophecy the wrong way?"

Uko gave me a level look. "I'm sssure whatever outcome of a wrongly fulfilled prophecy is not an outcome we want to witness. There would be problems for all paranormals."

Which meant what little breathing room we might have had while he wrestled with circumnavigating the prophecy's rules was gone.

"Riley." Jasper nodded at the skyline where the sun had begun to vanish over the rooftops. I understood. We needed to be out of here before the Deathless arrived for their shift at the Loft.

"I told you what I know," I said. "What have you got for us?"

If Uko understood our urgency, he didn't show it, staying quiet until Kaia nudged him. "Uko…"

"One moment," Uko said at last. "I must process your new information."

He stepped back into the darkness beneath the bridge, until I could only see his outline. I heard him say something in that rattling voice of his, and then heard voices answer, hundreds of them, like an angry, hissing nest of snakes. The sound sent a chill shivering up my arms.

"Ari, head back to the Loft," Jasper said. "It's unlikely, but if Lukas or the Deathless try something else, I want you there in case we're late getting back."

Ari hesitated before nodding. In a blink she'd shifted into her cheetah form and took off so fast she kicked up rocks that pelted painfully against my back.

"How likely are they to give us anything?" I asked Kaia.

"Not sure," Kaia said honestly. "Uko's been like that more and more lately. Untrusting, I mean."

"We don't have any more time to waste," Jasper said. "If they won't help then we need other options."

"Just give them a chance. I'm sure they'll come through," Kaia said. "They've got as much to lose as anyone if the Pack or Deathless somehow takes control of this prophecy."

"You should come back to the Loft," Leon said. "The rest of the Outcasts need you there. Especially now."

Kaia shook her head. "Uko's trust in me might be deteriorating but I feel better out here, trying to help."

Leon grunted. "When all this is over, we'll have smoothie night again. Try not to miss it this time."

"Only if Ari doesn't try to make all of ours kale," Kaia said, grinning.

Leon shuddered.

At last the hissing voices died away and Uko re-emerged from the shadows.

"Anything?" I said.

"There are those among the Horde who have knowledge of the things you speak. They said this: follow the markings to find the Dead City. There you will discover what you seek."

"They can't be more specific than that?" I said as Leon scoffed. Uko was silent.

"Okay, then what is the Dead City?" I pressed.

"A myth," Leon said, annoyed.

"All myth has basis in truth," Uko said calmly.

"It's a legendary city lost among the Dying Lands, the paranormal realm hidden amongst the mundane. It's a place where paranormals were supposed to exist in the times long ago," Kaia said. She looked doubtfully at Uko. "Though it *does* sound unlikely..."

"Magical city, lost creatures, pools of untapped magic, that place is supposed to have it all," Leon said. "Nothing but a fairy tale."

Uko still said nothing.

"Jasper," I asked, noticing he'd been as quiet as Uko. "What do you think?"

Jasper held Uko's unflinching gaze. "If the time comes when we need allies, will you be on our side?"

"We will see when that time comes," Uko said. "We will see you to this prophecy's end. After that..."

"Then we're done here. Kaia." Jasper gave her a jerky nod, and he and Leon began heading back to the road we'd come in on. The sun was sinking fast now. We probably had less than an hour.

I gave Kaia an apologetic smile and turned to follow them.

"There is something that would make us more likely to take your side," Uko said.

I paused. So did Jasper.

"And what's that?" I asked.

"Your allegiance. Pledge yourself to be a champion of the Horde, to return us to our rightful status, and I will ensure that when the time comes, we will be your loyal subjects."

"I can't do that," I said immediately.

"Oh?" Uko cocked one rotting eyebrow in what I could only assume was mock surprise. "And why not? The vampire has already pledged himself to his own kind. It seems only fair that each race take their piece of the Outcasts while there is still time. And we want you."

So did a bunch of paranormals. It seemed the gremlin was out of the bag now.

"Jasper pledging to the Deathless is exactly why I won't pledge myself to the Horde, or to anyone. I'll do right by you, Uko, I promise. But I won't get into a binding agreement."

Uko's eyes narrowed. "I urge you to reconsssider."

"The Deathless threatened us to get what they wanted," I said, standing straighter. "Are you willing to do the same?"

Uko held my gaze as Leon and Jasper flanked either side of me.

"Please, Uko," I said after we all stared each other down for an uncomfortable amount of time. I didn't want to come off as desperate but we were reaching that point. I just couldn't give myself up. Not if I—we—were going to lose Jasper. "I give you my word that I'll do what's right for every paranormal."

My skin prickled. And then I saw them: dozens, no, hundreds of red eyes peering at me from the darkness beneath the bridge. There were so many that each pair bled into the next, creating the illusion of a single red pupil fixated on me.

"Your word may not be enough," Uko said sadly. "We wish you all the best, Child of the Prophecy."

He turned and was swallowed by the red. One by one the eyes went out, until the bridge was empty and dark.

"I'll talk to him," Kaia promised. "I'll make him understand."

I nodded, trying to look hopeful. But I wasn't. Not anymore.

❧

I DREAMED I was in that magical tunnel; the stupid one that'd appeared once and then decided to play magical hide and seek ever since.

In my dream the tunnel looked brighter than before. This time I could make out the markings on the wall. Had those been there before? They glowed as I ran my fingers across them. I felt a similar warm glow on my shoulder, where I knew my birthmark was probably coming to life.

I heard a noise at the end of the hall. A door had appeared, one made entirely of stone and looking so big I knew even Leon wouldn't be able to push it open.

That was where I had to go. I knew it.

I ran toward it. If I wasn't quick, it'd disappear like last time, but the door immediately shrank away, growing more distant the faster I ran.

"No—you—don't!" I growled. I could feel my body heating up. Could feel the magic inside building to the surface of my skin where it began to boil. I gasped as flames exploded outward, splashing across the walls, consuming the floor.

The door vanished but I couldn't stop. The fire was too much. I *was* fire.

I screamed as I snapped awake.

I could immediately tell something was wrong. It was hot, way too hot.

And then I looked down to find my covers were burning. My curtains too.

I'd set my room ablaze.

CHAPTER TWENTY-TWO

I screamed and hurled myself out of bed, thinking that would stop the worst of the spread, but when I looked down I discovered another shock: my skin was practically see-through, and beneath it pulsed veins of magma. The flames sprouted from the veins and continued to grow the more I stared until I couldn't tell what was me and what was fire.

Water. I needed water.

I turned on the shower and threw myself into it, not caring how cold the water was. My skin hissed—actually hissed—as the spray hit. Steam quickly filled the room as I turned the pressure up, batting at my arms.

After what felt like an eternity the flames died down, but my body still felt overbearingly hot, my skin still molten.

I slipped a little on the tile as I stepped out, bashing my knees as I hit the ground. It hurt, but was masked by the new pain of my skin heating up. It felt like it was blistering.

There was a gasp at the door. I snapped my head up. Through my tears I could make out Jasper. Could make out his horrified expression as he took in the scene.

I must have looked like a wreck: soaking hair drenched like

wet noodles. The water that'd remained on my arms had started to steam again, making the air in the bathroom even more difficult to breathe.

"Jasper!" I pleaded. The burning on my insides was growing unbearable. "Help!"

He rushed to my side in an instant.

"Where's it hurt?" He looked over every part of my exposed skin, which I supposed was answer enough.

"I can't get it to stop," I said.

"Yes, you can."

"No, I—"

Before I could stop him, Jasper wrapped his hands around each of my upper arms. Not hard, almost gently. A small hiss of pain escaped his lips as the heat of my skin immediately began to burn him. I tried to jerk away.

"Stop! Are you *trying* to hurt yourself?"

"Keep yourself grounded here, with me." Jasper clenched his jaw but wouldn't let go. The palms of his hands were beginning to turn red.

"Jasper…"

"Breathe. Control it."

"I already told you I can't!"

"Yes you can," he growled. "You've done it before. This time is no different."

My skin was prickling with the heat and the growing force of his touch. He made it sound so easy. He sounded so sure that I could do this. If he was that confident, then the least I could do was make the effort.

I left behind the sensations of his skin against mine, the choking steam, the building, unbearable heat, and focused only on the core of power within me.

It'd become a raging inferno. Even approaching it from inside myself felt like stepping willingly into an oven. I forced myself to think of nothing else but tamping down its power.

The flames continued licking at me, begging for me to let them run wild. I brushed them away and continued fighting down the power. It took a couple more tries but at last it'd returned to its normal place.

I let out a grateful breath before examining my magic. Something about it felt different now. Its size and shape within me no longer felt uniform. It was as sporadic and unpredictable as an actual flame. I had no idea how I was supposed to feel about that.

"There. That wasn't so hard," Jasper said.

I nodded and slumped back against the glass of the shower. Jasper's hands remained on my arms. At last he pulled them off. I opened my eyes and gasped. Thick blisters and raw, red skin covered his palms.

"They'll heal," he said consolingly. "What matters is that you're all right."

My arms were fine. My entire body was fine. I didn't even feel that weak after all the water. In fact, the only thing that seemed wrong was that I'd nearly set my room ablaze. And hurt Jasper.

"See?" Jasper held up one of his hands. If I looked closely, I could see the worst of the burned parts beginning to close up. The blisters had already started to recede back into his palm.

He gave me a comforting smile that was probably more for my benefit than him actually feeling great. "Vampire perks. It's all right to be jealous."

"Lucky you," I said quietly.

It was then I noticed what he was wearing. Or rather, *not* wearing.

"Did I...catch you in the middle of something?" I managed to choke out.

Jasper looked down at his bare, muscled chest, flecked with droplets of water, then to the towel wrapped low around his slender hips.

"Yeah. I was in the shower. Could hear you through the walls. You scream like a banshee. And I've heard one before, so I know."

"Uh-huh." My mind had locked up, capable of only vague grunts. I had a brief image of our almost kiss. His bare chest was so close I could see a pink scar in the shape of what might have been a claw mark, running from his collarbone down toward his heart. "That's...uh..."

Jasper stood. "I'll be right back."

"Back," I echoed dumbly, watching his back flex as he walked out.

I shook my head, overwhelmed with embarrassment. That'd been...amazing? No! Unexpected. Definitely unexpected. In the best way. And Jasper hadn't seemed fazed by it in the slightest. Not that I'd expect him to be. A soaking wet girl with magma for skin on the floor of a bathroom did not the most romantic scene make.

I reached over and pulled a towel down to me. I was completely drenched but hopefully I could get my hair into a somewhat presentable state. I did another body check. I still felt...good. Really good. Though I knew showers didn't affect me like the rain did, I hadn't expected to feel this energized. The warmth of my magic spread outward, filling me with a new strength. I wouldn't say I felt more in control of my magic— quite the opposite, really—but something had definitely changed.

I hoped it was for the best.

"Riley!" Ari—frazzled bed-head, bleary eyes and all—rushed in, followed by Jasper, fully clothed now, holding a cup of water.

"I'm okay—" I started.

"Drink this." Ari snatched the water out of Jasper's hand and practically forced it down my throat. "I'm sorry I didn't come sooner. I would have except I was asleep."

"Like the dead," Jasper said, crossing his arms and leaning against the vanity. "Usually takes an act of God to wake her."

"Or a vampire who bothers to tell me what's happening," Ari snapped.

I finished off the water. "Jasper did fine." Very, *very* fine. "He helped me control it. I'm sorry I screamed and worried you guys."

"It's not a worry," Ari said firmly. "If anything at all is wrong, you tell us."

Jasper jerked his head to my bedroom. "Or we take a big sniff and figure it out for ourselves. I put out the fire. It'll probably smell singed for a week."

I put my face in my hands, mortified.

"What happened?" Ari said, rubbing my back. "Seems like the spring worked to unlock some latent magic. You have any idea what triggered it?"

"I was dreaming of the tunnel," I said. "The one supposedly leading to the throne. I kept trying to get closer to it, but it kept getting farther away and then..."

I gestured to my arms like that finished the story. "I don't get it. Does out-of-control magic like that happen a lot?"

"Not often," Ari said. "But it's not that uncommon, believe me," she added at my crestfallen face.

"Mostly to those just coming into their powers," Jasper said. "Not those who have had them for a little while like you."

Ari shot him a look that said, "Not helping!"

"So what does that mean?" I said.

"It means Lukas really wasn't lying. You're an elemental—an incredibly strong magic user—and you're getting stronger. More of your powers are starting to manifest."

I balked. "Great, does that mean I have to sleep in a metal box? Does that—"

I cut off, suddenly remembering the pictures Sawyer had pulled up on his computer. Giant. Soulless. Monstrous.

"I think this might be a one-time event," Jasper said to the first part.

"And what about after that?" I couldn't get the images out of my head. Couldn't get what they might mean. "What if this keeps happening and I turn into a full elemental?"

"Then we won't have to worry about the Deathless or Lukas," Jasper said. "Or having a home, or a city, or a world..."

"Jas, I swear..." Ari bit out. "That won't happen," she said to me. "You'll have us here to help you. I know!" She stood. "I'll blend you up a broccoli and garlic smoothie. It's an amazing immune boost. You'll feel tons better."

And she was gone before I could tell her no. Or vomit at the thought of a broccoli smoothie anything.

"It won't happen," Jasper said firmly. His eyes were arresting, staring deeply into mine as though imploring me to believe him. "Whatever you're thinking, it won't happen. For one, you're not a full elemental. Just part."

I rubbed at the puddle of water with my big toe. "Part might be enough."

"For two, you're going to learn to control your magic before anything gets too out of hand again."

"Control it with who? With you?"

"With me. Or with a much better teacher if we need it."

I didn't want any other teacher than Jasper. I didn't want to need another teacher, period. I wanted all of this to start making sense and for the world to stop just for a moment and let me breathe.

"It won't end with the prophecy, will it?" I said.

"What won't?"

I gestured to my arm. "This power. Finding the throne. I'll have to become queen, won't I? Otherwise it'll just keep getting worse—all of it—until I do whatever that stupid prophecy wants." I threw the towel into the sink. "I hate it! I hate how it keeps pushing me to where I don't want to go. I don't want any part of this."

"'A person often meets their destiny on the road they took to avoid it,'" Jasper said.

I looked up at him, confused. "What?"

"Jean de la Fontaine. French poet. I *do* read, you know," he said, arching an eyebrow.

I closed my hanging mouth. "That wasn't what I was most surprised about."

Jasper crouched beside me. "This destiny thing sucks, but you know what? I think you're one of the only ones who can do it."

"Liar."

"Shut up and listen for second: Lukas is willing to do anything to get this power. Farrar and Valencia are slowly trying to take it for themselves and the rest of the Deathless. And then there's you, someone who doesn't want it, who only wants to help out her friends and protect her family. I'd say those are qualifications for a good leader right there."

I still didn't believe it. Even though deep down I could feel a strange *rightness* with the idea. A rightness that could have been tethered to my very soul much like the calling I'd felt in the magic tunnel. That, and Jasper's confidence was infectious.

"What if the others don't agree with me becoming a queen?" I said. "Not just the other races but even the other Outcasts?"

"They might not. Actually, they probably won't. We'll deal with that when the time comes. Together."

"Won't be together if you're with the vampires."

Jasper gave a jerky nod. "Maybe not exactly. But we'll figure that out too."

His eyes flickered down to my lips. I could feel my breathing tighten, wanting to touch him now that he was this close, even knowing what had happened last time; knowing that this strange, new, unlocked magic I now had would be nothing but an irresistible feast to him.

I almost didn't care.

Before I could do anything monumentally stupid, Ari came back. She was smoothie-less (thank you, thank you, thank you) and looked pissed.

"Something wrong?" I said.

"There's someone here to see you," she said. "You'd better come quick."

§

AFTER JASPER and Ari had left to attend to our uninvited guest, I quickly threw on some dry clothes and followed them out, trying to ignore the pieces of charred curtain and covers scattered around my room. I'd have to pick them up as soon as possible and not just for cleanliness sake. I didn't want any more reminders about what had happened. I had to believe that Jasper was right and I'd get my new powers under control. I didn't want to consider the alternative.

I came downstairs to the living room and stopped, mouth falling open.

"Yo." Hayes waved to me from where he lounged on our couch. He looked totally at ease, even with Leon in full lion form eyeing him dangerously, and Jasper and Ari looking ready to tear him apart if he so much as twitched the wrong way. Maybe he really didn't feel like we were a threat, or maybe the person keeping him in place was Sienna, sitting in a chair across from him, looking like she wasn't sure if she wanted to hex him or kiss him.

"What are you doing here?" I said.

"I've only asked that about five dozen times," Sienna said. Her glare deepened. "He won't answer."

Hayes winked at her. "Normally I'd love to answer you, but I wanted to make sure Riley heard it first. And your couch is so comfy."

"Why'd you even let him in?" I asked Ari.

"*Let him try something,*" Leon flashed his enormous teeth. "*Please.*"

"I'm here now," I said. "What is it you so desperately need to tell me?"

"I got word an hour ago that Lukas found some kind of markings he was apparently searching for. He seemed excited about it."

"In the tunnels?" Ari said.

"Yes."

"So?" Jasper crossed his arms. "There are hundreds of ancient markings all over the city."

Hayes looked right at me. "You sure about that?"

I knew at once what he was saying. Uko told me that I needed to follow the markings to reach the end of the prophecy. The only reason Lukas would be excited was if he truly believed he'd stumbled onto something big.

"How do we know you're not lying?" I said.

"Yes, *please* be lying," Sienna said, leaning closer. "I'd love the chance to get a little payback. Even if you're telling the truth it'd be worth it."

For a moment, Hayes looked crestfallen. "Believe it or not, I didn't mean for any of you to get hurt at Lukas's. Though if you were trying to win the Darwin Award for most pointless risk, congrats, you did it. You're lucky you got out when you did."

"So that was you who helped us, then?" I said.

Hayes just smiled. I took that as a yes and turned to Jasper. "I'm not sure he's lying."

"I don't think he is," Jasper said. "And honestly, we can't take the risk if Lukas found something important."

"Where is Lukas now?" I asked Hayes.

"In one of the older tunnels on the north side. I'm supposed to meet up with him soon. He's only taking a small group of shifters. Strangely enough he doesn't trust everyone in his Pack."

"Gee, I wonder why?" Sienna said.

"Leon, help get ready to go," Jasper said. "Ari, show our 'guest' out."

"I'm not leaving until he's gone," Leon growled.

"Don't worry, I'll show him the door," Sienna said. A small

spark shot off her finger and snapped at Hayes, making him jump. "Off your butt."

"Whose side are you really on?" I said as Hayes walked past.

"The right one," he said.

"If you're leading us into a trap, I'll personally hunt you down and castrate you," Sienna said sweetly.

Hayes gave her a charming smile. "I guess I wouldn't mind if I got to see you again—"

Sienna slammed the door in his face.

"Guess you're over him," I said.

She shrugged. "Maybe. Maybe not. He's still cute."

"Ari, Leon, Riley, let's go," Jasper said. "No telling how far Lukas has gotten already."

Sienna looked like she was about to argue but squeezed me in a tight hug instead. "I should stay. Keep this place locked down while you guys are gone, you know? But I swear, if something happens and you all die, I'll kill you."

"That sounds fair," I said.

I spotted Collette watching us from the top of the stairs. She sneered at me.

"Off to save us poor, helpless Outcasts again I suppose?"

"I'm sure there are ways you could help, if you wanted," I said. "Nothing poor and helpless about that."

Collette flipped her hair over her shoulder. "And leave the Loft and my morning workout? As if." She turned, giving me a lazy wave. "Don't die."

I'd try my best. I hoped it'd be enough.

CHAPTER TWENTY-THREE

I hurried down to the garage beneath the Loft to find Jasper straddling a motorcycle, playing with the straps of a helmet.

I paused. The guy had enhanced speed and strength and yet apparently had one of these sitting around in the garage.

Not that I was complaining…

He saw me and patted the back of the seat.

Nope, definitely not complaining.

"Why didn't we use these before?" I asked as I tentatively swung my legs over and took the helmet he offered me.

"We weren't in a hurry before," he answered. "And Cliffside traffic's normally terrible."

He turned the bike on and the engine roared to life. The entire garage rattled with the power.

"Pretty cool, right?" Jasper yelled. "Ducati Monster. 208 horsepower, custom trim."

He glanced back, clearly expecting this to be something I should be impressed with.

"Sorry, what?" I yelled back.

He frowned. "At which part did you stop listening?"

"Right after you said 'pretty cool, right?'"

Jasper grunted and faced front again.

"I have an idea of the place Hayes was talking about," Leon said beside us. "Follow me."

I nearly burst out laughing when I saw him. "Dude, really?" I teased.

Leon finished clipping his helmet and strapping on the tiny goggles over his eyes. Then he somehow maneuvered himself onto an electric scooter that looked comically small for him.

"You laugh, but mine's planet-friendly, you gas-guzzling Neanderthal," Leon said.

"Don't listen to him," Jasper said, revving the engine.

"You boys done comparing your toys?" Ari said, hitting the button to open the garage door. She shifted to her cheetah form. *Try to keep up this time.*

Then she took off, Leon throttling his handle and screeching after her.

"What about the vampires outside?" I said. "Won't they follow us?"

"Not if they can't keep up," Jasper said, leaning forward over the handlebars. "Hold on."

I looked for a handle of my own.

"Around my waist, Riley." I could hear the laughter in his voice.

"Of course. Obviously."

No sooner had I wrapped my arms around his stomach then Jasper gunned the engine. It would have thrown me off if I hadn't been holding on so tight. Gravity gave me a solid yank back, then we were screeching up the garage's incline and exploding onto the street above.

Jasper put out his leg and skidded us to the left before gunning the engine and accelerating after the forms of Leon and Ari.

"We needed to give them a head start," Jasper yelled as the

passing buildings bled into a blur. "I wasn't kidding about holding on."

This time I had no problem following his advice.

※

WE SKIRTED through the narrow streets for a short time until Ari was convinced we weren't being followed and led us onto the highway. Thankfully it was still super early and dark. I didn't want to know what people might think if the African savannah suddenly wound up on I-90.

"This exit!" Leon yelled after a few minutes. We took the next ramp, past the Yansaw Center where most of Cliffside's Mighty Eagles basketball team played their games. Leon routed us around Northside Mall until we ended up in a somewhat nicer looking street lined with closed shops. Even the bar at the end was closed, but across the street from it was another, open one.

Only...there was something funny about it. Whenever I looked at it straight on it shimmered, as though draped behind a veil of water.

"Magic concealment," Jasper said when his engine was quiet enough to speak normally again. "Lots of places around the city have it. Spots known only to the paranormal world."

Ari appeared in human form beside us. "Stash your rides. We'll go in on foot."

I took off my helmet and slipped from the back of the motorcycle. Jasper and Leon wheeled their rides to the backside of one of the closed shops, well out of sight.

"What do you think?" Ari asked. "You think that Hayes guy was playing us?"

"I'm not sure," I answered honestly. Part of me knew better than to believe him, and yet part of me wanted to.

"Not sure why Leon thinks a night club is the place to start," Ari said. "Going in there cannot be a good idea."

"That's why we're not going in," Leon said, returning with Jasper. He jerked his head for us to follow.

I heard the thump of bass mingled with the cluster of excited voices as we approached. A sign with "Dusk 'Til Dawn" on it hung above a bouncer periodically ushering people inside. From amongst the crowd I could pick out the inhuman beauty of some vampires, the rough, gruff exterior of a few shifters. Even the glimmer of glamour. Fae or faerie. Had to be.

"Everybody here seems to be getting along," I muttered.

"Have to," Leon said. "House rules. You cause trouble you get kicked out. Or worse."

That made me feel a little better as we approached. But right before we hit the line to get in, Leon cut sharply right and led us down a narrow alleyway between the two buildings.

"When Hayes mentioned tunnels in the north side I knew there was a good chance it was this place," he said. "Though no one here would ever explicitly say it, on my deliveries I caught word of a back part of the lot where tons of shifters congregate. Those from Lukas' pack supposedly."

"You ever confirm it?" Ari said.

"Never needed to. Guess we'll find out if it's one of these tunnels Lukas was using."

We reached the corner and Leon put a hand up. He peeked around, then sharply jerked back. "Well if the pack *doesn't* use it, then it's kind of strange that they have two shifters guarding an old cellar door."

"Let me look." Jasper checked himself, then retreated. He paused to think for a moment. "Here's what we'll do: I'll strike from the top. Ari, take that second one on my signal. Hit them hard and fast before they make any noise. One howl and we'll have a dozen more to deal with."

"I want in on this," Leon said, pounding a giant fist into his palm.

Jasper patted him on the shoulder. "You're many things, but subtle isn't one of them."

And then, quiet as a breath, Jasper leapt, easily making it to the top of the roof where he vanished into the shadows.

"Subtle," Leon grunted. "Says the guy with a bike that wakes up half of Cliffside every time he drives past."

"I think it's pretty cool," I said.

"Course you do. It's the whole bad boy persona, isn't it? Girls love that sort of thing."

"I didn't say that," I countered, my cheeks heating.

I heard the faint sound, barely louder than a cough, of flesh hitting flesh.

I blinked and Ari's cheetah form had slipped around the corner. There was a short cry, quickly cut off.

"We're good," Ari said. *"Come on, you two."*

The small door the shifters had been guarding was inset into one of the walls of the narrow alley running between the back of the shops. It was honestly amazing Lukas had made anyone guard it. If no one had been here, I probably would have walked right past.

"Did you kill them?" I asked Jasper as he finished dragging the second shifter out of sight.

"No," Jasper said. "Though between the headache they'll have and Lukas' wrath, they'll probably wish they were dead."

Ari pawed at the enormous steel lock securing a dead bolt across the door. *"Jasper, could you—"*

Leon stepped forward, shifted one hand into an enormous lion's paw, and ripped the lock clean off. "Subtlety, thy name is Leon."

Jasper glared at him. "Are you going to let that go anytime soon?"

"Probably not," Leon said, grinning. He gestured to the door. "After you."

"I'll go first," I said, brushing off the remaining piece of the deadbolt and pulling open the door. I was immediately hit with the smell of mildew and a musty odor I could only describe as "old." Though Lukas apparently used this tunnel too, much like the last one we'd been in he clearly hadn't bothered with air fresheners or a scented candle or two.

I took the slick steps carefully, summoning a ball of flame to light my way.

I'd been afraid of what my magic would do after the mishap in my bedroom, but it answered no problem. It did feel a bit more eager, a bit more difficult to keep at bay, but that could have been my imagination.

We hit the bottom and were immediately presented with three tunnels splitting off in different directions.

"Which way?" Leon said.

I briefly extinguished my fire, plunging us into darkness. "Anyone see another light?" I whispered.

"No," Jasper said. "Ari, what if you—"

"On it."

I cast another flame in time to see Ari sniff the air. Her nose wrinkled in what I could only describe as a cheetah's disgusted face.

"Right tunnel. Stench of dirty fur and rancid breath. Has to be them."

"We need to hurry," Jasper said. "Lukas cannot reach the throne first."

"We know," I said. "Trust me, we know."

"Good." Jasper nodded. "Can you keep up?"

I sent my ball of fire out into the tunnel ahead of us. "Can you?"

Jasper grinned and took off running, Ari loping at his heels.

"Stay a little behind us."

I jumped at Leon's giant lion form suddenly beside me. *"Something seems off about this, but I'm not sure what,"* he said.

He took off after the others. I sprinted close behind, trying to keep from running into the walls as the tunnels narrowed, then widened again with frightening regularity.

I could still make out the others ahead, lit up by my firelight, but they were pulling away fast. My shoes slipped a bit on the next turn as I tried to speed up. I swallowed the urge to shout at them to slow down. We had to stay quiet. No telling where Lukas and his crew were down here. I understood that we wanted to ensure Lukas didn't reach the throne first, but I had my doubts he'd even be able to do anything with it. Heck, *I* didn't know if I could do anything with it, and I was supposedly the super special chosen one.

The white of what I really hoped wasn't a skull reflected the fireball I'd cast for myself. I forced my gaze forward and kept running. This tunnel was just as creepy as the first. It'd be the perfect place to wander around and die in.

My firelight suddenly rose up and I emerged at another small chamber with a three-way split. I paused to catch my breath. "Which way—*pant*—this time?"

I looked up to find I was alone. Panic immediately clenched my heart. "Jasper? Ari? Leon?" I hissed.

No response. No sign that they were even close by.

"Guys?" I said, louder. My voice echoed back to me, sounding thin and desperate.

"Riley!"

Jasper's voice came from the tunnel in the dead center.

"Way to leave a girl behind!" I snarled as I started running toward it. He sounded so far ahead, I couldn't believe how much they'd gained on me, paranormals or not.

"Hurry up!" Jasper called back. "We ran into some of Lukas' pack. He's close!"

The tunnels flickered crazily as my firelight bobbed to keep up. "Slow down! How am I supposed to freaking follow you?"

I heard other voices. Maybe Ari and Leon. They were too faint to make out, and the stone walls distorted all noise. They might have been ahead of me, or in the passage I'd just passed, and I'd never know. But I did know that if I didn't hurry and they got hurt...

Best not to think about that.

At last my firelight zipped ahead and ascended again. I was coming up on another open space.

I curled my fists, bracing myself for a fight as I rushed out into the broad chamber.

No one was there.

I spun in a circle, looking for the others; even looking for any sign of Lukas or his pack. A sense of déjà vu was taking me over. High-vaulted ceiling. Empty stone stands circling a sunken center floor.

I'd arrived in the Conclave chamber. But how...?

"It's amazing how all these tunnels connect, isn't it?"

The silky voice crawled up my spine and sent shivers down my arms.

I turned to look up at Farrar perched in the first row of stands. His eyes glittered hungrily down at me.

"So easy to tease you away," he said. "And now here you are, completely defenseless and alone."

CHAPTER TWENTY-FOUR

Farrar leapt down, barely making a sound as he landed.

I took a step back. "Where's Jasper? Where are my friends?"

"Pointlessly wandering the tunnels, I suppose," Farrar said. Then, in an eerily similar impersonation of Jasper's gruff voice, he said, "They'll probably be doing that for hours, thanks to the false information I fed Lukas' lap dog Hayes."

I took another step back as Farrar began circling, driving me toward the center of the chamber. This close, I could tell the voice wasn't Jasper's. But distorted by the tunnels it hadn't needed to be perfect. It'd done its job and drawn me right to Farrar like the gullible idiot I was.

"So Lukas really doesn't know where the tunnel and the throne are," I said, stalling.

"Oh, he's around here and searching," Farrar said. "I doubt even with Lukas' single-minded determination they'll find it. But that doesn't matter. They're missing the *point*."

"And what point is that?" I was nearly in the center of the chamber now. There was no cover anywhere. I couldn't trick my way out of this, and as one of the leaders of the Deathless I knew Farrar was strong. Possibly stronger than Jasper.

"The point is that the throne doesn't matter," Farrar said, clearly enjoying himself. "According to the prophecy, only an elemental can claim the throne and from it wield power over the other races. But that power comes from you. All of that power in the hands of a little girl who doesn't know the first thing about using it."

I ground my teeth together to keep my magic from rising. I'd need it, but not yet. I had to time my magic perfectly. "I won't be your puppet to use. You might have forced Jasper to join the Deathless, but you can't force me."

"The Deathless?"

I held in a gasp as Farrar moved, suddenly gripping my chin and twisting it up to look him in the eyes. "Forget the Deathless. This is for me and my little secret. You see, I'm a Forsworn vampire, too."

I stilled in my struggling, the implication hitting me.

"It wasn't easy, pretending you didn't matter to me. Pretending I had no interest in you," Farrar said. "But now all your magic will be mine alone. I'll draw it from you like a needle from a vein. And then I'll use its power for my own."

I let out a sharp cry as he gripped my chin harder, pushing my lips tight against each other. I shoved against him, but it was like trying to move a steel beam.

"Be still, please..." Farrar cooed. "This doesn't need to be difficult. I am not cruel. I do not wish to cause your last moments more pain than is already necessary."

The red in his eyes glowed brighter, filling the edge of my vision and creeping to cover it. I could see only him and nothing more. I could feel my will to resist fading, even while I simultaneously felt his magic slowly taking me over.

"Let me drain your magic," Farrar said, his voice turning silky smooth. "You wouldn't use it to its full potential anyway."

"I..." I gasped.

"Yes?" Farrar leaned in, until his bulbous lips were inches from mine. He sucked in a breath and an orange layer of my magic disappeared into his mouth. I felt a low, ferocious growl from deep inside me, growing stronger. "I am listening," Farrar said. "Is there anything you want to say? Anything you wish to confess to me before you die?"

"I...."

The growl grew, until my entire body rumbled with its force.

"...wouldn't do that if I were you."

My magic burned away his vampiric compulsion at the same time I swiped at his face, a tiger's claw of flame leaving seared marks across his skin.

Farrar screamed and his hold on me broke. He tried to grab me again but I called on my magic and hurriedly cast a blazing wall of fire between us.

"You little witch!" Farrar screeched, clutching at his face.

"Nope, but you're close!" I yelled, running backwards, trying to put as much space between me and him as possible, my heart thudding a million miles an hour. Farrar tried to follow, but each time he did I cast my magic like a flamethrower, covering the ground and driving him back again. The tactic was working, yet already my magic was starting to weaken.

"You can't fight me forever," Farrar called over the flames. "Eventually you will tire and I will win. It's inevitable."

He leered at me from the other side of the fire. "Please be reasonable, Riley. What would you do with the throne? With all that power? Lead us? You know *nothing* of our world and yet the witches' prophecy chose you. Can you not see the folly in that?"

I was out of breath, every space around me covered in flames. Sweat coated my skin. Farrar paced outside the nearest circle of fire, watching me, waiting for the instant I let my defenses wane. "Admit it, we would all be better off if the prophecy remained unfulfilled."

"I don't know much about this world," I agreed. "But I have to try to fulfill it. And I'm not going to let some ugly fang face like you take that chance away."

Farrar's expression turned sad, as though he'd truly hoped I'd submit and let him kill me that easily.

Then he leapt higher than I thought possible, seeming to hover over my flames. I screwed my feet into the ground like Jasper had taught me, bracing myself for an attack. Farrar came down right on top of me, driving his arm down into my shoulder. I blocked the worst of the blow, but Farrar's other hand snapped sideways, clipping my jaw. White exploded in my eyes. I tasted copper and sweat.

"Not strong enough, I'm afraid," Farrar said.

He hit me again and I was suddenly face down on the ground in the center of the chamber. Farrar's faint footsteps approached. "I never wanted this to be distressful. It may seem unbelievable, but undue suffering puts me off my appetite. Now please hold still..."

My body screamed in agony as I pushed myself up. I had to stand. Had to face him and—

I finally got a good look at the floor.

Smooth grooves had been carved in flowy, circular patterns crossing beneath my hands and expanding in a circle to take over most of the chamber's center. The circle ended in a single point in the middle with a symbol in it. The same symbol I had on my shoulder. Elemental.

Follow the markings.

It couldn't be possible. A trick of the light caused by fatigue and too many blows to the head. Yet the symbol wasn't disappearing, no matter how many times I blinked. I didn't have anything to lose by trying.

I pulled my exhausted magic to the surface and plunged my palm into the middle of the symbol. There was a sizzling sound.

Veins of orange began to spread along the lines, branching where they met others.

"No more tricks." Farrar grabbed my shirt and easily lifted me up. "This is over."

I drove a fiery fist into his gut, putting all my weight behind it. His eyes bulged. He dropped me and stumbled back, the flames coating my fist continuing to spread where it caught the delicate fabric of his coat.

"No! *No!*"

Farrar's entire body was alight now, no matter how much he batted at it. I could only watch in fascinated horror as his skin flaked away like ash. His bleached white skeleton went next, splashed with red and orange, turning to smoldering black. The last thing I saw of him was a single red eye before it, too, was incinerated with the rest of him.

I gaped at the spot where Farrar had stood moments before. Then gaped beyond it, where Jasper, Ari, and Leon had just entered the chamber. They all looked shocked to find what had once been a leader of the Deathless now taking up space no bigger than a shoe box.

Then I saw the movement in the stands surrounding us.

Vampires. A dozen of them. Every single one having probably just witnessed what I'd done to their leader.

"She killed Farrar!" one of them seethed. Angry hisses filled the chamber.

I put my hands up. "No! Well, yes, but he attacked me first—"

"Kill her!"

I barely had time to make out Jasper and the others moving to intercept the group before the first vampire was on me.

Survival instinct kicked in. I took a shallow cut to the shoulder with a sharpened claw but paid it back with a punch to the throat. The vampire staggered away, choking, only to be replaced by two more.

"He attacked me!" I yelled. "I was only defending myself! You have to—Stop!"

Couldn't they understand that I was the victim here? Or did they not want to?

I nearly tripped as the first vampire leapt again, sinking his fangs into my arm. I screamed as I pulled on my magic. The vampire let go, mouth steaming where my fiery veins had burned him. I ducked the next vampire's strike, but he moved too quickly, pinning my arms to the floor. His fangs sank toward my neck.

Right as another pair of fangs wrapped around his midsection and hurled him off me.

"You good?" Leon said. He nimbly swung his lion form around and smashed another in the chest with his back paws.

"I'm good," I said, sucking in air and trying to reorient my spinning vision.

"Stay beside us. We're getting the hell out of here."

Jasper was nothing but a blur outmaneuvering the other vampires. Ari ran circles around a couple others, darting in every so often to bite one and send them flying against the walls.

I slid my way in between them as Leon joined Jasper's side. I crouched, trying to reorient myself. Warmth spread across my hand. I looked down to find the orange markings I'd filled had spread and begun to glow even brighter. So bright it was starting to hurt. The center of the floor had begun swelling upwards, as though something was trying to push its way up from below.

"Watch out!" I yelled as Jasper and Ari almost backed into it. "At your feet!"

Jasper looked down a moment too long and three of the vampires latched onto him. He managed to reach through the tangled mass of tearing limbs, grab one, and hurl them off him. The others weren't relenting. Blood sprayed and my stomach went weak. I sprinted at him, fire burning through me with renewed strength. They wouldn't hurt him—they wouldn't hurt any of them. I wouldn't let them.

"Get *off!*"

I grabbed the first vampire by the arm and threw him, his skin sizzling where I'd touched him. Jasper now had enough time to put a hand between the other vamp's tearing claws. I saw him grit his teeth and *push*. The other vamp went soaring off, slamming into his companion. Neither one got up.

"They nearly had me." Jasper shot me a grateful look, blood leaking down the side of his face. "Some teacher I turned out to be, huh? Can't even fight off a few underlings."

"You're hurt," I said.

Jasper glanced down at the deep gouge marks in his forearms. They'd already stopped bleeding. "I'll live. We need to get out of here."

He nodded to the stands where I could make out a growing number of red-eyed shadows. I couldn't make them out super well, but for some reason I didn't think it was Uko and the rest of the Horde come to save the day.

"Ari! Leon!"

"Had enough fun?" Leon said, smashing down another vampire with his paws. *"Or are we staying for seconds?"*

"We'll back you up," Ari said. *"Head out the way we came. And maybe stick together this tim—Watch it!"*

Jasper reacted before I could, shoving me aside as one of the vampires we'd thought was down sprang up again and tackled him. Before I could cast a single attack, a force like a wrecking ball slammed me from the side.

"Hold on, Riley!" Leon roared.

I tried to yell back but an impossibly strong hand squeezed my throat, cutting my scream to little more than a gurgle. I looked up into the hate-filled eyes of a vampire.

"Die!"

The grip tightened and I threatened to black out. The tiger

within was trying to come to my defense but it wouldn't be in time. These vampires didn't care if I had power or was a special key to anything. They'd seen me kill one of their supposedly perfect leaders and so now I had to die.

Spots danced in my eyes. My thoughts were sluggish as I fought for breath.

Then I *could* breath. Great, gulping lungsful of amazing air. My feet touched ground again and my legs immediately gave way.

"Hands off, bloodsucker. She's mine."

"Jasper?" I managed.

I blinked until I could see. Not Jasper.

Lukas.

"Hello, *queen*," he said.

Hayes dashed into the chamber behind him, followed by about a dozen other shifters. He cast a spell that toppled one vampire but was soon lost among a swarm of others as the two groups collided.

"You didn't think I'd lose my prize that easily, did you?" Lukas said.

He grinned as I scrambled backwards. My hand struck something hot. One of the orange lines. The floor had cracked extensively in some places, revealing a dark chasm below. I could see now that something wasn't bubbling up from below. Something was giving way.

Lukas' smile faltered. "What did you...?"

"Riley!"

Jasper tore through the fray toward me, hand reaching for mine. "Watch—"

The center of the floor collapsed. The solid ground beneath me was suddenly gone and I fell into darkness.

CHAPTER TWENTY-FIVE

I awoke with a splitting headache.

I immediately shoved away the pain and tried to get my bearings. I couldn't see or hear anything. The memory of what had happened before I'd blacked out came back to me and I resisted the urge to call out for the others. I was in a place I didn't know, probably somewhere deeper in the tunnels. With all the vampires and shifters I'd seen fighting, it was likely I wasn't the only one down here.

It was even more likely I was very much alone amongst them.

At last I moved my arms and legs to make sure they weren't broken and sat up. I hissed as sharp pain in my ribs let me know it was there. I tenderly touched the spot and bit down another hiss. Probably broken. After all…

I looked up from the pile of rubble I'd landed on, through the hole in the roof of some house, way up into the darkness.

I'd fallen from up there? If it hadn't been obvious before, that proved it: I *must* have been part paranormal to survive that. Either that or—and I was no geologist—I'd landed on the rare pillow rock.

I slid off the pile onto my jelly-like legs and cast firelight so I could finally see. My injured rib gave me a little knife-stabbing reminder every time I breathed in too deeply, so I kept my breaths as shallow as I could as I forced my way through the wooden front door and outside to a street.

I looked around, utterly confused.

The house I'd landed in—and I was just realizing I'd landed in a flippin' *house*—looked like something out of Disneyland's Ye Olde Time of Knights and Dragons theme park. Thatched roof, mud sidings, rough stone foundation. I wouldn't have been shocked if a peasant came toddling around the corner.

The rest of this place wasn't like that at all. Sure, there were a couple more cottages, but I stood on a paved road, complete with cogworked lamps, like something I might have seen in a steam-punk movie. Large, multi-tiered buildings, some collapsing but most of them in decent shape, rose in front of me.

A city. A dead city. *The* Dead City. Had to be.

Follow the markings to find it...right. More like "have the markings drag you down below the surface of the earth and there you'll find it."

I looked up again at where I'd fallen. I could see only dark-ness. If the collapsed part of the floor was still there, it was closed over now.

With no other options and no clue how to get out, I started walking. My footsteps were eaten up by the quiet. It was almost lucky I couldn't breathe too deeply. Much louder and I was afraid I'd disturb something. I wasn't sure what, but the Dead City probably hadn't gotten that name because of anything good.

Unlike Cliffside that (I hoped) was above, this city was built on hills. After struggling through a gate right off the street, I was able to get a better look around. Hundreds more buildings undu-lated like waves across the uneven underground landscape. More skyscrapers, too, and winding networks of streets that criss-crossed in no particular order.

It wasn't the easiest to make everything out, but from what I could see, it all looked stuck somewhere around the 19th century, with a few signs of more modern buildings. This must have been one of the main places the underground tunnels led to. A place where paranormals had lived before emerging to live alongside humans.

I squinted at a large, circular building on the next hill over. It reminded me of a parliament building or city hall. A plan clicked into place. I needed to find a way out, but if the Horde was right, then the throne should be down here, too. I had no clue where, but the building in the dead center of everything seemed like a pretty good place to start.

I took the stairs down to the road below and picked up the pace. I hoped Jasper and the others were okay. It was painful to think of them still up above. I was confident they could outmaneuver a fight between the shifters and vamps, but with Lukas there…

My stomach knotted tighter. First I had to get out of here. Then I could deal with the consequences.

I stopped at the next street. I couldn't see anything that immediately alarmed me, but all the same I had an unsettling feeling that I wasn't alone.

I quickly closed my hand to extinguish the light, staying motionless while my eyes adjusted before stepping quickly up the street. I could pick out a faint noise up ahead. Someone talking.

I slipped toward them as quietly as I could. Here the road diverged in two directions. The talking came from the left, around the corner of another house. I peered around.

A single vamp walked aimless in the middle of the street, muttering to himself. I ducked back around, trying to calm my beating heart in case that gave me away. He must have fallen down with me, though I wasn't sure how we'd ended up so far apart. If he was here, that meant others could be also.

I took a painful, steadying breath. I had to go around him. If I tried to fight and screwed up, I was done for.

I took one final look. The vamp's head snapped around to look right at me.

I backed up, terror seizing me. A hand clamped over my mouth.

"Quiet," Jasper whispered.

Jasper!

He held me close while we waited, my mind going crazy. Him being down here as well was obviously bad since we were both trapped. But I couldn't pretend I wasn't overjoyed to see him.

Jasper eventually uncovered my mouth. When the vamp didn't pop around the corner, he jerked his head for me to follow him down the other side of the house.

Right as the vampire dropped in front of us.

"I thought I heard some rats!" he hissed.

I threw a fireball as Jasper lunged. My magic missed but Jasper didn't, intercepting the vampire as he went straight for me. The vampire's unconscious body slammed into mine, taking me to the ground. Intense pain raced up my side and I bit on my lower lip hard enough to bleed, desperate to not scream and give ourselves away to anyone else.

Jasper heaved the vampire off. He must have seen how agonized I looked because he immediately scooped me up, careful not to touch the side I was clutching, and leapt onto the roof of the nearest building. "Hold on. We're going somewhere safe."

❧

JASPER FOUND one of the taller buildings that didn't look too broken down and busted his way inside.

"We need a better vantage point," was all he said before he took the stairs.

Just when I was beginning to feel truly useless, we emerged in a small, empty flat. The only items left over from the previous occupants were a stray sock and what might have been a bowl like the kind Sienna used for combining magical ingredients.

Jasper set me down. His fingers immediately went to the side I clutched.

"Watch it!" I hissed as he tried to prod at it. "How about *not* poking the painful place?"

"I need to see if it's broken," he said without remorse.

"It hurts. That's all we need to know."

I couldn't help grimacing as I sat up. Jasper watched me, concerned.

"Push some of your magic into it."

"What?"

"You can move your magic to different parts of your body, right? Do that and move the magic to where it hurts."

I wasn't sure how fire magic was supposed to heal, but I trusted that Jasper knew what he was talking about.

I straightened up as much as I could and concentrated on diverting some of my magic toward the tender spot in my ribs. A moment later I felt the spot grow pleasantly warm.

"Huh." I raised my arms over my head and twisted, testing the limits of my movements. The pain was there, but it'd retreated to a dull ache. "That helped. Thanks."

"I didn't do anything. It was all you." Jasper stood to look out the cloudy window. "Can't do a fire. Too risky if we don't know who else is down here."

"Are Ari and Leon okay?"

"Not sure," he said, voice grim. "Let's not worry about them. They can take care of themselves. What we do now is the question."

He returned and took a seat across from me. "I need to know what happened after we entered the tunnels."

I recalled in as much detail as I could remember about getting split apart from them and running into Farrar. About the markings and how I'd activated them.

"Farrar, that backstabbing piece of trash." Jasper looked angry enough to bite off someone's head. "Lucky you incinerated him before I got to him. I had no idea he was a Forsworn. Or that he had it out for you."

"I think we can safely assume everyone has it out for me, unless they're in the Outcasts," I said drily.

Silence hung between us, heavy with implication. "So what now?" I was almost too afraid to ask. "Before I ran into you, I was heading to the center of the city. There's a building there I thought may hold the throne."

"Maybe..." Jasper drew the word out, deep in thought. "I don't know as much as Sawyer, but I'm pretty sure this Dead City isn't the original. It only looks a few hundred years old. I can't imagine it having a throne of any kind."

My spirits sank. "You think this isn't the right place?"

"No, I think it is. The Dead City has only ever been in one spot, so the buildings we're seeing must have been built upon others for years. Thousands of years. And since the Horde said you had to go here, then we can be pretty confident we're on the right track. And yet..."

"You're not so sure."

"It doesn't make sense. Why would a city that never had any monarchy have a throne?"

I sighed, unable to come up with an answer. "Even if we find the throne, what can we do about the shifters and vamps?"

"The Deathless will act like Farrar's betrayal was no big deal," Jasper said. "Valencia will try to use you to focus their anger once she gets them under control. She'll frame you to feel justified."

"Just like they're going to use you once you join them."

Jasper gave me a fierce look. "I'm not joining them until you're queen. Until then I'm yours and the Outcasts'."

The proclamation sent a warm feeling blooming in my chest, though it didn't last very long. "That'll happen sooner rather than later. Unless I can't reach the throne. Unless..."

"Stop thinking negatively." Jasper stood and offered a hand to me. "You feel better?"

I checked that my magic was still masking the pain in my ribs. "Yeah. It's fine."

"Good. Then get up. We're down here. Throne has to be close. I'm not letting you give up now."

He said it like it was the easiest thing in the world. I wasn't so sure. There were still a dozen problems to fix. A dozen people who wanted me and my powers for different reasons. What did solving one prophecy matter in the face of all that? What did any of it matter?

"Hey."

Jasper was giving me a look of such fierce determination I couldn't help but feel jolted in place. "I see you giving up. That crap's not going to help anyone, so cut it out. Yeah, we have problems, but there are things we can still do. And I and every one of the Outcasts will fight with you until we solve them."

I took his hand and in one move he easily pulled me up to him.

"You're right," I said. The prophecy might be the only chance we had. I'd have to take it. To hell with whatever happened after.

Jasper grinned at me. "There's that fire I saw the first time we met."

"You mean when you basically assaulted me and accused me of conspiring against you?"

"I...may have been a little overzealous. To be fair, if I'd known how much trouble you'd be, I would have acted even worse."

His hand didn't let go of mine. His other hand slid around my back to steady me.

"Jasper..." My voice was hoarse. "Do you think we could ever...Do you still think...?"

"I don't know." He didn't look away, but there was a sadness and uncertainty in his eyes. "I want to."

"I get it." The words killed me to say, but what else could I do?

If kissing him hurt us both, if what he *was* was a danger to me, then there wasn't much we could do now.

"I'll find a way to make it work, Riley," Jasper said. "I promise."

It wasn't what I wanted to hear, but it was the best I was going to get right now. "Good. Now, let's go make me a queen and finish that stupid prophecy."

❦

IT'D TAKEN the better part of two hours, but the circular, center building we'd both seen was close. Just a few more streets and I'd be inside and learn if this impromptu side quest was worth it.

But as the enormous front came into view—looking like a cross between a football stadium and a Roman coliseum—I felt a pull on my senses. I stopped, trying to place whether I had just imagined it or I was feeling a tug from the magic covering my wound.

"Jasper...Hold up."

His expression was concerned. "Your rib hurting?"

"No. I..."

There it was again. A sixth sense. A pull I couldn't put into words that spoke to something deep inside me. The same pull I'd felt right before...

"This way."

I turned off the street, following the tugging that grew with every step.

"Riley, wait." Jasper caught up with me. "We're nearly inside. We should check it out first."

I wasn't sure he was wrong. I wasn't sure we were right.

I *was* sure this was a feeling I couldn't ignore.

I picked up the pace, turning down another slender street, excitement building until—

I stopped, breathless, and pointed. "Found it."

The magic tunnel I'd seen in the Conclave chamber stretched

out before us, the mouth of it literally opening in the dead center of a brick wall.

"I don't get it," Jasper said. "I thought that was leading us to the Dead City."

"I don't get it either, but I'm not losing it."

I grabbed his hand and together we dashed inside.

I almost expected it to be an illusion, like those old road-runner cartoons where Wiley E Coyote runs face first into a painted wall. But the tunnel was very much real. The glowing markings following us along the walls and ceiling felt even more so.

"I think we're near the end!" I said, giddy. "I think we can reach it!"

"Sure hope so!" Jasper said, glancing back as though the tunnel would collapse on us at any moment. But he couldn't feel what I did. This was different than the first time. The tunnel knew I was ready to face where it led, even if I didn't feel like I was.

The longing feeling grew and grew until it was nearly unbear-able, until I was going to punch the wall if we didn't reach the end soon.

And then we had.

"Wow." Jasper sounded in awe. I had to agree.

We'd wound up in a gigantic vaulted room—not unlike a throne room. On the right side were thick sandstone pillars standing guard before a sudden drop off. Far below the edge was a view of pretty much the entire city.

"There." Jasper jerked his head toward a door on the opposite end of the chamber. "I get it now."

"Get what?"

"We were right: the Dead City never had a throne. This is new. The throne of ancients is reestablishing itself, creating a new order in a new place, atop something dead."

I looked through the pillars, at the silhouetted remnants of the almost-modern city contrasting with this fantasy-like throne room. Creating a new legacy? Was that true? Was I the first para-normal in a millennium, possibly ever, to take this spot?

Jasper nudged his head toward the door again. "You ready?"

I squared my shoulders. The longing feeling was gone. I'd reached the place where I was needed. "As I'll ever be."

"Good. I'm right behind—"

He gasped. I whirled around as bloody claw tips emerged from his stomach. My mind froze, unable to believe what I was seeing.

"So close," Lukas said as he removed his claws and let Jasper collapse. He looked at me hungrily. "Now, let's get that door open."

CHAPTER TWENTY-SIX

"I'll kill you!"

Fire flared in my core but Lukas moved before I could strike, clamping down on my hands and twisting my arms so far back I felt like my tendons were tearing.

"Let's not make this harder than it needs to be."

I gasped as he threw me to the ground. He was nearly fully shifted, his golden eyes slitted, narrow mouth filled with sharp teeth. "I've had more than enough games. You'll give me what I'm owed. Come here, Hayes."

I hadn't noticed Hayes behind him. He was looking uncertainly at Jasper, then at me.

"Hayes!" Lukas roared. "Bind her magic. I don't want any more surprises."

"She won't fight any more," Hayes said. "Will you?" he asked me, almost pleading for me to say yes.

"I gave you an order," Lukas growled. "Bind her magic or I break her hands. Then I start breaking the rest of her before I move onto you."

Hayes reluctantly raised his hand. I started scrambling back.

"Wait—"

My magic surged, right as a feeling not unlike a door slamming shut closed me off from it. I tried calling on it again, but it barely offered a whimper.

"No. Nonono..." I reached deep inside but the fiery core of my magic was dulled. A sheath of Hayes' magic prevented me from reaching it.

Jasper still lay unmoving, and a different sort of cold fell over me. I scrambled over to him and cradled his head in my lap. "You killed him!"

"Nearly," Lukas said. "Think of him as collateral. You do what I want, and if you're lucky we all get out of this in one piece. For the most part."

"Don't...help him, Riley..." Jasper wheezed.

His eyes were clouded with pain. He tried to sit up but only managed to get halfway before his body shook and he fell back exhausted.

"Don't move," I said. "Let me look."

I pulled up the bottom of his shirt and held in a breath. Five neat, bloody holes had punctured through the smooth skin of his abdomen. I waited for them to close up like all the other injuries he'd had, but they refused. What had Lukas done to him?

"Enough wasting my time."

My scalp screamed as Lukas grabbed my hair and started dragging me toward the door. "I didn't follow you all the way through the Dead City just to be turned away now."

"I won't do it!" I said through gritted teeth. I battered against the sheath covering my magic. I could feel it starting to break but at this rate it wouldn't be in time. "I won't!"

"You will." Lukas let go of my hair and crouched beside me. Even his halfway shifted form was positively immense, like he could swallow me up in two swift bites. "I won't just kill your little boyfriend and hurt you, I'll finish off that traitorous lion and cheetah shifter still above. Oh yes," he said, a delighted smile spreading across his face. "They're still alive. I can change that.

Same with that witch boy and faerie girl in the Loft. After all, I don't need to play nice with the Conclave rules if I'm about to have the power of the elemental throne."

"*You'll* have the power?" Hayes sounded genuinely confused. "You mean Riley. That was your plan. You were going to put her on the throne to rule in your place."

Lukas jerked me around to face the door. "There's been a change of plans."

"You can't take the throne," I said. "That's why you wanted to keep me. You need me to finish the prophecy."

I sneered triumphantly up at him, but Lukas' grin only grew. He reached into his pocket and produced a smooth, black stone about as big as my hand.

Hayes sucked in a sharp breath. "A transference stone? Where did you get that?"

"Only the weak put all their hopes in a single way to accomplish their goal," Lukas said. "I went looking for an alternative plan and a seller of mine happened to have exactly what I needed. A rare, newly acquired magical artifact that would give me everything I wanted."

"The museum," I said, the pieces clicking together. "They broke into the museum and you— It won't work."

"We'll have to see, won't we? All it takes is a little magic to prime it. Easy enough for Hayes here to perform."

"No."

Lukas' smile slowly slipped. He cocked his head as though he'd misheard. "What did you say?"

Hayes took a nervous step back as Lukas stood. "I said I won't do it."

"You'll do as I say," Lukas said. "You work for me. I *own* you."

"You told me Riley would take the throne. That was supposed to be the plan."

The sheath surrounding my magic cracked. A bit of it leaked through and reached for me. I desperately urged it on.

"Plans change." Lukas stepped toward him. "Now I'm taking it."

"Riley's meant to take the throne. She's an elemental. That's how it's supposed to be."

Lukas paused. He sniffed the air and somehow, crazily, I knew he was picking up more than just scents.

Lukas took another large breath and spat on the ground. "Double-crosser! I knew there was something not quite right about you. How many times have you sold us out?"

Hayes trembled but stood his ground. "The prophecy says that she's—"

There was a crack of bone as Lukas swiped. Hayes went sliding across the floor and lay still.

"The *prophecy* will not decide what I do!" Lukas snarled.

But the second he hit Hayes, I felt the sheath he'd cast over me shatter. Magic rushed to my call, filling me so fully all I could see was orange. All I could feel was the power of the fire begging to be unleashed.

Lukas turned as I stood. His maniacal grimace dropped. "Damn—"

I hurled a fireball at his chest, sending him flying back. I channeled the flames to crawl across my body like armor, covering me but not burning.

"You've hurt my friends," I said as I stalked toward him, leaving a seared trail in my wake. "You tried destroying our home and using me like a puppet. Not anymore. I'm not going to let you hurt them or me ever again."

Lukas chuckled as he pulled himself into a crouch. "You'll certainly try. If it's not me after your power it'll be someone else."

Too late I realized why he'd let me get close as he leapt up, shifting entirely into his wolf form. I threw another fireball but it merely glanced off his fur. He hurdled my next attack and lunged in to snap at my side. I felt the brush of sharp teeth pierce through the fiery armor covering my arm. I fought down a surge of panic. He might still want to use me, but that didn't mean he needed me *intact*.

Lukas lunged again but I barely evaded him, bracing my feet against the ground as I waited for him to face me. Instead he kept running.

Straight at Jasper.

"No!"

A column of fire erupted from my hand, narrowly missing Lukas as he cut out of the way just in time. I sprinted to cover Jasper.

That was exactly what Lukas had been waiting for.

He darted back in, his massive weight driving into me. I heard my injured rib pop. Lukas' jaws closed around my shoulder and shook violently before tossing me across the floor.

I felt the tiger deep inside me growl.

"Friends are a luxury you can't afford," Lukas said as he stalked toward me. *"Especially if you ever became a queen. Consider this a lesson."*

I pushed myself to my elbows. The flames covering me sputtered weakly, receding to little more than a thin film across my skin. The tiger uncurled.

A little help, I begged.

Lukas shoved me onto my back and pressed a crushing paw onto my chest.

"Now I'll drag you to that throne, and then I'll take it and your magic both. And you can die knowing that I'll do a much better job ruling than you ever could."

He leaned forward and the pressure on me increased. His claws created bloody punctures in my chest. I would have screamed if I could have breathed.

I heard a tiger roar.

It came out of nowhere and blindsided Lukas, sending him careening off me. I gasped sweet air. I latched onto my retreating magic and held it, commanded it to surge to life once again, to give me as much power as I had left.

Lukas snapped at the tiger, then tried to leap around it. I hurled a fireball at him. He moved to dodge it and wound up straight in the tiger's path. It brought a fiery paw down across his muzzle so hard I could hear the impact from where I lay.

Lukas stumbled back. My tiger struck again and this time there was nothing to stop Lukas from sliding between the sandstone pillars and disappearing off the edge of the room.

After staring at where he'd vanished for a moment, I at last struggled up and carefully approached the edge. A few small rocks dislodged and bounced down the sharp incline, vanishing into the black far below the base of the building. I looked for any sign of Lukas. I was sure that no one, not even a paranormal, could survive a fall like that.

I tried to muster some sort of sympathy; maybe some guilt. After all, it had been my magic, my tiger, that'd killed him, but I felt nothing but relief. Lukas would have killed my friends without hesitation. Even if I'd kept him alive, I was positive the Conclave wouldn't have been on our side. He wouldn't have faced proper judgement.

I felt the warm brush of the tiger against my back. It gave me what I could only describe as a chastising growl. I couldn't help giving a tired grin. "Guess you saved my butt again, didn't you?"

My tiger's growl turned into a rumbling purr.

I took a deep breath and felt the tiger rejoin my magic, taking with it some of my strength. I teetered on my feet and shut my eyes until I was sure I wouldn't black out. I couldn't afford to. I still had things to do.

The transference stone sat where Lukas must have dropped it during my tiger's final attack. I smashed it with my heel until it shattered, and then scattered the broken pieces across the room.

"Riley…"

Even though he was a vampire, Jasper had never felt cold. But he felt cold now as I knelt and took his hand. The spot where Lukas had stabbed him looked even worse than before, the holes leaking even more blood.

"Don't sit up," I commanded as he tried. "I'm going to fix this."

"I don't….think we can fix this."

"Shut up." My eyes burned. "You're not dying a second time. You can't get away from me that easily. You just need a little magic, that's all."

"Maybe if Sienna or Collette was here—"

I leaned down and kissed him.

What little fire still covering my body wrapped us together as I opened his lips with mine and kissed him harder. It was cold and burning and awkward and *amazing*. I didn't just want one. I wanted a hundred. A thousand. I wanted to kiss him until I grew tired of it.

And then I felt my magic jerk toward him. The flames were sucked into his mouth along with the rest of my magic.

Jasper tried to pull away. I felt his lips attempting to form words, trying to stop me, but I held on, not wanting it to end even as I felt myself grow weaker. I had to give him as much as I could. Enough to know that he'd be all right.

At last I did pull away, but still my magic flooded into him. I grew weaker with every passing second and I knew I'd gone too far.

"Enough!" Jasper growled.

He pushed me onto my back and at last I could think clearly again. I blinked up at the ceiling. I felt weak—weaker than I'd ever been—but hopefully I'd given enough of my magic to him to make a difference.

"Are you okay?" Jasper said. Out of the corner of my eye I watched him roll himself over to face me.

I did a mental check. "I'll live. And you?"

Jasper checked his wound. The bleeding had stopped. The

holes weren't closing up yet, but I was confident they would, given time. He glowered down at me.

"That was the stupidest thing you've done yet. And that's a high bar to clear."

I found myself grinning. "Admit it, you liked it."

Jasper continued to glower, even as he took my hand and squeezed. "Never said I didn't."

My stomach did a little flutter that had nothing to do with my sluggish, slowly recovering magic. I tilted my head around to look at the door.

"Stay here. I'll be right back."

Jasper kept hold of my hand as I weakly stumbled up. "Whatever's beyond that door, whatever happens when you finish the prophecy, you'll still have me, and you'll still have the Outcasts."

"I know."

I squeezed his hand before pulling away. He would be safe, for now. Lukas was gone. Hayes was nowhere to be found. Maybe now that he'd double-crossed both sides, he'd scampered off to lie low somewhere. Sienna would be disappointed.

I limped to the door. I searched the roughly worn exterior, seeking what I already knew would be there. I found it in the dead center: the symbol of the elementals.

I reached toward it, feeling a slight tingle as the matching symbol on my shoulder came to life. The markings on the door filled with answering light. There was an enormous groan, a *thunk* like the earth itself was moving, and the door opened just wide enough for me to walk through.

The chamber on the other side was nearly identical to the first but much smaller. More intimate. The chamber of a queen and only her trusted few.

The throne—the thing that'd caused this whole mess—was at the other end. It was simple and somewhat blocky, made of deep black onyx stone with a laughably high back that fanned out at the top, inlaid with cold ribbons of sleek metal.

Maybe I should have felt reverence. Or awe. Or anything other than bone-deep exhaustion flavored with bits of stabbing pain. This was the thing—my destiny—I'd been unaware of for so long, but which had changed the trajectory of my entire life. And probably would keep doing so, no matter what I wanted. The throne of an elemental queen.

I limped over to it and reached out to touch the chair arm— hesitating only slightly—before my fingers touched the cold stone.

A buzz of magic immediately shot up my arm. Dust fell from the ceiling as the entire room shifted, seeming to come awake from a millennium of slumber.

Bright lines of orange magic shot from the base of the throne, filling the inlaid metal until the entire thing glowed a powerful orange. The lines continued outward, running through the floor before vanishing over the lip of the chamber in the direction of the city. A moment later the entire city came alive. The street-lamps flickered on. The roof of the cavern glowed with magical light, washing everything in a warm yellow glow.

The Dead City was alive again.

"Quite a welcome home party," I mumbled. I looked down at my hands. Despite the massive changes around me, I didn't feel any different. Had I fulfilled the prophecy and broken the curse? Were we now free to see our loved ones, or...?

I turned back to the throne. I still hadn't sat upon it. Maybe I needed to do that in order to—

"You can't go in there." Jasper's voice was loud and command-ing. My first feeling was relief that he'd healed well enough to sound strong again. The second was heart-clenching fear that Hayes had returned to finish us off. Perhaps he hadn't learned his lesson after all.

I sprinted toward the door. Jasper was still yelling at someone and I ran faster. If anything happened to him because I'd been careless....

I'd just reached the door when Iris stepped through.

"Riley!"

I was too stunned to move, too stunned to speak. Iris threw her arms around me and hugged me close. "You finally found your destiny. I'm so, so happy!"

"Iris...how...what?" I couldn't seem to form a coherent sentence. Not when one of the most precious parts of my old life and the beginnings of my new had just smashed together.

"Hayes told me where you were," Iris said, pulling back.

"I...I don't get it."

"Better tell her." Hayes leaned in the doorway, wincing as he clutched his side. "Waiting won't make it any better."

I looked between them. "Make what—What is *happening?*"

Iris was nervously gnawing at her bottom lip. She looked *scared*. "Riley, there's so much to tell and I don't think we have the time right now. Please understand that I...I never wanted..."

"Out with it," Hayes sighed.

Iris waved her hand. My stomach clenched as my killer—hooded, face like clay—materialized beside her. I braced for him to attack me, but with another wave of her hand he vanished. I looked, unable to believe it, from where he'd stood to Iris then back again.

"I'm the one who started your prophecy," Iris said, voice trembling. "Riley, I'm the one who killed you."

❧

Riley and Jasper have found the throne, but Riley's true trial has just begun...Continue the adventure in book 2, **Elemental Trial!**

Get two free YA urban fantasy books and stay updated on my newest releases, giveaways, and more by **joining my author newsletter!**

Please Leave a Review

Every single review helps authors like me find new readers and continue doing what we love: writing great books for you to enjoy. If you get a second, could **you leave one on the platforms above?** Thank you so much for your help and support!

Author's Blathering Note

Thank you for reading *Elemental Outcast*!
Be sure to come hang out in the **Fantasy Fiends Reader group** on Facebook! We chat, recommend YA fantasy reads, and get into mischief. It's the best place to learn about new book releases, exclusive ARCs, cover reveals, giveaways and more.

Want to make extra sure you never miss a new release? Follow me on **BookBub!**

I'd also love to hear from you on social media:

- facebook.com/seannfletcher
- bookbub.com/profile/sean-fletcher
- amazon.com/author/seanfletcher
- instagram.com/seanfletcherauthor
- goodreads.com/seanfletcher
- twitter.com/seannfletcher

In the Depths of Darkness

Shadows of the Swarm

Website:

https://seanfletcherauthor.com

ACKNOWLEDGMENTS

So you've made it to the acknowledgments...Congrats! You get to learn about the incredible people who helped make *Elemental Outcast* a reality.

You see, as much as my introverted self wishes I could do every aspect of publishing alone, I can't. I'm many things, but an omniscient, all-doing publishing savant I am not. If it takes a village to raise a child (or however the saying goes) then it takes an incredible horde of awesome people to raise or a book.

So:

Thank you to Becky Johnson for her consulting prowess and helping me wrap my thick head around the direction of my author career

A big thanks to Analisa Denny for her developmental editing eye, brutal honesty, and forcing me to admit that, yeah, some parts of the first draft kinda sucked. Fix them.

Thank you to Jessica Nelson for her proofread so I won't get emails raving about how riddled with errors my books are.

Thanks to Christian for his incredible cover designs, and for taking my jumbled mess of 'the cover should look like this but not like that' vagueness and turning into something drool-worthy.

To Gwen Jarvis for being an upbeat and go-getting VA, and being my second brain when mind decides to desert me.

Finally, as always, thanks to my friends and family (if they're reading this). They may not read my books, they may not even *like* my books, but they usually like me, and their love and support helps make this possible.

Sean

ABOUT THE AUTHOR

 Sean Fletcher was born in the broiling, arid state some people lovingly refer to as Texas. He is the Amazon bestselling author of YA fantasy, in addition to other forthcoming books whose characters will not give him a moment's peace until they get their turn in the spotlight. When not making things up and putting them on paper, he can be found hiking, biking, or traveling, sometimes all at the same time.

COPYRIGHT

Made in the USA
Las Vegas, NV
04 December 2021

36086668R00163